"HOGAR BLOODSWORD, HEAR THY QUEST...

"Go to the Cold Waste of the Sorcerers who dwell beyond the ice-troll caves. There, in rune-built Nardath-Thool, are kept the treasures thou must seek.

"Know thee, for the RAVENSWORD thou shall shed both blood and tears, and to win it thou must best both sorceress-queen and dragon's spawn in the city of thy quest."

The light faded and Hogar found himself standing alone in the cave. The vision he had so vividly beheld was gone with the gray mist.

He was not alone for long.

A roar from the mouth of the cave gave Hogar but scant warning of the prowling cave lion's presence. . . .

① SIGNET SCIENCE FICTION

COME OUT OF THIS WORLD

(0451)

☐ **CHILDREN OF ARABLE by David Belden.** In a distant future where males and females seem interchangeable, and babies are grown in labs to meet the needs of society, one *real* woman in search of love could launch a revolution that will alter the universe forever... (146603—$2.95)

☐ **THE GLASS HAMMER by K.W. Jeter.** Ross Scyuyler is a hero—a racer driving black market computer chips through hostile and dangerous territory. But when this microcomputer starts warning of conspiracy and doom, he must choose between familiar dangers and the perils of an all-seeing, yet faceless enemy.... (147669—$2.95)

☐ **INFERNAL DEVICES A Mad Victorian Fantasy by K.W. Jeter.** George Dower, a proper London gentleman, is the victim of his father's plans to destroy the earth with an automation. "Jeter is an exhilerating writer who always seems to have another rabbit to pull out of his hat."—*The New York Times Book Review* (149343—$2.95)

☐ **TIES OF BLOOD AND SILVER by Joel Rosenberg.** To David, stolen from Elweré as a baby and raised as a thief of the Lower City, it is a dream of paradise, a treasure trove to which he must find the key, no matter what the cost. That is, if Eschteef—twice the size of a human, with glowing eyes and rows of needle-sharp teeth—doesn't get to him first... (146212—$2.95)

Prices slightly higher in Canada

Buy them at your local bookstore or use this convenient coupon for ordering.

NEW AMERICAN LIBRARY,
P.O. Box 999, Bergenfield, New Jersey 07621

Please send me the books I have checked above. I am enclosing $_____ (please add $1.00 to this order to cover postage and handling). Send check or money order—no cash or C.O.D.'s. Prices and numbers are subject to change without notice.

Name_____

Address_____

City_____ State_____ Zip Code_____

Allow 4-6 weeks for delivery.
This offer is subject to withdrawal without notice.

HOGAR, LORD OF THE ASYR

John Rufus Sharpe III

A SIGNET BOOK

NEW AMERICAN LIBRARY

NAL BOOKS ARE AVAILABLE AT QUANTITY DISCOUNTS
WHEN USED TO PROMOTE PRODUCTS OR SERVICES.
FOR INFORMATION PLEASE WRITE TO PREMIUM MARKETING DIVISION,
NEW AMERICAN LIBRARY, 1633 BROADWAY,
NEW YORK, NEW YORK 10019.

Copyright © 1987 by John Rufus Sharpe III

All rights reserved

SIGNET TRADEMARK REG. U.S. PAT. OFF. AND FOREIGN COUNTRIES
REGISTERED TRADEMARK—MARCA REGISTRADA
HECHO EN CHICAGO, U.S.A.

SIGNET, SIGNET CLASSIC, MENTOR, ONYX, PLUME, MERIDIAN
and NAL BOOKS are published by NAL PENGUIN INC.,
1633 Broadway, New York, New York 10019

First Printing, December, 1987

1 2 3 4 5 6 7 8 9

PRINTED IN THE UNITED STATES OF AMERICA

*For my wife,
Josephine Tumminia Sharpe
And for my grandson
And granddaughter,
Geoffrey and Nicole Hales*

CONTENTS

	Foreword	ix
I.	The Sword in the Oak	15
II.	In the Queen's Cause	34
III.	The Dweller in the Woods	41
IV.	The Weird of the Gods	50
V.	Fomors!	56
VI.	Witch Storm	64
VII.	Runulf of Dorn	68
VIII.	Starulf Rides Forth	74
IX.	Hired Sword	78
X.	"Berserkers!"	85
XI.	Half Beast, Half Human	93
XII.	The Sword from the Howe	101
XIII.	Ragnahild	106
XIV.	"Valkyrie!"	114
XV.	The Rallying of the Jarls	119
XVI.	Tidings and Good Counsel	124
XVII.	Death Stalks the Marriage-Fest	130
XVIII.	Trouble with Hromund	137
XIX.	A Long Black Galley	140
XX.	The Road to Arn	144
XXI.	Street of the Wind Sellers	147
XXII.	Siren Song	152

XXIII.	The Cold Waste of the Sorcerers	158
XXIV.	Glikka	163
XXV.	The Chamber of Goom	168
XXVI.	Nardath-Thool	173
XXVII.	Tha	178
XXVIII.	"This Is Treason!"	183
XXIX.	The Moonrath	186
XXX.	The Doom Ring	191
XXXI.	"Put Not Thy Trust in Sorceresses!"	197
XXXII.	The Smell of Dungeons	201
XXXIII.	The Queen's Pleasure	204
XXXIV.	"Kill! Kill! Kill!"	208
XXXV.	The Field of Nardath	213
XXXVI.	"I Have Given Thee a Son."	219
XXXVII.	Fair Wind for Tarthiz	221
	GLOSSARY	224

FOREWORD

The antediluvian world of the Hogar Saga is a primeval era preexistent to the dawn of written history, when time-forgotten empires and kingdoms thrived in an elder age; when the merchants of fabled Ophur and Havilar loaded caravans and ships with silks, and jewels, monkeys, peacocks, ivory, and gold, that found their way to Tarthiz; when the opulent city-kingdoms of Shennaar, in the Land of the Two Rivers, flourished in barbaric splendor east of the sun; when the Nemedian magi ruled sinistrous Nardath-Thool, that fey city in the trackless waste beyond the Finnamark, rune-built on the charred ruins of ancient Asgarth. An age when a warrior people subjugated the Nordland, thirty-five generations after Ragnarok.

This great cataclysm, the twilight of the gods, passed down by knowing skalds, is said to have caused the sun to darken, the earth to tremble and sink beneath the sea and the flaming heavens to fall upon the bloody battlefield where the gods lay slain.

One might liken the Hogar Saga to a Norn-woven tapestry, worked on the warp of conjecture, and presupposing the existence of man and his gods in the post-Ragnarok Age, when the seed of Odin, Thor, and Tyr brought forth kings.

The get of this god-born race who survived that wrathful day of doom begat generation upon generation, venerating the gods of their fathers. But as they began to raise walls of felled timbers about their garths, they were conquered by invading Aryans who called themselves Kelts.

It was some twelve thousand years ago, with the wane of the hunting tribes, that this new people appeared; drifting north from the Caucasus, they skirted the Sea of Tethys and moved up through the fertile lands later to be called Europe into the northern regions below the ice-capped Frozen Lands of the Finnamark. Here they settled, driving the Reindeer People before them, and taking the god-born to husband and wife.

This new people were a tall, blue-eyed race of warriors and warrior women, red or yellow haired. At the start of their drift, the Kelts were a tent-living, goatherding, horse-keeping people, moving ever northward with the spread of the forests that replaced the grassy steppes; their grazing stock and wagons pushed up the great Ister valley and across lands of belligerent pre-Teutonic tribes, who drove them farther north to where they settled.

They called their new home the Nordland, after the god-born, who called themselves Nords, and their gods the Asa. There, below the Great Ice Marsh, they built the greatest of the Nordland rikes, or kingdoms. This they named Nordgaard. The skalds and priests of the god-born chanted runes of many-mansioned Asgarth, the home of the Asa, as it was before Ragnarok; and so they eventually came to call their conquerors the Asyr, meaning "godlike." And they taught them to revere the old gods. Thus it was that the mortal descendants of Odin mingled the god-blood flowing in their veins with that of the blue-eyed Keltic Asyrfolk, and their get rose to be kings.

But all was not idyllic. Into the Nordland came warring strangers, likewise tall, blue-eyed Kelts (some with darker hair and beards), calling themselves the Vandir, and worshiping other gods. They raised their own rike of Vandirheim, so that it marched on the border of Nordgaard. Vandir and Asyr plundered each other, and their generations were hereditary enemies.

The map of the antediluvian world was vastly different from today's. The prevailing animals in the spreading forests of future Europe were the royal stag, the bison, and the aurochs—or great ox—which stood a majestic eleven feet high at the withers; deer and the great wild boar abounded. There were lions in what is now Germany. These were twice the size of the modern lion, as were the cave lions of the Nordland. The great white wolf and the snowy saber-toothed tiger roamed the Cold Waste. Here, too, were found the last of the hairy mammoth. There were elephants and lions in the Shennaar, as well as the Nilotic nomarchies in the Land of Khem, and the Black Kingdoms of Kush.

Southwest of the Nordland was the Kymric Wilderland, with its rugged coastline and highlands. West of this lay the island stronghold of the Fomorian pirates. Across the river later to become the English Channel, throve the pre-Frankish kingdoms. To the south lay the Tarthizian peninsula, with its landbridge of hills that closed out the waters of the Outer Sea (now the Atlantic), and joined what is now Spain with North Africa. An ingenious system of locks and canals connected the great harbor of Tarthiz with both the Outer Sea and the landlocked waters of the Middle Land Sea, which the Egyptians much later called the Great Green.

The antediluvian world as thus conceived and partially outlined here, is conjectural. It is not intended that this preface be accepted as an accurate account of a bygone age. Rather, it is a prehistoric time frame, within the parameters of which the Hogar Saga was set down; and as such, it concerns a time about twelve thousand years ago, when a man named Hogar lived and fought his way to a throne.

The Norns who tie the threads of life
Embrangle as they weave;
The knots of destiny must Man alone
Untangle to achieve.
—*Ketil the Skald*

1

The Sword in the Oak

The stallion had cast a shoe and was limping badly. All night the outlawed thane had braved the driving snow to elude his pursuers; the wind cut through his bearskin cloak like the cold blade of a knife. The stallion was blowing hard. Hogar, the king's thane, reined to a walk to breathe the beautiful black animal. From nearby, he heard the eerie hunting cry of a wild dog pack. The stallion's ears pricked up with a nervous twitch. It sidled skittishly on the ice-clogged slope as the chilling cry echoed again and again amongst the thinning snow-clad timber through which its rider urged it on.

Grimly, Hogar knew the cry was that of the leader, the first of the pack to show itself, now silhouetted against the flush of dawn on the crest of the snow-whitened ridge above; then two more appeared; then another. They had scented man and stallion. Soon the whole pack would be gathered to close in for the kill. With a thought-plagued mind, Hogar awaited the charge, tensed and ready.

Proscribed!

He swore vengeance by the Asyr gods he denied, for the wrong done him—banished for life by the false-king, Hothir Longtooth, he who was both stepsire and uncle; he who had him stripped of weapons and trappings, and thrown naked in a guarded cell, charged with slaying an unarmed karl. Fortunately for Hogar, there was no dungeon at timber-built Grimmswold. From that he could not have so readily escaped. The bloodiest night of his young life flashed before the weary thane's troubled mind as he surveyed his surroundings for a defensible position where he could hold off the pack and face one wild dog at a time with a protecting tree at his back. The baying of the gathered pack traced an icy finger down Hogar's spine. He drew the broadsword that swung from his baldric, in readiness.

The stallion's lame leg made it clear he could not make a run for it when the pack broke. Far better for the beautiful animal to fall under the ravening fangs than he. Hogar's decision was made for him; at that moment, the pack raced down the icy slope in full cry. He whipped his mount into a stumbling gait with the flat of his sword, diverting the attack from himself. The pack took the stallion in the throat and breast as Hogar slid over its croup and eased himself onto the hard-packed snow by letting the tail slip through the fingers of his left hand. He landed catlike on both feet, steadying himself with his sword blade plunged into the icy surface to break his fall. The momentum carried him down; he rolled over once, then regained his footing with his back against a tree.

The stallion was screaming now; it struck out with flailing hooves at the slavering jaws that tore its flesh. Hogar thanked the gods he denied that there were but six of the vicious spotted beasts in the pack, five of them bringing the stallion to earth. The sixth had taken a glancing blow from a hoof that sent it tumbling and yelping, kicking up the snow. As it scrambled on all fours the voracious brute saw Hogar afoot and bared its fangs. Here was easier prey.

Hogar crouched for the springing attack, sword point extended. The charging carnivore took the blade up to the hilt through the chest before it was dead. He barely had time to withdraw the sword before another of the pack was upon him with a savage leap. Stepping to one side, Hogar brought his sword around in a sweeping circle. The wild dog's head fell one way, its carcass another.

The courageous stallion was down. Three of the snarling brutes were in for the kill. A fourth met Hogar halfway; then as though forewarned by the blood drip from his sword, it made a wide berth around him, growling viciously, and fell upon the headless carcass of its kind with ravening fangs. The other three greedily tore at the dying stallion's flesh, too blood-crazed to stop feeding as Hogar approached. He dispatched them quickly, and mercifully drew his sword across the stallion's torn throat.

Hogar waited for the last of the pack to charge. Instead, the surviving canine bared its fangs over the headless carcass on which it was feeding, then licked its chops and cravenly slunk away. Hogar's thrown dagger brought it down.

The outlawed thane again appraised his surroundings. He was not at all certain where the disputed Marches lay. It was Helmer Bloodsword, his father, the late Jarl of Valhelm, who had built Grimmswold keep; here he had garrisoned seven score fair-haired Asyr warriors to patrol the border. The heavily timbered stronghold, so named after a loathsome troll once said to inhabit the woods, had long been defended against both weather and Vandir attack, in the ongoing quarrel between the Asyrfolk and their warring neighbors. Beyond the ridge began the tundra of the Great Ice Marsh the skalds called the Frozen Lands—the Finnamark of saga and song. That way offered no escape. Turning back the way he had come meant discovery and capture by Asyr or Vandir patrols.

Had the stallion not thrown a shoe, it would not have gone lame; events might have taken a different turn. But the big black stallion was dead, and Hogar was afoot in surroundings that offered every chance he would freeze to death before nightfall should he fail to find suitable shelter and the means of making a fire.

The question of which way to turn before the cold chilled him to the marrow was answered by the appearance of two Vandir lancers far below on the road he had previously left. He knew from their wahooing that the riders had sighted him; there was no possible way to evade them as they urged their mounts up the icy slope, long spears couched.

Hothir's henchmen had turned back earlier from pursuing the outlawed king's thane. They now stood warming themselves with mulled mead and a blazing longfire at Grimmswold keep, dismissed by their liege after reporting their quarry lost in a blizzard.

Ketil the Skald, seated to one side of the darkened great hall, overheard the returning patrol make their false report to Hothir Longtooth. He had caught the remarks the warriors passed between themselves, that the young outlaw could perish for all they cared; they had more sense than to follow anyone deranged enough to ride deliberately into the frozen arms of the Ice Goddess, Hel.

The grizzled skald did not miss the dark look on Hothir's brow; nor how wroth the false-king grew when told that Hogar had eluded his pursuers. Ketil had witnessed the sorcerer's trick that led to Hothir acclaiming himself King of the Asyr, and the trumped-up bloodshed that brought about Hogar's banishment. The skald's mind churned with the events of the previous night, when the jarl had drawn the spurious sword from the oak and made himself king.

Ketil remembered well how the snow had been falling half the day, with the wind piling heavy drifts against the pales. It was well on toward the evening meal; the returning patrols soon would be clip-clopping through the gate. Jarl Hothir was not yet home from hunting the great wild boar that roamed the forest. Blund, the sentry over the gate, still posted his watch, grumbling to himself, impatient to be relieved to fill his belly with roast deer meat and gut-warming mead. The huge karl shouldered his crossbow resolutely. His steaming breath rimed the straggly yellow beard he buried in the folds of his great cloak, away from the biting cold.

A moment before, he and the ground guards had challenged the chariot of the Vandir king's emissary in the common tongue. The magnificently harnessed Lord Drakko had been passed through to the jarl's great hall in the longhouse, under a white shield of truce on king's business; for Thorodd Fairhair, the jarl's brother, the King of the Asyr, was a royal guest within, albeit taken to his bed with a sudden malaise. Drakko's lathered horses and his charioteer were left to brave the elements beside a miserable, small fire; no Vandir was ever afforded the shelter of Asyr stables.

Entering the great hall, Drakko pulled up a side bench before the blaze crackling in the longfire trench laid along the center of the vast room. Trestled oaken boards were being set up, soon to groan under trenchers of hearty Asyr fare and horns of heady drink. From the walls were hung a thousand war shields, gleaming bright between crossed battle-axes, swords, and long spears. Pillars of hewn oaks with defoliated limbs supported the roof. These were carved with the figures of Asyr kings as gods, locked in battle glory with fabulous beasts, and glowering trolls and fiends. The longfire filled the chamber with smoke reek, slow to rise through the smokehole in the roof. A thrall came and fussed with the logs to no avail, and presently was waved away with an imperious hand by Drakko on the entrance of the jarl's lady.

Ermengard was royal Rhenish; the daughter of the King of Skaane, long dead in his howe. Her braided tresses were red gold; though now in her middle years, she was still beautiful. Her throat tightened at the sight of Drakko, whom she loathed, lolling boorishly on a bench before the fire's welcome warmth, with no intention of rising.

"Lord Drakko," she said, her voice as cold as the night, "you make bold indeed to enter this house, knowing your presence is unwanted. I regret Jarl Hothir is not present to welcome you in the manner you so well deserve."

Drakko flushed.

"Lady, I come on king's business," he protested, with a poor attempt at rising. At a clap of Ermengard's graceful hands, a girl thrall brought a flagon and cup on a salver.

"Now, if you will excuse me—" Ermengard let her voice drop in a tone of dismissal.

"By the gods!" Drakko cried angrily. "You Asyr do put on airs. Barbarians, the lot of you!"

"Nay, it is you Vandir who are the barbarians," said Ermengard icily. "And lechers."

Drakko purpled as though struck across the face.

"You will serve the mead yourself, lady." He gritted the words.

"Pour," Ermengard told the thrall. In a bound, Drakko was at her side, grasping her roughly.

"Out!" he shouted to the frightened thrall, who put down the salver and fled. "Now, lady," he said through clenched teeth, "taste the mead, and I will taste it from your lips."

A clank of metal from behind them froze the leer on Drakko's lustful face as he beheld the cause of the sound. Jarl Hothir, yellow maned and bearded, trapped in hunting jerkin and cross-gartered breeks, with a bearskin draped over his shoulders, stood framed in the open doorway unannounced, naked sword in hand. A fresh wound in his right thigh dripped blood on the rushes through makeshift swathing.

Behind the jarl stood Hogar the king's thane, red of hair and smooth-shaven, shouldering a broad-ax. With it he had brought down the charging boar as the vicious tusks rent Hothir's thigh; indeed, saving the life of him who was both stepsire and uncle to the young thane.

"Unhand her, Vandir swine!" thundered the jarl.

Ermengard struggled free of Drakko's grasp.

"My lord husband," she cried, swaying a little, "you are hurt!"

" 'Tis but a scratch, lady," said the jarl lightly. Such a wound nearer the groin was called a royal death. "I lost both footing and spear as the boar charged." He scowled darkly. "Vandir dog, I hold you to answer. Draw!" he said contemptuously, casting aside his bearskin.

"But I come under white shield," protested the emissary, sweating visibly. "On king's business." Drakko faltered, weakly. Cursing himself for having lusted after the jarl's wife, even but momentarily in anger, he took a step forward with both palms upraised, almost in supplication.

"Draw!" demanded the jarl, his cheek muscles twitching with wrath. Drakko had no alternative. His rash behavior had invalidated sanctity of truce. He drew reluctantly. With a clash of swords, each attacked with a fury, both aware the quarrel would end only when one or the other lay dead on the rushes.

Hothir Longtooth was a young man no longer; but powerful indeed was this chieftain of the Asyrfolk, who stood second only to his brother, the ailing king. Aye, and ambitious as well. Hothir's eyes were ever on the Raven Throne. He coveted the royal chair of the Asyr kings with all his scheming heart and soul. His pain-twisted face was dark with hatred under the heavy scowl that beetled his brows; he closed ground quickly, his sword weaving a circle of iron around his adversary.

Parrying each stroke in his mind, Hogar appraised the Vandir's sword style. Drakko was no match for a swordsman of Hothir's mettle. But the gored thigh was a grievous handicap. The jarl was tiring fast, weakened by loss of blood. Drakko, sensing this, moved in for the kill, not counting on the young thane's interference until he heard the battle cry of the Asyr.

"Odin! Odin! Odin!"

With the ancient watchword roaring in his throat, Hogar put aside the ax, dropped the bearskin from his shoulders, and drew his broadsword. He stepped to Hothir's side, his rusty and unruly locks falling about his neck like a red lion's mane. Parrying Drakko's slashing blade, he took over with all the expertise Ketil the Skald had taught him from boyhood; for the grizzled warrior-bard was equally adept at both swordplay and skaldcraft. Hothir gave him but a stiff nod and stepped back, sheathing his own weapon.

"The boar's tusks have slowed my hand," was all he said.

Not a word of thanks, thought Hogar angrily. His vexation quickened his attack; with furious blows, blade ringing on blade, he forced Drakko backward between the trestled boards.

Ermengard came at once to her lord's side, offering her arm for the jarl to lean upon; for Hothir was now bleeding freely.

"Come, lord," she said gently, "you must rest. I've had the leech summoned to attend your wound." But Hothir's mind was on the swordplay. He watched every move of Hogar's flashing blade, and that of his opponent with hard, calculating eyes.

"Here is something to watch indeed," he told her. "Leech or no leech, 'tis your son's first duel, lady—I shall watch the kill. Attend!"

Hawk-nosed Ketil the Skald stood watching his protégé's swordplay from the doorway.

"Praise Odin!" he said quietly as he joined the jarl and jarless. "Hogar has learned well all I have taught him. Mark you, Hothir. He will one day be the greatest swordsman of his time."

Hothir cast the grizzled skald a dark look as Ketil and Ermengard helped him to a bench beside the longfire. Hogar, meanwhile, had his adversary cornered like the last opposing piece on a game board, leaving no possible move for escape. His point was pressed against the Vandir's throat, poised for the thrust home. Drakko cravenly threw his sword onto the rushes and extended his empty hands above his head. Cold sweat beaded his pallid brow.

"I am unarmed!" he cried out for all to hear. "Hothir, I come on king's business."

"So I perceived as I entered my hall," said the jarl with heavy irony. Drakko sweated under the atheling's sword. Hogar's words were cold and deadly as a serpent as he spoke.

"Drakko, you swine, unarmed though you be by your own doing, I shall kill you for daring to lay a hand on my lady mother." The thews of his sword arm flexed; his knuckles whitened under their grasp upon the hilt.

"Stay your sword, Hogar!" Ketil the Skald called out in dire warning. "Must you force the jarl to banish his lady's own son for slaying an unarmed man in cold blood?"

"Spare me that sorrow, Hogar," Ermengard pleaded.

"The skald is right," said Hothir Longtooth sternly, his eyes unfathomable beneath his craggy brows. "As lawgiver, I must counsel you, Hogar. King's thane, or nay, you are not above the Law of the Asyr. Put up your sword. Let us see what business of Valhelm's lion the jackal brings."

Hogar narrowed his fire-blue eyes at the craven Vandir with utter contempt, and lowered his point.

"State your errand, emissary," growled the jarl. It had not gone well, Hothir thought darkly. Drakko was clever enough a swordsman to have given the lad his death, had not Ketil been so thorough in his teachings.

The emissary's droned greetings from his king grated upon Hothir's dark thoughts; he was motioned to silence as the leech entered the great hall to attend his lord. Drakko was humbled to wait upon the jarl until his wound was dressed; the probing of it brought a vile oath to Hothir's grim lips.

"Out, clod!" he roared, wincing in pain. "Send me the shaman, Klavun Thorg." He directed his eyes to Ermengard. She left the hall with the ousted leech to do her lord's bidding.

The prize of the hunt had meanwhile been brought in, stripped of pelt, hooves, and tusks. Skewered on a spit over the longfire and turned by a surly kitchen knave, the boar carcass dripped its angrily hissing fat onto the bed of hot coals. Hothir's favorite hunting hound came in from the kitchens and lay down on the rushes, pretending to sleep with one eye watching the spit.

As though summoned by the savory aroma, the winding of battle horns and the hoof crunch on rime announced the returning patrols as they rode through the stockade gate eager for the longfire warmth. Soon they were shaking the snow from their great cloaks in the foreroom. Ridding themselves of ring mail and horned helms, they took their places at the board still armed; for so was Hothir Longtooth wont to sit at meat.

"I see you bagged a boar, my jarl," cried a bull-necked, one-eyed warrior happily.

"And if you had two eyes in that thick skull of yours, Ari Oxmain," replied Hothir with a deep-throated chuckle, "you would see that the boar came nigh to bagging me." There was a roar of laughter at the jarl's jest.

Nay, thought Hogar bitterly, he'll not tell them it was I who brought the boar down with my broad-ax, I who saved him from being gored to death. We have never been close, Hothir Longtooth and I.

The jarl's coldness made Hogar more and more certain that he who was both stepsire and uncle bode him naught but ill will; too frequent were the dark and guarded glances the jarl directed his way to be taken otherwise.

Hothir held up a ringed arm for silence, and the laughter subsided. At this juncture, Klavun Thorg entered the great hall robed in scarlet as a Nemedian priest of Tha. His shaved pate shone with the reflected fireglow. He hurried to his master's side, and fell to treating his wounded thigh; with mysterious unguents, arcane mutterings, and strange passes of the hands, he quickly staunched the flow of blood.

As the Nemedian plied his sorcerer's skills, Hothir Longtooth's thoughts idly dwelt on the day the shaman fell into his hands . . . in a sea skirmish with a slave ship off the rockbound Kymric coast . . . how he had cut Klavun Thorg free of his galley chains and the oar that had all but pulled the heart out of his frail body. Hothir remembered, too, when renewed strength once again flowed through the Nemedian's veins, how fascinated he had been by his new thrall's spellcraft (for all Nemedians are sorcerers, they say); and thus had he acquired himself a personal warlock for life. Brushing this idle musing aside, Hothir called out to his shield karls.

"My lady sends word by the shaman that she has retired with her women so that we warriors may freely bouse ourselves at the board, as is our wont." He gave the waiting Drakko a scathing look. "You may speak now, Vandir dog."

Scarlet-faced, the emissary delivered a burthen of words. Jarl Hothir heard him out, scowling when Drakko concluded with a demand to see Thorodd, the king.

"What all your puffery boils down to is this," the jarl summed up gruffly. "The borderland dispute between our peoples is settled, provided I agree to abandon Grimmswold keep and leave the Marches henceforth patrolled by you Vandir alone. This," he roared, "is not king's business! I am overlord here. Grimmswold is not a crown-fylke, but my own, inherited with the jarldom on my brother Helmer's death; fiefed to my atheling, the king's thane, when he comes of age. All this you know, Drakko. Also, that my royal brother lies here sick unto death." He turned his eyes on the shaman. "Tell the dog," he said.

"It is the wasting sickness," whispered the Nemedian, prolonging the last word in a hiss.

"Aye, Thorodd's taken his death within this very longhouse," said Hothir. "Unable to be moved, even by horse litter; never again in this life to set eyes on fair Nordgaard. Nay, Drakko, you sly and oily dog, your business here is indeed not king's business, but your own; to take, if you can, another man's wife in his absence from hearth and home." The jarl turned angrily to Hogar. "Get this swine's offal from my sight. Ari Oxmain!" he shouted down the hall. "You and the shaman will help me to the board."

Ashen with humiliation, the Vandir king's emissary grated, "We will meet again, atheling." Eyeing him in cold fury, Hogar sheathed his sword.

" 'Twill be your bane when we do," he said. As he took a swinging step forward, his dagger struck out quick as a serpent's fang. "Let this remind you I shall kill you when next we meet, Vandir."

With a sharp outcry, Drakko clapped a hand to his left ear and fled the hall, blood dripping through his fingers.

Taking a gold ring from his arm, Hothir broke it in two. He tossed one half to Ketil the Skald and bade him begin the chanting and carouse. At a strum of the bard's harp, tankards banged on the oaken boards; the great hall rang with boisterous staves. The mead flowed freely. Midst it all, Hothir Longtooth and his sorcerer put their scheming heads together, knowing full well they would not be overheard above the din. Hothir natheless kept his agitated voice low.

"You fool!" he whispered harshly. "The accident during the hunt—you were to arrange it! What went wrong? You said it was in the stars."

"The stars but incline; the gods impel, master," said the sorcerer humbly.

" 'Tis Hogar I want dead, not myself," Hothir rasped.

"A thousand pardons, master."

"Go you now, and prepare the final potion for my royal brother lying in the tower room. 'Tis time the supposed wasting sickness took him." Hothir smiled cruelly. "You saw the Vandir's frightened face at the mention of it. He believed, as all will believe. See to it Thorodd Fairhair breathes his last this night. Make ready for that of which we have spoken."

"May the hand of the incomparable Tha touch thy heart, O Hothir," said Klavun Thorg, retiring with his shaved pate louted low.

"Go," whispered Hothir fiercely. "Go sacrifice whatever it is you sacrifice to your white goddess, shaman, and have done quickly! I have waited long enough to be king."

While Ketil the Skald's resonant voice led the carouse, in a secret room in the tower Klavun Thorg intoned weird incantations in the Old Tongue, invoking the Oirrin-Yess, the White Gods of his homeland, and Tha the incomparable, Queen-Goddess of Nardath-Thool. And in the great hall below, the bored kitchen knave kept turning the spit, wishing to Thor the boar carcass was roasted, carved, and trenchered, and he was tumbling the scullery wench who earlier had let him feel her thigh.

Hothir at length called out to Ketil, tossing him the other half of the ring he had broken.

"Hear me, skald! Have done, and give us instead Thorir Treefoot's lay."

Ketil deftly fisted the piece of gold and, striking a chord, replied brazenly, "Half a stave for half a ring."

Hothir grinned wryly at this licensed boldness and threw him a finger ring set with stones that glittered in the rushlight. Nimbly catching his jeweled reward with one hand still holding his harp, Ketil began the lay of Hothir's valiant sire. From his place beside the jarl, Hogar the king's thane listened to the oft-told saga of how his grandsire, the undaunted Thorir Treefoot, long dead King of the Asyr, lost an eye and a leg against the pirates of Thairm in the Orkna Ey; and how from them he had won the Ravensword.

It was in the midst of the rollicking battle staves that from the doorway there came a cry of alarm that silenced the hall.

"Master, I bid you come at once!"

It was the sorcerer, Klavun Thorg, who stood there, the look of a bearer of ill tidings etched on his crafty face.

"What now, shaman?" asked Hothir idly, playing out the hand. The Nemedian approached the high seat before speaking further.

"Thorodd Fairhair is dead," he said, for all in the hall to hear. "But a moment since, he died in my arms as I gave him to drink of a cup of water to wet his fever-parched throat."

Hothir faced his garrison masked with feigned sorrow.

"Your arm, shaman," he said loudly. "Steady me while I do what I must do." With Klavun Thorg to lean upon, he painfully made his way from the hall. Pausing at the doorway, Hothir called out to Ketil, "Sing them of the valiant Thorodd Fairhair, skald, till I am returned to receive each karl's fealty to his rightful liege." He tossed Ketil another arm ring, not bothering to break it.

It was a grief-stricken figure Hothir Longtooth presented, had curious eyes observed the jarl and his sorcerer making their way to the tower room, where lay his royal brother. Once within the chamber with the door bolted, the jarl erased the bereft look from his face and took a chair.

"Well done, shaman," he crowed happily, casting an indifferent glance at the still form across the room. The Nemedian bowed low with a crafty smile.

"In Nemed all things are possible, master."

"Tell me, how did the po—" Hothir cut his words short with a sharp intake of breath.

Was that a whisper from the deathbed?

Pushing the sorcerer aside, he hobbled unassisted to the couch and leaned over the body, searching out any sign of life.

"Mother of Odin!" breathed the jarl, aghast as the eyes in Thorodd's pallid face opened and gazed into his own; and there came from the king's lips the whispering of a word and a name.

"First Helmer—"

Thorodd Fairhair gave a deep sigh of surrender, and death closed his eyes. Hothir Longtooth stood trembling as with an ague. Why should Thorodd look into my eyes and whisper an accusation with his dying breath? he asked himself uneasily. Thorodd knew naught of the happening in the canebrake at the hunt—that it was I who loosed the bolt that slew Helmer twenty long years ago. Was he about to say, "First Helmer—now me" as he died? How could he have known? Merely guessed at the truth? Who could have told him? Ermengard? Ketil the Skald? Even so . . . I must silence them—silence them all—even to the last man jack of the garrison, if need be! Hogar must be next. He must not live to claim the Raven Throne against me now that Thorodd, too, is dead. . . .

Aloud, he cried out at the sorcerer angrily, "You blundering fool! What means this? You bade me come at once—that Thorodd was dead. And here I find him still alive. Have a care, shaman. If all goes not well in this game we play, I shall cut out your black heart and feed it to my hounds."

Klavun Thorg transfixed the irate jarl with a will-binding stare. Momentarily glamored, Hothir felt a wave of calm wash over him; his anger abated, totally forgotten. His words bespoke his grim satisfaction.

"You have done well, shaman." With cold, unfeeling eyes, he stood by the bedside looking down on his royal brother's mortal remains. "Did you summon the leech?"

"Nay, master. I came to you at once," said Klavun Thorg, his voice fawning. "When I left Thorodd, I swear to you by Tha, the king was dead."

"Faugh! You have botched it. You dolt! You fool! You lied! You swore your foul incantations would materialize the Ravensword long enough to be seen held aloft in my hand to proclaim me king. Show me the sword, I say! Can you or can you not raise it from its secret place by the sacrifice of a human life? Must I march on Nardath-Thool myself to gain it?"

Under the Nemedian's continued stare, Hothir felt his anger cool again. He cast another glance at the couch where the dead king lay.

"Think you, then," asked the jarl, "the magic was too weak?"

"Nay, master."

"Why, then, have your filthy gods not spoken?" Hothir demanded. The shaman intensified his spelling stare; but Hothir was strong-minded and difficult to control with the eye alone.

"Defile not the Oirrin-Yess with angry words, I beseech you, master. They are everywhere. Even in this very room. And they hear. Heed not Thorodd's last words. The gods sometimes will the mind to live after death long enough for a last word—uttered in the right presence." He sucked in his breath and let it out in a slow hiss.

"Unless he were only fevered," Hothir mused. "Fevered, but not yet dead." The Nemedian shook his head in silent denial. It was a moment before he spoke.

"The wasting sickness fevers the mind, yes. But the draft I gave him would not," he said. "Thorodd's last words were spoken as though from the grave. The name he named was that of one already dead. 'First Helmer,' he said. Perhaps it means—"

"You talk overly much, shaman." Hothir's voice was low and harsh. "Mark you well. It was the wasting sickness that did Thorodd Fairhair in, not an ensorceled vial. As for the name 'Helmer,' Thorir Treefoot sired three sons. Helmer was the second born, the first to die. In his last fevered moment, Thorodd thought of Helmer—long dead these twenty years of a hunting accident—such as you were to arrange this day. He spoke not from the grave, as you imply your foul gods willed him to do. Dead men speak not. Cover his face, and help me to my hall, that I may be acclaimed king by my own falchion—since you twice have failed me. Make sure, then, that you cast a spell in the eye of every man jack present, so that all will believe that which they do not see. Be certain, shaman, it is I and no other who draws the sword from the oak this night!"

An expectant roar went up amongst his warriors

when Hothir again appeared in the great hall on the shaman's arm. Painfully he took his place at the high seat. With Hogar on his right and the sorcerer on his left, the jarl unsheathed the false kingsword at his belt and held it aloft. For a moment it caught the longfire gleam. Looking round the trestled boards, Klavun Thorg fixed each karl's eye with a spell-binding gaze.

"Behold the Ravensword of Thorir Treefoot! Lo, the one and true king's falchion!" Hothir cried out the lie, his voice exultant. "Behold the Kingsword of the Asyr!" With both hands grasping the hilt, he drove the spurious blade deep into the oaken pillar nearest the high seat, declaiming the ancient ritual question:

> *"Who shall first then try his might,*
> *And wrest the sword from oak this night?"*

One by one the warriors rose as they were bade by the shaman's stare-spell and stood forth to draw the sword. Hogar felt the hot words of protest rise bitter in his throat. But when he would have cried out, Ketil the Skald, who had come to sit beside his protégé, laid an arresting hand on his shoulder.

"All thrones come not easily to them who plot and scheme," he whispered. "Patience, Hogar."

"Only the Ravensword is the true king's falchion," said the troubled thane.

"The shaman caught not your eye? Good."

"Fools!" muttered Hogar. "Like a gaggle of geese they are, pecking along a trail of corn, at the end of which waits the butcher's ax." True, he thought, Thorodd had become king without holding aloft the Ravensword, long lost since the battle of Skaanè, where Treefoot fell against the Vandir. Aye, but Thorodd had not driven a spurious kingsword in the oak!

"What game does Hothir play?" he asked the skald.

"That we shall know," said Ketil, "when a false move at last reveals his game plan. I counsel you to be patient, lad." Hogar nodded, eyeing the clamoring warriors. Each of them, he knew, felt in his heart it was he and he alone who could best Hothir Longtooth in the drawing of the sword; each saw himself as king.

One-eyed Ari Oxmain was first to try. Ari was a mighty warrior. He grasped the sword hilt in both hands, his corded back bowed; his thews bulged, the sweat rolled; but draw the sword he could not. Those who followed also failed, strong and mighty karls though they were. Hothir's lips curled in a secret smile as he beheld the garrison confounded by the Nemedian's spellcraft. None could draw the sword. Not Donar, not Helgi Hotblood; not Val; nor Rorik Bloodaxe, champions all. When all had failed, a respite was called by Hothir, and the mead flowed; the competing warriors drank deep. Those able to continue rose on unsteady legs. Blund the sentry weaved drunkenly toward the oaken pillar for a second try. He brushed against Hothir as the jarl rose from the high seat and hobbled forward to take his own turn. Hothir would have fallen had not Hogar helped him recover his balance. Blund glowered red-eyed at the king's thane. One word could have settled the incident peacefully, but Blund did not court talk. What he sought was a brawl, and he had found one. He drew.

"Keep the peace!" cried Hothir, secretly delighted with the turn of events. "Take their swords. Let them battle with their fists."

It took a bit of doing to disarm both men. Once freed from restraint, Blund seized Hogar in a fierce bear hug meant to crush his heart against his ribs. The redhead, though dulled with mead, was ready for him. They fought with fists, feet, and teeth; they wrestled each other to the earthen floor, rolling in the rushes amongst scraps and bones thrown to the hounds. The garrison gleefully urged them on; forgetting the drawing of the kingsword for the nonce, they shouted for more to drink. Hothir reseated himself to watch the outcome, his lips curling in the same secret smile.

"All goes as planned," he whispered in Klavun Thorg's ear. The Nemedian gave him a knowing nod.

"The giant will crack Hogar's back like a soup bone," he ventured, "given the chance."

Blund was a huge brute of a man. When sober he was a likable enough sort, but it was a bitterly cold night, and he had stood watch above the gate overly long before his relief. He had drunk much, quickly, and eaten little. He prided himself on his physical prowess, that he could stand up to any karl in the garrison, bar none but his brother, Rorik. Now for the first time he was tasting the bitter wine of humiliation, fighting with his fists like a lowly thrall, bested by a mere youth of nineteen winters.

The two brawlers regained their feet. A powerful blow sent the drunken Blund stumbling backward against the hanging shields and weapons. A madness crept into his eyes as he grasped the haft of a war-ax and tore it free. Swinging the ax wildly in a circle, he advanced on the wary redheaded thane who had beaten him fairly with bare knuckles, forcing Hogar back, perilously close to the blazing longfire trench. The ax fell. Hogar reeled away from the blow aimed at his skull, falling backward against the high table boards. Like a madman, Blund rushed in for the kill, bringing the ax down in a vicious arc.

In a haze, Hogar spun away from the descending ax blade; it missed his head by scant inches, driving deep into the wood. The spinning movement brought him stumbling hard against the oak pillar nearest the high seat; his back to the hewn tree, he faced his crazed adversary with both arms flung above his head. Blund struggled to tear the ax head free. Hogar's fingers instinctively closed about the sword hilt they touched. Gripping fiercely with both hands, he brought his whole might to bear with such force his torso and arms continued forward, with the downward sweep of the falchion he unwittingly drew from the oak. There was a sickening sound of metal shearing through bone, and Blund fell away, a bloody thing cloven to the chin.

While Hothir sat aghast at his carefully laid plan gone awry, the sorcerer Klavun Thorg, with a pass of his hands, cast a mote in the eyes of Hothir's warriors, so that they momentarily saw nothing.

Hothir's eyes were hard, and cold as the wind whipping around the longhouse eaves; then a burning rage melted the icy hatred in his look as he turned his wrath on the atheling he wished dead. For a moment Hogar stood stunned with realization. He had drawn the sword which he as atheling was forbidden to touch. Handing Hothir the blade hilt first, he knelt for the death blow.

"You berserker fool!" Hothir ground the words between clenched jaws in a rasping whisper. With a meaningful glance at the Nemedian, he drove the spurious king's falchion in the oak. Klavun Thorg, with a pass of his hand, drew the mote from the eyes of the shield karls, so that they saw only what they were meant to see, as Hothir cried out, "Behold the sword in the oak drawn forth by your rightful king!"

A moment of silence hung over the great hall. Ketil the Skald had been feigning drunkenness and witnessed the jarl's base trickery. He struck a chord on his harp and improvised a stave lauding Hothir Longtooth. Beakers were raised high with the shout of "Skoal, Hothir, King of the Asyr!"

"They believe!" the jarl whispered to his sorcerer. He felt the hot blood pounding in his temples. "The Raven Throne is mine!" he exulted. Peeling off a ring, he tossed it to the skald.

"Forget not your pact with the Oirrin-Yess," Klavun Thorg warned in a low voice. "Let us give thanks to Tha—"

"Some other time, shaman," said the jarl impatiently, pushing the Nemedian aside. "Hear now Hothir Longtooth, your king!" his voice boomed across the hall. "He who stands before me with guilty hands that slew an unarmed comrade-in-arms in cold blood, shall be justly punished for his crime. I, Hothir the King, do proscribe and banish Hogar the king's thane from Nordgaard for life. Take him away!"

11

In the Queen's Cause

When Ketil the Skald heard of Hogar's escape and how he had eluded Hothir's manhunt, he knew what he himself must do. Slipping unobtrusively from his place by the longfire, quickly he made his way to the women's bower. At a certain door he listened a moment with his ear to the panel, then knocked softly. There came a sound of slippered feet, and a whispered challenge through the door.

"Who knocks at this hour? Begone!"

"Fjaerlda, 'tis I, Ketil the Skald. Open guickly!"

With the grating of unbolted locks, the door was opened a crack. An owlish eye peered out cautiously and fixed itself on Ketil's face; the door was opened a few inches more to reveal an exceedingly ugly hunchbacked female dwarf in nightdress. She held a lighted taper close to his hawk nose.

"Is it you, then, Ketil the Skald?"

"I told you through the door it was I. Will you open, Fjaerlda?" he asked with an urgency in his whisper. "My message is for Ermengard—for the queen; not for the ears of this hallway."

Fjaerlda barely opened the door enough to admit the skald. He slipped past her into the unlit chamber beyond. The door was closed quickly behind him, and a bolt shot into place. The ugly little woman with the twisted back held up her light to lead the way, then turned to her late caller with a suspicious air.

"What hide you under your mantle, Ketil the Skald?" she asked.

" 'Tis a gift. For you, Fjaerlda, and no other," said Ketil. "My harp." He brought forth the small stringed instrument and presented it to her. " 'Tis yours to care for the while I live; and yours it will be when I am gone to my grave; which might well be soon, for what I am about to do. I see you sense something is in the wind, that I would part with my harp. Well, then; I go tonight—I must!—and quickly, ere commanded to chant staves for Hothir's cover, the while he plots our doom with the evil one he calls shaman."

"You mentioned a message for the queen."

"I may not see her, then?"

"At this hour of the night? Do you think me twisted of mind as well that I would waken her?"

"Tell her, then," he said tersely, "Ketil the Skald rides to rally the jarls in her service. Quickly, now, let me out; and be quiet with those locks. One more word. Tell the queen my sword is at her feet, forever in her service; that I ride this night to find her outlawed son, who one day will sit the Raven Throne by right of blood and his good sword arm—not by sorcery."

"He is proscribed then?" Fjaerlda asked with a sharp intake of breath, her owlish eyes wide with the question.

"You didn't know?"

"The king has told the queen nothing. What mean you by sorcery? Indeed, something sinister is come over Hothir. The jarl has become king, and the man a beast. Sorcery? Quotha! It is as though he had changed skins with a snake by trickery or witchcraft. The wife knows not her husband; a stranger he has become, silent and unfriendly by day; an insatiable troll who summons her to his bed by night."

"Witchcraft and trickery, forsooth," said Ketil. "Only thus did he draw the sword from the oak to make him king. Yet who knows what dark things a man who wants a throne so much will not do? We know this: Hogar is proscribed by the man he knows to be his uncle and stepsire. And once I ride out of Grimmswold gate this night, I, too, will be outlawed by my own act of treason to the false-king. Bolt the door after me," he warned. "To no one but the queen say I have seen or spoken with you this night. Fare thee well, Fjaerlda."

Going quickly then to his own quarters, Ketil clad himself in ring armor. Broadsword swinging at his side and a dagger at his belt under his skald's mantle, he made his way unseen to the stables. There the sagaman, who was as renowned a warrior as he was a teller of tales and a chanter of staves, saddled his big roan. He rode through Grimmswold gate on the wings of a trumped-up lie to the sentry, about bearing the news to Nordgaard how Jarl Hothir had drawn the sword from the oak and claimed the Raven Throne as king. It would be the last time Hogar's mentor and everfaithful friend since his toddling days rode out of Grimmswold keep as Hothir Longtooth's sworn liege man.

As Fjaerlda closed and bolted the door behind Ketil's departure she placed the harp he had given her in a chest; then she tiptoed to a closed door on the opposite side of the room lit only by her taper. Carefully lifting the latch and knocking ever so gently, she entered the chamber and approached a shut-bed.

"Dost sleep, my lady?" Fjaerlda asked softly.

"Is it you, dear sister?" The words came sleepily.

" 'Tis I, the Ugly Cygnet, Swan Maiden."

"Surely it is not morning? The lark has not yet sung. Why do you awaken me now?"

"I bring a message from one you can trust." There was a rustle of silks. The shut-bed opened. "Concerning the son who will one day be king," the dwarf woman concluded.

Queen Ermengard sat up at these words and whispered, "How fares he then, my son?"

"Outlawed. Proscribed by Hothir," Fjaerlda replied.

"Is he imprisoned?" asked the queen breathlessly.

"Nay; no longer, at least," said the hunchback. " 'Tis Ketil the Skald's message I bring, Queen sister. He rides to rally the jarls in your service, to set the rightful heir upon the throne which Hothir usurps by witchcraft and trickery. The skald said also to tell you he rides this night, an outlaw himself of his own making, to find—"

"Speak not that name within these walls, nor where he may be hiding out, lest ears beyond them carry tales," the queen cautioned. "Ketil is a renowned swordsman as well as a singer of staves. He will find the one he seeks. And you, dear sister—"

"I am known only as the Ugly Cygnet. The dwarf with the crooked back, sister and constant companion to the Swan Maiden," Fjaerlda interposed wryly. "A maker of songs, a twanger of harp strings—"

"Tush!" said the queen. "Listen to what I say. None but Ketil and I are aware how well he has taught you both his arts." Ermengard smiled. "Aye, Fjaerlda, it has been kept a secret between the three of us that you are indeed a mistress of the sword, tutored by a master swordsman for my protection, against him to whom poor, well-meaning Thorodd Fairhair gave me in marriage as the king's ward; me, just got with child by my husband so soon dead—"

With a sharp outcry, Ermengard was on her feet, a look of sudden revelation in her eyes; they glowed with the newfound truth as she took the twisted figure before her by the shoulders and hugged it to her heaving breast.

"I know him now! In this dream I have dreamed all these years," she whispered fiercely. "I know the hunter at last!"

"Give me air, I pray you!" Fjaerlda worked herself free of the smothering embrace.

"A boon, sweet sibling! Grant your sister and your queen this boon!" Ermengard cried out. "Go as I direct you with this message . . ."

Once through Grimmswold gate, Ketil the Skald put the big roan into a thunderous gallop down the road by which Hogar's pursuers had returned to the garrison empty-handed. With the wind and snow in his face, he drove his mount hard, hooves pounding against the rimed road. It was harsh weather, but scarcely an excuse for Hothir's horsemen to have turned back. Ketil knew the road well. He had crossed the frontier into the Marches, the disputed fylke that lay between Nordgaard and Vandirheim. Soon there would be a border patrol to contend with; Asyr or Vandir made no difference. He was an outlaw, even as Hogar. He sought to find the lad (for so he thought of him) before he boarded a ship into exile—if indeed somehow he had eluded his hunters.

Ahead of him, in the change of wind that drove the snow away from his face, Ketil saw the patrol. Blocking the road stood a lone Vandir lancer.

Why only one?
Was this a trap?

It was too late to detour or turn back. He had been seen. The lancer gave challenge.

"Halt! State your errand."

The canny skald thought rapidly for a plausible answer. He slowed the roan to a walk and let it blow. Only twenty paces lay between him and the enemy horseman. Ketil halted the roan. The Vandir walked his chestnut stallion closer, long spear couched.

"Be off, Asyr dog. This is Vandir land," he warned. "What do you here?"

"I ride to Vandirheim on a mission of life and death," lied Ketil the Skald glibly. He was at his best when making up preposterous tales. "Thorodd Fairhair, King of the Asyr, is dead. Hothir the usurper has banished the true and rightful heir and claims the Raven Throne. He is in league with the Thalmanda Fire Lords of Thool, who are on the march again with their Black Legion, threatening to burn every Vandir garth and steading as they burned Skaane. I ride to warn your king Hern, to beg him to let bygones be bygones; to join arms with the Queen of the Asyr against Hothir and his cohorts. We must stand together at last, or fall."

The Vandir had continued to walk his mount closer. He snorted aloud at Ketil's obvious fabrication.

"You expect me to believe that pack of lies?" he demanded. Lowering his long spear, he doubled over in his saddle with raucous laughter.

Ketil dug his heels in the roan's flank.

"Then believe this!" he cried, sweeping past the lancer on the gallop. His sword flew into his hand as though by sorcery; he brought it downward in a slashing blow that sent the Vandir's head rolling.

Ketil dismounted. Tethering both horses off the road, he exchanged metal and trappings with the slain lancer. Untying the roan, he gave it an affectionate caress on the muzzle, a word in its ear about the oats that waited in the stables at Grimmswold, and a sound slap on the flank to start it on the way home. For all appearances an armored Vandir lancer on patrol, Ketil kicked his new mount into a trot along the road down which his vanquished foe had ridden to his sudden demise.

Presently, he caught up with a second lancer. From his gruff manner and pomposity, Ketil took him to be the slain Vandir's superior. He gave Ketil a dressing down for being late on patrol. The skald muffled his face in the dead rider's great cloak and wisely said nothing. Having had his say, the patrol leader bristled his reddish mustaches, coughed importantly, and broke his bay gelding into a smart canter with a testy sign for his subaltern to follow in close order.

With his naked sword in hand, Hogar faced the two horsemen as they urged their mounts up the icy slope with long spears couched. The lead rider reined in a full spear's length from the outlawed thane and motioned his companion to a halt. Brushing his mustaches free of snow, he sat his mount, coughing importantly.

"What do you on Vandir land?" he barked.

"You can see he is a hunter of wild dogs," spoke up the second lancer, his face partly concealed by his great cloak. " 'Tis a fine *kettle* of fish to *scald*!" he exclaimed in a loud voice. "Have you no eyes in your head?"

"I can see that under his bearskin he wears the trappings of an Asyr warrior, you dolt!" was his superior's angry rejoinder. "What kind of a question is that?"

"One that requires this for an answer!" cried the other. Like a flash of lightning, his sword was drawn and thrust through his comrade's throat. "For Odin and Nordgaard!" he shouted, revealing his face for the first time.

"Ketil!" exclaimed Hogar, scarcely able to believe it was he. "So it was a kenning of yourself you meant by the play on the words 'kettle' and 'scald.' "

The skald laughed heartily.

"Did you not know my voice?" he asked. "Or at least, this hawk beak of mine? Mount up, lad, and let us begone from here."

With Hogar astride the bay, leaving the lancer's corpse to redden the snow, Ketil and his young lord regained the road and turned their horses in the direction chosen by the skald.

"This road follows the seacoast," Ketil told him. "At Koben you will find a ship. You must take passage from the Nordland. Meanwhile I ride—" The skald's breath quickened as he saw the patrol ahead.

"Vandir!" he cried, wheeling the stallion. "Be quick, lad! We are seen. Make a run for it!"

Hogar saw it would profit them nothing to stand against eight horsemen with long spears, only to fall in the end. The patrol had spotted his Asyr metal, and was riding them down hard. He turned the gelding.

"Make haste, lad! Retreat is sometime the better part of valor, say I. You are destined for greater things than taking a spear through the body on this lonely road. At the gallop!" Kicking their mounts, they raced breakneck down the road with the pound of hooves in their ears, hearts pounding in their throats. Riding close, Ketil shouted over the thunder of the galloping horses.

"Not far yonder is a snow-covered thicket to hide in. Dismount when I tell you, before the patrol clears the bend behind us. Lie low till the Vandir are out of earshot. I ride to rally the jarls in the queen's cause against Hothir.

"War it is, lad; to put you, Helmer Bloodsword's rightful heir, upon the Raven Throne. Hothir must be stopped! Here, take this purse. Make your way to Koben. Stay at the Blue Dolphin till I join you. Wait two days, no more. If I am not come by then— Now! *Quickly!* Here's the thicket. We part here, lad. The gods speed you!"

Hogar tossed Ketil the reins as he rolled from the saddle. From the thicket he called out, "Odin ride with you!" as Ketil thundered down the road leading the big bay. Well past the spot, Ketil dropped the gelding's reins. He knew the riderless bay would turn about to head home and foul the tracks, causing his pursuers enough momentary confusion for him to cross safely into desolated Skaane. There, in Queen Ermengard's homeland, he would find the first of those he sought.

III

The Dweller
in the Woods

Fjaerlda reined her mare as she approached the first destination on her errand for her sister the queen. From the wain-rutted road she had traveled hard, doggedly skirting the craggy Nordland seacoast, a private lane led through a small forest. Here, set deep in a stand of pines that rose majestically above the highest chimney pot, spread a great estate. The gatehouse was fallen in and abandoned; beyond was a chieftain's hunting lodge of timber and stone.

Entering the gate, the hunchback walked her mount slowly with sword drawn, as though something sinister was about to befall her. Past the gate, she put the mare into a sudden charge, sword point extended above the animal's ears and well beyond its muzzle. There was a tinkling of shattered glass as the barrier of the illusion was broken. Reining up, Fjaerlda again slowly walked the mare. Instead of a great estate, there now lay before her the smoldering ruins of a burnt-out steading.

Again the charge at sword point; again the tinkling of shattered glass. Before her now rose the ramparts of an ancient fortress. Through the massive gates, with the heavy clip-clop of iron-shod hooves striking upon stone, came a body of mounted yellow-haired women warriors armed with spears and swords, their battle girdles and breastplates of silver and bronze, and winged helmets flashing in the moonlight.

Again Fjaerlda put the mare into a gallop, sword point extended as before; again the tinkling of shattered glass; the third illusion vanished as had the two before it. In its stead was a craggy rise of barren rock, exposing the dark sea-carved mouth of a cave, at the lip of which a lion stood paused to yawn its intention of bedding down for the night.

Fjaerlda again urged the mare; again the shattering of glass at sword point. The fourth illusion dissolved in a like manner. Before her now, on a crude bench by the doorway of a forest hut, sat an old man skinning a plump hare for his supper. His long gray beard kept getting in the way as he worked. His soiled blue robe was embroidered with runes and magical symbols. His long gray locks hung about his shoulders in tangled disarray.

"Welcome, Ugly Cygnet," said the Wizard of Lom. "Behold your supper. I have been expecting you. What greeting bring you from the Swan Maiden? But you can impart all that as you transform this little fellow into a delectable ragout." He eyed her warily. "You *can* cook, can you not? It's so hard for me to remember everything. I weary of my own culinary delights. Cooking by magic has its limitations; nothing compares to a woman's touch with wine and herbs. By the by, Fjaerlda, did you enjoy the illusions I cast up for your amusement? All real, you know; a bit of the past, a glimpse of the future. As long as one knows how to break the barrier, no harm can come. I'm pleased that you remembered. Not knowing, or forgetting, can prove hazardous, even fatal. Come, let us go in. You can talk to me while you cook."

"O Great Wizard, lucky will I be to get a word in," said Fjaerlda, looking up at him impishly, "if you hold not your tongue. It is loose in the middle and waggles on both ends, O Seer-of-All."

After seeing to the mare, she put aside her byrnie and her sword and began preparing supper. While she did so, she related the events that had transpired so recently at Grimmswold; of Jarl Hothir, who now called himself king; of Hogar, proscribed for life, an outlaw on the run; of Ketil the Skald, and where he rode, and who it was he rode to find; of Ermengard, now Queen of Nordgaard, and the boon she asked of her sister; of the killings done, and the slayings yet to come, until on the Raven Throne at last there sat the rightful king.

After supper, the wizard took down a harp that hung on the wall of the humble one-room hut. Fjaerlda strummed the melody of a lay she had composed long ago at Skaane Hall, the while he spread the table with sand foretelling the past.

"Well do I remember that song," said the wizard wistfully, "and the old days when Ogmund was King of Skaane, and you and your sister were young."

Fjaerlda nodded and kept playing.

"You called Ermengard 'Swan Maiden' then."

" 'Twas but a game we played as girls. Nay, I have not come to speak of that," said Fjaerlda, "but of sorcery and treason—"

"And a hunting accident twenty years past, that at long last begins to smell of murder," he finished for her.

"You read my very thoughts as though I were casting runes," the hunchback whispered in awe. The Wizard of Lom smoothed the sand he had spread on the table. When he spoke, his voice was charged with magic.

"Behold what is writ upon the sand."

Fjaerlda saw the sand become a mirror of water. Rings rippled outward from its center, like a pool into which a pebble is dropped. The mirage reflected the wizard's face as he bent over it, peering intently.

"O Mirror of Truth," he intoned, "reveal to us the secret of the hunt, twenty long years gone."

Fjaerlda gazed deeply into the still surface of the mirage. What she saw caused her to cry aloud. It was the cold-blooded slaying of brother by brother, conjured out of the long dead past by the Wizard of Lom. . . .

Stepping forth from concealment in the canebrake where he had lain in ambush, crossbow cocked, awaiting his prey, a tall, yellow-maned and bearded hunter strode to where the man he had just slain lay facedown in a pool of blood. A feathered quarrel protruded from a ghastly hole in the dead man's skull behind the right ear. The tall hunter crouched down to examine the death wound. A secret smile played about the corners of his mouth, the cruelty of it hidden by the soft yellow beard. A dark look beetled his craggy brows, a look of both satisfaction and excitement from bringing down his kill with a well-placed bolt. He turned his victim over, and looked with cold eyes upon the dead face of his own brother. Then he rose, waving both arms to summon help.

Fjaerlda grasped the wizard's arm.

"Ermengard's dream!" she whispered. The wizard nodded.

"Now you, too, know the face of the hunter," he said. Her owlish eyes went wide with the sudden knowledge.

"Hothir!"

The name was scarcely audible on her lips. The wizard took her hand and pressed it gently.

"True, true. Only in Ermengard's recurrent dream the hunter was faceless," he told her. "She never was sure until the banishment of her son was made known to her."

"Hothir!" Fjaerlda spat the hated name. "Surely, his motive for murder was more than lusting after Helmer's new-wed bride, already with child?"

"Sooth," said the Seer-of-All. "He lusted after the Raven Throne. Ambition and greed drove him to murder his brothers. But Hothir's lust for Ermengard took him down the dark path into dabblings with black magic."

"You mean Hothir seduced my sister by sorcery?"

Again the wizard nodded. "Yet in her secret heart, Ermengard was never his. Which accounts for her recurrent dream of Helmer slain." He made a pass with his hands over the sand. "Attend closely, Fjaerlda," he urged.

As one mirage dissolved into another, the hunchback next saw a portion of the deer forest she remembered from childhood. Beyond it, over the treetops, rose the stronghold of her Rhenish father, Ogmund, King of Skaane. There in the forest under a great spreading oak, she saw her sister Ermengard lying in the final throes of labor. The mirage, she knew, was a part of Ermengard's recurrent dream . . .

The heavens clashed with lightning and echoed the

roll of Thor's thunder cart as Ermengard brought forth her firstborn, unattended save for a gray wolf-bitch that licked her hand and bit the cord. With the birth cry, a red-haired boychild stood forth from his mother's womb hero-born, full clad in shining ring armor. From the forest depths came three gray-mantled Weirds with hoods drawn over their faces, bearing a wondrous sword graven with ravens and rist with elfin runes. They bent low with whisperings to the young mother; they crooned over the newborn bairn. In his right hand they placed the wondrous Ravensword as his birth gift. They cast the runes to choose him a name. From the distaff of spun flax carried by one, they drew out the bairn's life threads and tied the knots of destiny . . .

Fjaerlda clutched the sage's arm; in her mind she heard the cry of an eagle, and in the Old Tongue the words *"Hogar be he named."*

With that the three Weirds turned and left as they had come. Presently by another way from the forest, there came four grief-laden karls bearing the slain body of their young lord on a blazoned shield. Ermengard mouthed a scream as the retainers lowered the shield with its sorrowful burden beside her where she lay . . .

In her mind, Fjaerlda heard Ermengard cry out weeping, *"Oh, Helmer, Helmer!"*

It was then the yellow-maned and bearded hunter strode from the forest. At the sight of the byrnie-clad bairn, the hunter drew his sword. As the boychild stepped forth armed they were met in a fierce clash of iron on iron. The hunter staggered under a telling thrust, and fell slain. Ermengard clasped her newborn son to her breast; the byrnie became a swaddling cloth, the sword an infant's rattle. The child mewled, and Ermengard gazed through her tears upon the dead face of her lord husband . . .

Again in her mind, Fjaerlda heard her sister weeping, *"Oh, Helmer, Helmer!"* The strange mirage dissolved into nothingness. There remained only the table spread with sand.

The Wizard of Lom broke the silence.

"Ermengard's dream will trouble her no more," he said. "Now tell me—bother! I keep forgetting things—

tell me, what is the boon your queen sister asks of you?"

"To seek out Starulf," Fjaerlda told him, "and bring him word that Ermengard of Skaane—for so he will remember her—enlists his aid in righting a great wrong; to raise an armed host against the false-king Hothir, and place her son, the true heir, upon the Raven Throne."

"The Old Warrior would leave his place amongst the feasting valiant in Valhalla to be of service to Ermengard," mused the wizard. "Even as I; albeit I am no man of arms. Well, Fjaerlda, shall I produce him out of thin air, an it please you?" Rising from the table, the sage made a sign toward the door, now closed against the darkening night. He cried out harshly, and the door stood open.

"Starulf! Your presence is commanded!"

Lightning lit the night. And in the hut doorway there stood the ring-mailed figure of a tall, black-mantled Rhenish warrior of old; laden with years and bearded gray, he wore the blazon of the House of Skaane. From under the bull-horned helmet, his old eyes flashed boldly. He stood a moment not saying a word, then strode to the table.

"Who calls Starulf?" the Old Warrior demanded gruffly.

"Is he dead, then?" whispered the hunchback with a shiver; for the armored figure before them shone with an eerie transparency, as though summoned from the grave.

"Nay," said the wizard. "I have called forth his mental image. He appears now in his shadow form as he sees himself in memory." To the mantled warrior he said, "I, the Seer-of-All, have summoned you, Starulf. Ermengard of Skaane, now Queen of Nordgaard, enlists your service."

Starulf's sword hand went swiftly to his hilt.

"Who would harm Ermengard of Skaane?" he cried. The sword at his side was halfway out of its scabbard as he spoke. Prompted by the wizard, Fjaerlda related the burthen of her errand, and told of the events leading to Hogar's banishment. The Old Warrior's eyes blazed from under his horned helm and fixed themselves intently upon her own. When she had delivered the gueen's message, he shot his hilt home and spoke gruffly as before.

"When Skaane fell before the Vandir and the Fire Lords, I swore on Ogmund's howe that whenever called upon, I would defend his daughters to the death. Then I had the strength of ten. My prowess was legend. But now I am an old man—" His voice quavered; his throat rattled with phlegm. Fjaerlda beheld an eerie change come over the byrnie-clad figure before her. Instead of the great Rhenish hero of Ogmund's reign, the conjured shadow wraith became that of the humble karl he now was, living in obscurity, the self-appointed watchdog of the burnt-out walls of Skaane Hall.

"Alas, what can an old caretaker do to aid the Queen of Nordgaard?" he asked unhappily. "Even if Ermengard were not now queen, what can this old warrior do? My sword arm has lost its cunning."

"Once it was told," said the wizard, "how your genius for strategy was unequaled. What of that, Starulf? Has your head lost its cunning as well? Queen Ermengard sends for a chieftain she can trust to lead her army against the false-king."

"Is there an army, then?"

"There will be. For you, Starulf, shall levy one!" the wizard exclaimed.

"In the heat of battle, Hogar of Valhelm shall be your good right arm." Fjaerlda's voice was exultant. "Don your armor and helm again, Old Warrior!" she cried.

Starulf's old eyes blazed with the glory not yet forgotten; an old war horse answering the battle cry. With Fjaerlda's words, there came again the eerie change; he stood once more byrnie clad, drawn sword in hand.

"Sound the lurs!" he roared. "Tell the queen I ride in her service. Tell Hogar Helmer's son I sing him of Bloodsword, his doughty sire:

Storm the walls, and carry the moat;
Or tear the lion out of Valhelm's coat!"

Without another word, the Old Warrior vanished as he had come. The open door of the hut stood empty a moment, then swung shut. For a long while the wizard and the hunchback remained silent, absorbed in their thoughts.

"Come, Fjaerlda," he said gently at length, for he saw she was moved by all she had witnessed. "We know what we must do, and speedily, ere the queen's cause is lost. Where is your trysting place with Ermengard? Bother my forgetfulness!"

"She awaits me at Arn."

"The fortress of the Red Swan," he murmured, remembering. " 'Tis well. How many shields defend her?"

"A hundred battle maidens."

"Get you then to Arn posthaste," cried the wizard, his eyes bright with the adventure. "As for myself, I ride at once to Skaane to fetch Starulf in the service of his queen. The old rogue by now has gone back to sleep."

"Ride, did you say?" asked Fjaerlda, puzzled. The stable had been empty when she saw to her mare.

"Aye, little cygnet. On the wings of night," said the Wizard of Lom. Fjaerlda strummed the harp strings, as though resolving her mind with the chord. About to say something as she put the harp aside, she saw the door open slightly of itself. She was aware of a soft whispering sound, like a soughing breath of wind. The door closed then, as though someone invisible had stolen quickly out into the night. Fjaerlda looked over at the kindly old man in his chair. Where the rush light should have cast his shadow, none was there. She knew his shadow self was gone from his body, riding the wings of night to Skaane.

The little hunchback stood slack-mouthed in wonder a moment. Girding on her armor and sword, she closed the door of the hut behind her, went to saddle her mare, and rode hard from Lom Woods to Arn.

At Grimmswold keep, in the early hours before dawn, Hothir Longtooth rose up from his shut-bed in a rage at the word brought him by the shaved-pate Klavun Thorg.

"What mean you, shaman, by these unseasonable tidings?" The sorcerer louted low before his liege as he spoke.

"All is even as I have said, master. The queen has departed Grimmswold. Even now, my familiars tell me, she makes her way posthaste to Arn, seeking sanctuary with Queen Astrith of the Swans."

"Surely she rides not alone," said Hothir with a scowl. "Who then of my company rides in her train?"

"Ari Oxmain, for one."

"That one-eyed traitor!" cried the false-king bitterly. "Of all my shield karls, did I wis Ari Oxmain ever true to his sworn oath. Let him go, then, and may it be his bane. Who else rides with the queen?"

"I know not their names, master," Klavun Thorg answered. "Only that they number a full score and ten."

"Then sound the lurs!" Hothir commanded. "Roust every man jack from his bed, and to arms! Here, shaman; busk my byrnie. Summon Rorik Bloodaxe to me at once. Say I ride not after the wayward queen, but to Nordgaard; there by strength of arms will I sit the Raven Throne!"

IV

The Weird of the Gods

Past the snow-piled thicket where the outlawed king's thane lay concealed, the Vandir horsemen rode hard. As the pounding hooves receded, Hogar brushed off the snow and appraised his surroundings. The craggy seaward side of the road, rising above where he stood, was naked rock. The steep, rugged coastline thrust granite fists up at the glowering sky and fell in sheer cliffs to the sea below.

Hogar knew that by now, warriors with whom he had grown up would be turned out in force against him at Hothir's command to ruthlessly run him to earth, a hunted outlaw. Beyond the Asyr border, sharp-eyed Vandir lancers patrolled the Marches. He chose to avoid the Koben road and make his way over the crags. Quickly scaling the jagged rocks, firm of foot and well booted, he made it to the top of the nearest rise. He lay on his belly, his eyes following the curve of a half-hidden cove below, where a black promontory jutted into the frothing surf at the end of a sea-licked finger of sand.

It was from here he first spotted the sea cave and climbed down to where its mouth opened on a flat shelf of rock that protruded like a pouting lower lip. Hogar crawled deep inside the cool darkness, grateful for the shelter the cave afforded, and surrendered to the spent feeling that welled up within him. Much had happened overnight since leaving Grimmswold; the long hours of hard riding and fighting for his life had finally taken their toll on his strength. He lay on the cold floor of the cave, with his great bearskin cloak pulled about him. It was a while before he sensed a presence other than his own within the cave.

Turning cautiously on one side, so he could draw his broadsword, Hogar peered into the half darkness. Of a sudden, he was filled with apprehension; he grasped the hilt and silently inched the blade from the scabbard in readiness against the unseen thing that shared the unlit cave. His first thought was he had entered the lair of some wild beast. Bears and cave lions were known to roam the Marches. But there was no fresh spoor. Instead, a sea-wrack stench pervaded the cave—or was it the scent of some loathsome sea troll about to return? Faint at first, the stench grew stronger.

As his eyes compensated for the darkness, Hogar saw the source of the sea stench. In the far recesses of the cave, a heavy grayish mist billowed up from a wide and jagged crevice in the floor near where he lay. He shuddered to think a few more steps in the dark would have hurled him to his death. The noxious vapor made him feel drugged. He needed air. He would move toward the mouth of the cave. It was then he saw something unbelievable. His senses told him he was hallucinating. Either that, or he was awake within an ensorceled dream. He could not bring himself to believe what he saw and heard. . . .

Not since Ragnarok had such things been seen!

The gods were slain, he reminded himself. They no longer existed—except in the staves of the skalds. The keening voice audible in the cave was but the woeful cry of the wind, howling up the creviced passage from the sea below . . . that, and the sob of the surf breaking upon the rocky shore.

Yet even as he argued all this to himself—awake or bewitched; whichever, he knew not—Hogar became aware of a weird glamour that shone through the billowing mist, revealing the presence of the very gods whose existence he denied. Materialized in armor and trappings of an age long past, they sat silently enthroned in awesome splendor—silent since Ragnarok.

On the highest seat of all, raised above the others as befitted the chief of the gods, sat one-eyed Odin, bearded gray in shining armor; his golden helm was plumed with eagles' wings. On his shoulders intimately perched were a pair of ravens. In one hand was grasped his great spear. A round battle shield resting against one knee bore his blazon of three golden horns.

Seated next below Odin was red-bearded, mighty Asa-Thor, with his foe-destroying hammer held ready; below Thor in turn, sat one-handed Tyr, his braided yellow hair crowned with stars. Lastly, dolphin-helmed Ægir sat leaning on his three-tined sea spear.

On yet a lower tier stood a glowing forge, attended by a swart half-dwarf, half-elfin figure in yellow, puffing a great bellows. Close by, an anvil awaited the iron bar the hybrid creature was heating to a malleable redness.

Entrapped in this eerie enchantment—if sorcery it was—Hogar beheld himself rise from the floor of the cave and stand sword in hand facing the silent gods. Above the keening wind, there arose a chanting in the strident voice of a woman he at first could not see. Presently, half-shadowed in the eldritch light, he made out a voluptuous female figure seated high on a witching stool. Her flowing golden hair partially clothed her nakedness.

That she was the Weird of the Gods, he was certain; still he denied her existence as well as that of the gods in whom he no longer believed. In his fey trance he heard the Volva chant in the Old Tongue a prophecy of his days to come.

"Hogar Helmer's son, king's thane, true heir to the Raven Throne; outlawed atheling of the Asyrfolk sprung god-born from Odin's seed; one day Lord of the Asyr; son of Bloodsword, stand thou forth!

"KNOW THEE, thou wert goaded into drawing the false-king's falchion from the oak. By plans well-laid, and a warlock's trick, wert thou proscribed and banished to serve evil ambition and greed.

"KNOW THEE, vengeance shall be thine against the false-king Hothir, who slew thy father and took his bride.

"KNOW THEE, the son of thy loins shall sit the Raven Throne as king in thy stead; and his son, and his son's son after him, shall rule in Nordgaard. Thy throne awaits thee elsewhere; for thou shall fare afar to the Four Reaches of the World. Henceforth, Hogar

Bloodsword be thou known! Lion, Dragon, Eagle, Warlock, Caldron, Stone, Spear, Sword, and Ring shall thou encounter. Thy fame as a swordsman shall proceed thee wheresoever thou may venture. Thy good fortune is borne on a fair wind to far-away and splendored Tarthiz, where there shall await thee a great winged ship flying thy standard."

The eldritch light dimmed; the awesome tableau of the silent gods faded; and the cave was filled with the roar of the sea. Through a breech in the mist, above the glowing forge, there appeared a black-hulled longship with its oars shipped, the gunwales hung with bright painted battle shields; its single mast flying three ravens on a scarlet sail that bellied in the wind. Hogar found himself irresistibly drawn to the galley, felt the sturdy oak planking of the deck underfoot. Yet he knew he remained in the cave, as above the roar of the wind and the sea he again heard the strident chant of the Volva.

"Behold, Hogar the Asyr, how thou dost walk thy longship's deck. The angry sea beneath thee swells; the storm clouds strike. 'Tis witchcraft makes the sea to roil. Not e'en the gods themselves could weather such a gale. Above yon point on Utgarth's shore, in mounded howe thy father lies. There seek snug harbor ere thou founder. The wind grows stronger, and moves the sea to fury now; thy deck is awash; thou canst not see, blinded by the witch storm. The stalwart warriors, pirates born, who ply thy ship with mighty oars, stand bailing. Salt stings their eyes; their stout arms fail; their oars stand still against the swell; their backs and hearts are breaking. Ask no quarter of the gods who cast thee now on angry waters for thy disbelief. Yet behold how the billows calm. The gods are appeased by thy offering. For thou dost offer up thyself on the horns of the storm.

"KNOW THEE, thou shall battle against great odds, and win both sword and ring of wondrous power. The sword, with ravens graved, shall make thee king; the other, Odin's ring, shall make thee one day Master of Runes."

The Volva paused in her chanting of the strange

prophecy; for the iron bar glowed red in the bellows-blown coals. The yellow half dwarf placed the sparkling bar on the anvil. With one great hammer blow on the hot metal, he wrought forth a magnificent falchion which he held aloft, flaming in his gloved hand. The Volva resumed her chant.

"Behold the sword of thy grandsire, Thorir Treefoot, Lord of the Asyr! Behold the RAVENSWORD, dwarf-forged and elfin-fashioned of iron and flame by Hrokk the Halfling. Behold three ravens graven black are perched upon the battle blade, oft crimson-beaked by their appetite for the flesh and blood of the slain. Behold Thorir Treefoot's raven mark, rist between the elfin runes from point to hilt that knew his mighty hand. The bloody dying-day he fell upon the field of Skaane, then did the RAVENSWORD fall from the sight of all men."

The half dwarf thrust the flaming replica of the true King's Falchion into a water trough beside the forge. Sword, anvil, forge, half dwarf, and longship vanished in a hiss of steam; only the Weird of the Gods remained. Seated on the witching stool amidst the billowing mist, with her long hair flowing like molten gold between her voluptuous breasts and thighs, thus spake the Volva:

"The gods counsel thee, Hogar Bloodsword; heed thou their rede. Great will be thy gain if thou dost. *Follow thy weird*. Quest for the RAVENSWORD, and with it wreak thy vengeance! For thus were the threads of thy destiny spun out and tied by the Norns who named thee, a bairn newborn amidst the thunderclaps and lightning crash, and the scream of an eagle.

"GO THOU, THEREFORE; seek out the RUNE-RING OF ODIN, lost on the field at Ragnarok.

"KNOW THEE, this is thy quest: Go thou beyond the Finnamark, to the Cold Waste of the Sorcerers who dwell where many-mansioned Asgarth once did stand; beyond the ice-troll caves, where winds the River Skaa, where flows the Sea of Nemed. There, in rune-built Nardath-Thool, are kept these treasures thou must seek.

"KNOW THEE, for the RAVENSWORD thou shall

shed both tears and blood. With it thou shall win a throne, and a breathtaking queen to bear thy sons.

"KNOW THEE, for the RUNE-RING OF ODIN, thou must best both sorceress-queen and dragon's spawn, in the sinistrous city of thy quest.

"VOW THOU, now, Hogar Bloodsword, to follow thy weird with the blessings of the gods. Henceforward, deny them not! Solemnly swear after me, as I tell thee. . . ."

The eldritch light faded as the Weird of the Gods came to the end of her prophecy, and the oath was taken. Hogar found himself standing wide awake, sword in hand, alone in the half darkness of the cave. The vision he had so vividly beheld was gone with the gray mist. All had vanished, leaving only the pungent smell of the sea permeating the cave.

He looked about him in bewilderment, pondering what strange spell had brought him face-to-face with the Weird called the Volva, and the awesome silent gods themselves.

Of one thing he was certain. The crevice remained; it was real. Below the jagged hole in the cave's floor, a brackish pool clogged with sea wrack slushed back and forth with the ebb and flow of the tide; it was from this, he realized, that the sea stench had risen in the noxious mist of his fey trance. He stood looking down upon the murky waters, alone in an empty cave with his troubled thoughts, and a solemn vow to the gods to fulfill the Volva's prophecy.

He was not alone for long.

A roar from the mouth of the cave gave Hogar but scant warning of the prowling cave lion's presence.

V

Fomors!

As the great cat sprang, Hogar braced himself in a crouch on the far side of the crevice, his broadsword grasped firmly in both hands, the blade held upward for the thrust like a short spear.

The cave lion had only its dinner in mind. It leaped for the kill, momentarily unaware of the jagged opening in the cave floor. It raked the air with its talons, catlike, in a futile effort to gain traction and avoid the gaping hole that suddenly yawned beneath its contorted body. From the cave's mouth to its prey, the lion's leap was a long one, but not long enough. It was short of bridging the crevice by inches. As the big cat twisted upward, Hogar's carefully timed thrust ripped open its exposed belly. The lion fell screaming through the yawning hole, with its bloody entrails spilling. It was dead before the gutted carcass broke the murky waters of the tide pool below.

Wiping the blade on his breeks, the outlawed thane sheathed his sword and stepped quickly to the mouth of the cave and peered out. Satisfied the lion had been hunting alone—neither a female nor a pride was in evidence—Hogar threw his bearskin over his shoulders and put the hairsbreadth moment behind him. Rather than risk further attack from predators on the prowl amongst the fells, he made his way down toward the cove he had seen from the craggy rise.

The black promontory jutted into the surf below him. A ribbon of smoke rose from behind it on the strand, but the headland obscured the fire and whoever was cooking over it. The soft seabreeze brought the savory aroma of roasting venison to his nostrils.

He had not eaten since the night before, but his hunger was tempered by caution.

What if it were a patrol? What would a patrol be doing on the beach, though? What would they have done with their horses? There was no possible way a horse, not even the most nimble-footed Asyr pony, could negotiate those crags and boulders down to the sand.

Who, then?

A beach fire suggested fishermen. If so, he could bargain for passage in a fishing sixern to Utgarth, across the Cat's Throat, instead of continuing on shank's mare to Kōben. But fishermen would be cooking part of their catch, if anything; it was deer meat he smelled on the fire, not fish.

It was well on to supper time, and the aroma from the beach fire was tantalizing. He looked at the sun. It was halfway down the sky and would soon be falling behind the World's Edge. He had no choice but to vacate the cave, with but one way out, save for the drop through the crevice to a quick death, should some prowling beast venture in during the fast approaching night. He had two immediate problems to face. Food and shelter. The Marches were not grazing land. Where had the deer come from? The nearest reindeer herd was at Grimmswold, leagues away. Hogar smiled at the thought of some reaver poaching a stag from under Hothir's nose—

That was it, of course.

Reavers!

Hogar's hand moved instinctively to his hilt.

Sea wolves! Marauding barbarians who looted and slew for the sheer joy of it. Like the dreaded Fomors.

Fomors!

From boyhood, he had heard tales of how Fomorian pirates plundered the Nordland coast villages and steadings, burning byres and murdering tenants, carrying off livestock, and sometimes the womenfolk as well in their cattle raids, as they called these farings. All the way from Tor-a'Mor on the Green-Island-Under-the-Waves, as the Asyrfolk called the Fomorland below the World's Edge. From far beyond the pirate-infested

Orkna Ey, the seal islands off the northernmost tip of the Kymric Wilderland, they came plundering, cutting a swath of blood. Ogres and giant trolls they were, so it was whispered amongst the cotters, with animal heads to frighten a body half to death before they slit his throat and took his cows or sheep, or his woman.

If the deer roasting in the cove was soon to fill the bellies of a Fomorian pirate band, Hogar mused, it meant their galley was beached, perhaps needing repairs.

He grinned. The Volva had sworn him to a quest, foresaw that he would rove the Four Reaches of the World to fulfill his destiny. Now the gods offered him a ship for quest faring.

He moved warily down to the far side of the point, taking care not to dislodge any loose shales. Strange, he thought; no sign of a lookout. The pirates apparently knew this rugged cove well—if indeed they were pirates—not to fear a surprise attack from the crags above. A few yards from the beach, Hogar had his answer; the lookout he had failed to spot seemingly materialized out of thin air. A woad-dyed, pelt-clad Fomorian in a wolf's-head helm towered over him with a thrusting spear pressed to his gut. An answering hail to his captor's hair-raising yell came from the beach; Hogar was disarmed and urged along with gruff Fomorian monosyllables and an occasional prod, till they gained the strand.

A long black galley was beached high on the pebbled cove, where fifty frightful Fomors lay sprawled about a driftwood fire. A reindeer carcass turned on a spit, dripping fat and savory juices onto the sputtering charcoal that sent tongues of fire licking up the big black face of rock.

Tales of Fomors being ogres and giant trolls were easily believed on seeing them. They were frightful of mien, averaging seven feet or more in height. Each marauder wore a wolf's-head helm, and a wolfskin across one shoulder, with a murderous long-knife and a broadsword hung from his warrior's girdle. All were shod in coarse boots, midcalf high.

The lookout announced himself and his captive

loudly, and shoved Hogar toward the fire. He halted him before a great ogre of a pirate, bearded black, with a ghastly sword scar across his sightless left eye, where he stood warming his back at the fire. A nod from this formidable cutthroat dismissed the lookout. He surrendered Hogar's weapons and withdrew.

"Well, Nordsman," queried the one-eyed Fomor in passable Nordish, "what brings you to my camp?" Hogar recognized the resonant voice that had answered the lookout's halloo.

"The inviting smell of roast deer meat on an empty stomach," he said with a bold grin. Untying the pouch that hung from his baldric as he spoke, he let the contents clink against the palm of one hand. "For the chief I would serve," he said, tossing the pouch to the one-eyed pirate, who caught it deftly in one hand and emptied its contents into the other.

"Damn my eyes! Ten gold rings, and a dozen halves!" he exploded with greed. "Who are you to have such a purse?"

"An outlaw, proscribed and banished, O Chief of the Fomors," Hogar told him truthfully, but with guile. "There is more gold where that comes from." Avarice gleamed in the cutthroat's good eye.

"Carve the meat!" he shouted. "And broach a cask! Sit, Nordsman. Here, beside me. While we eat and drink, you will tell me about this gold hoard at which you hint. How are you called, outlaw?"

"I am Hogar Bloodsword."

"A sea wolf, by Cromm Cruaich! Or my name isn't Lon Thoddrach. You at the spit! Fetch Hogar Bloodsword a juicy joint along with mine, and a cask of the water of life to wash it down."

As they gorged themselves Hogar spun out a yarn worthy of his warrior-bard mentor. After a few drafts of poteen, he was inclined to believe it himself. He told how he had been marooned by his mutinous crew on this very cove, five days since, left without rations or water, but allowed to keep his arms, and forced to watch his own galley sailed away from under his very nose, how he sought shelter in a sea cave, and lastly, how he had killed a cave lion that attacked him as he lay on the cold floor of the cave, trying to sleep on an empty stomach.

"And I would have eaten the carcass raw," Hogar boasted, "had it not fallen through a crevice. I was that hungry—and still am."

Lon Thoddrach's roar of laughter ended in a great belch.

"Damn me!" he said, wiping his greasy fingers on his beard. "But get to the part where you have all this gold stashed away."

"How is it you speak such good Nordish?" Hogar asked.

"That is another story," said Lon Thoddrach, with a great show of teeth intended for a smile. They gleamed white against the blackness of his beard. "Right now, Hogar Bloodsword, as you choose to call yourself, you are telling me yours. Go on."

Hogar continued his fabrication, borrowing from the Volva's prophecy. His facile mind wove a bold plan as he spoke; and so he began to spin the threads of the daring quest for a sword, a ring, and a sorceress-queen.

"The gold, O Chief of the Fomors," he lied glibly, "is well hidden, with no map save the one in my head. Kill me, Lon Thoddrach, you bloody reaver, and never will you find your way to the treasure vaults of Nardath-Thool."

"Nardath-Thool, is it? And no map, eh?" The one-eyed blue giant fingered his beard. "I once heard tell of a port by that name, a dwelling place of warlocks and dragons, it was said to be. Drink up, my bucko! Dragons and warlocks be damned! We sail for Nardath-Thool and your hoard of gold. And you, Hogar Bloodsword, shall chart our course, by Balor of the Evil Eye!"

Hogar took a long pull at the cask and passed it to the Fomor chief. The bait was taken. He had his ship!

"Let us drink on it, my blue-skinned friend. Half the gold of Nardath-Thool shall be yours, Lon Thoddrach, if ever we ship oars at the jetties of that warlock's nest. I swear it by Odin's good eye!"

"You dare mock me, Nordsman?" cried the pirate

chief, with a sour turn of mood. He cast Hogar a fierce look.

"You are no god, Fomor," said the redhead coolly. "If your gorge rises at my choice of oaths to swear by, hand me back my sword and we will soon see who is the better man."

"Let us not be hasty, Nordsman," said Lon Thoddrach. "Damn me! You and I could be friends, mate, if we but trusted one another better than I trust you with a sword in your hand." He roared at his own wit. "More meat, here, for both of us. Another cask! Now tell me more about the treasure we seek, while we eat and get drunk. Doubt me not, Hogar Bloodsword, or whoever you are. We sail to find your gold, come morning."

A ship! By Tyr, a ship!

Hogar's pulse leaped. No matter, a black-hulled Fomorian pirate galley instead of a sleek Nordland longship under his own command. He would sail as mate, with fifty fierce and frightful men led by this blue-skinned ogre at his side; he'd brave the perils of the Frozen Sea and storm the walls of that sinistrous city where ruled a sorceress-queen called Tha. Not for gold—nay, let this bloody reaver think there's gold! For the Ravensword and the rune-ring of Odin would he set sail on the morrow's tide!

Coolly, Hogar said, "Hand me my sword, Lon Thoddrach, that I may swear blood oath as vassal to his liege."

Hearing the turn of their talk, the drunken Fomor who served them spat beside where Hogar sat.

"Ye'll swear blood oath to an oar, Nordsman, when ye sail under my lash!" he said in passable Nordish, with a sneer. "I be the one ye'll take orders from at the oars. I'll have ye sweating and pulling the heart out o' ye, as is fitting for a stinking Nordlander dog."

"Stow it, Gwern," cried Lon Thoddrach with displeasure. "You sour my milk. No rower is flogged on my ship without my command; remember that, oarmaster though you be. Off with you, then, and have done with your truculence."

"Nay," grumbled Gwern. "Not till I have spit me a Nordlander dog on my blade."

"By Balor!" Lon Thoddrach roared. "Defy me, will you, you jetty scum, knowing the Nordsman is unarmed? Here, Hogar, if that be your real name—take your sword!"

As the outlawed thane again felt a hilt in his hand the Fomor chieftain rose, tossing a half-gnawed bone into the fire. "Fetch me my pipes!" he bellowed. "A brawl is brewing, lads! Stand away, and give the Nordsman room to breathe. Now let us see who spits who!"

Hogar tried his sword and stood facing his challenger, who had backed off to draw his own weapon. The pipes were quickly brought. Lon Thoddrach blew the goatskin full of air in one great breath, and primed the stops. A loud wailing arose as though the bag was filled with lovesick cats, as he skirled on the pipes of Tor-a'Mor. It was an eerie banshee wail, meant to put fear into the bellies of the foe and warm the cockles of the stout hearts rallying around the piper in the thick of the fray. Strangely, it was the Nordsman's pulse that quickened to the mad skirling beat and the oarmaster who was chilled by the cold glint in the fire-blue eyes of the outlawed thane facing him drawn, his tousled rusty locks falling about his shoulders like a red lion's mane.

Gwern cursed himself for a drunken fool to have provoked the Nordsman. He had the look of a master swordsman about him. But draw he must, or forever be shamed in the eyes of his shipmates. Gwern drew slowly, circling clear of his opponent's reach. Hogar, sensing his purpose, rushed him with his blade slashing, forcing Gwern to defend himself.

Slash! Parry! Counter!

Clang!

Gwern was no craven. He fought back blow for blow, but he had imbibed too much too quickly. He knew he was drunk. Unlike most Fomors, who fought like trolls under the influence of the creature, Gwern had no stomach for it. He retched as the fiery liquor rose in his throat, a billowing sea of bile. As he backed out of swordplay range, one hand raised to beg a moment's respite, his legs buckled under him. He crawled away, vomiting like a sick animal.

"By Balor and Bress!" cried Lon Thoddrach with disappointment. "I have not yet warmed up the tune." He looked at Hogar with admiration in his one eye. "I like the cut of your sail, Nordsman," he said with a fierce grin and a clap on the back. "Forget Gwern, mate. He will be too shamed to give you further trouble once he is sobered."

But Hogar natheless knew he had made an enemy on whom he must keep a weather eye.

VI

Witch Storm

Swiftly and silently, but for the steady dip of the oars, the long black galley sped through the choppy waters of the Cat's Throat, outward bound for the Nord Sea.

Some fifty-odd Fomorian pirates and one lone Nordlander with a rusty mane manned the ship. With their chieftain at the helm, they took their stints at the tholes. Those not pulling an oar saw to their weapons and trappings, burnishing metal bosses and sharpening iron blades and axes. There were other chores, like that of constantly bailing. All kept busy but one.

Gwern, the oarmaster, would normally have been treading the deck between the rowers amidships, cadencing the stroke and threatening the backs of any laggards with his knotted skeeg. But this dark morning found him leaning on the larboard rail of the stern deck, staring morosely into the galley's wake. Still slightly drunk from the night before, Gwern kept to the side for good reason, from time to time casting a malevolent eye on Hogar, where he sat lustily pulling on his oar.

"The time will come, by Cromm Cruaich!" muttered Gwern to himself, and spat contemptuously into the sea.

On the steerboard side of the stern, Lon Thoddrach stood at the helm, guiding the shallow, narrow-beamed raider through the hazardous shoals.

Well past the skerried waters, the weather changed. The squall struck without warning. It was as though the angry heavens had opened, loosing the torrent upon them that drenched both men and ship. The fierce wind split the single mast asunder; the heavy, square sail, which had been hoisted to spell the rowers, was torn from its rigging and carried away in shreds. Lon Thoddrach clung desperately to the steer oar, trying to ride out the storm, but the oarsmen were unable to make headway in the billowing sea that blinded them with salt spray and blotted out the sky. Hogar and his rowing mates were tossed like straws athwartship by the fury of the sea swelling over the side.

The galley was awash.

The men stood bailing.

Gaining his feet and clinging to anything he could grasp, Hogar fought the roiling waters pouring over the gunwales.

They were foundering!

He clenched his fists and shook them impotently against the rage of the gods. As if in answer, lightning split the sky, and Thor's thunder wheels rolled. Tyr ripped the heavens with a wind that moved the waters in great cresting swells.

"Odin damn you both! And the Volva!" Hogar cried out, no longer seeing; the salt was in his eyes, burning and blinding. 'Tis the prophecy she spoke in the sea cave come true, he thought futilely.

" 'Tis a witch storm!" he bellowed toward the sternpost, where the stalwart Fomor chieftain stood wrestling the tempers of the sea and sky with a helpless helm. "Take her about if you can. Make for the shelter of yonder point!"

Hogar rubbed the salt spray from his eyes for a bare moment, before the next wave hit the stern and washed over the helm, down the length of the ship. He saw Gwern coming toward him, weaving, clutching the lash, saw Lon Thoddrach struggling to hold the helm. He thought he heard the Fomor chieftain's shout; it was the roaring of the raging sea he heard, as a great rolling breaker struck the galley amidships, in a terrible cross current that threatened to capsize her. It spun him around as the skeeg struck him heavily on the head. The world went black inside his skull. His last conscious thought was of being washed over the side.

"Bail, damn your eyes!" shouted the Fomor chief to his panicked crew. "Gwern! Where are you, Gwern? You white-livered excrement, ship your oars, damn you! You can't row in this sea, you bloody fool! Bail, damn your eyes! We're foundering! Hogar! These are Nordland waters that rage about us. Call on your Nordland gods to spare us and our ship!"

A hand clutched him and clung as another wave hit.

"Is that you, Gwern?" yelled the spray-blinded Fomorian giant at the steer oar. "I can't hold this sea back alone. Help me steady the helm. Gwern! Answer me, damn your eyes! Is that you, Hogar? I command you to appease your Nordland gods!"

"It's Gwern," said the oarmaster, gasping out his words. He clung to his chieftain's arm for support. "The Nordlander dog was washed over the side when that towering wave took us amidships."

Lon Thoddrach rubbed the sea from his eyes with a growled curse. "Damn me! He it was, and his Nordland gods, that brought this evil down on us!" he cried out, grabbing his oarmaster's shoulder.

"Good riddance, say I," said Gwern. "See how suddenly the storm eases off? I tell you, my chieftain, it is good riddance!"

Lon Thoddrach scanned the sky, muttering to himself. A witch storm Hogar called it, shouting against the wind. And now, with the Nordsman washed over the side, the sea was calming. Were the gods appeased? Was death the penalty for damning the gods? He had heard Hogar cry out his blasphemy, saw him raise his clenched fists futilely at the sky.

By Balor and Bress! They had come perilously near going aground on the great jagged point yonder, with the salt of the raging sea in their eyes, blinding them. Lucky it was they had not, he told himself. It was called Loki's Rock. He knew well enough to avoid it like the plague. Jutting out from the Utgarth mainland like a giant's thumb, it was said to be the ensorceled haunt of demon trolls.

Utgarth!

By the gods, the witch storm had tossed the galley about like a pod in a pan, across the Cat's Throat!

"Oars out!" he shouted, looking over the still-restless but calming waters. "Take the helm, Gwern. I'm going forward." He called out as he passed those who stood bailing. "Keep a weather eye peeled for a redhead bobbing in the sea. Steerboard your helm!" he shouted aft; he felt his ship tack as Gwern brought it around. He stood at the bow, eagle-eyed as they circled.

"Hogar Bloodsword he called himself, did he?" muttered the Fomor chieftain. "By the Eye of Balor, he was no outlaw; neither rover nor reaver. He was a king's son, he was, if ever I saw one. It's a pretty ransom I've let slip through my bloody fingers, letting the lad get himself drowned. I should've chained him to the gunwale till we reached Tor-a'Mor. He thought we were off for Nardath-Thool, as I said we were last night in my cups. Eh! Nardath-Thool! And him with the only map engraved in his mind. I'll never find the gold without him, damn his eyes!"

The search was to no avail. At length Lon Thoddrach gave it up. We could circle forever and there would be no sight of him, he told himself. He turned to face the stern of his ship, bellowing, "Look alive, there! Mend that mast, and rig another sail!" He strode aft, shouting orders with every step.

"Gwern, you excrement, who taught you how to steer? I'll take the helm. Dip those oars, there! Gwern! Get their backs into it!" He put the helm about to face the open sea. "Keep bailing, there, damn your eyes! By Bress, how we shipped water! But we're afloat, lads, and I'm taking her into the Orkna Ey."

A cheer rose from every weary throat. The Orkna Ey meant snug harbor in a pirates' nest, with plenty of grog and wenches to pass the time, while the galley had her seams caulked and her hull tarred.

Thinking back to how he laid the butt of his skeeg hard against Hogar's head as the founderous wave struck, Gwern grinned evilly to himself.

"I said the time would come, by Cromm Cruaich!"

He spat into the sea.

VII

Runulf of Dorn

The field farthest from Dorn Hall extended to the edge of the cliff, on the seaward side above Loki's Rock; there a low dry wall had been laid of stones gathered in clearing the land. Not far below the cliff's edge, the jagged black boulders gave way to a long shelf of rock worn smooth by the relentless washing of the sea. Beyond this, the scarped cliff sloped down to a pebbled strand, where an aging dragonship long home from a-roving still lay in an old launching shed.

Dorn had never been an efficiently productive steading; its poverty began with its soil. Salted by sea air and poor at best, the fields were suited mostly to the growth of hay, for pasturing sheep and a milch cow or two. A few acres, cleared and planted in patches, yielded vegetables and enough grain for baking bread and brewing small ale. Most of the land was in forest, kept virgin by the thane for his hunting pleasure, and providing meat for the table.

The steading was neglected beyond belief, its longhouse a leaky ruin, except for the tower; the wattle-and-daub walls had not been whitewashed in years; its turf roof was a nesting place of mice and spiders. The byre and stables were a shambles of half-fallen-in roofs and moldering piles of fodder and manure. Thus they remained, thanks to the thane's pinch-fisted grudgery.

Near the cliff's edge, Hrapp the reeve stood appraising the damage wrought by the sudden storm. He was overseer of the thralls, numbering thirty-odd soil-bound wretches who provided labor in the fields and inside work to run the steading.

The field thralls idled about, knowing there would be no planting done now, not until the sun had dried out the soil enough to take the seed without it rotting. The plowshare had turned up numerous stones in the recently plowed furrows, now become puddles of muddy water. These stones Hrapp had the thralls carry and set in the dry wall at the cliff's edge, to keep them occupied.

It was in this way the naked body of a man was discovered. When looking down over the wall for a moment to watch the surf breaking against Loki's Rock, one of the thralls saw the body lying on the shelf below.

"Dead man!" he shouted in excitement. His fellows crowded about to peer curiously over the edge. Hrapp, too, saw the body.

"Some poor fisherman washed up by the storm," he said, and decided to let the tide return to the sea what it had given up.

And then he saw the body move.

"That man is alive!" he cried, and detailed four stalwart thralls to fetch him up the cliff.

"Press the water out of his lungs, and get him up safely," he ordered as they began the descent. "Then carry him to my hut. You there, boy! Run and tell my old woman to have a fire on the hearth to warm him."

It was many hours later when Hogar woke out of the deep sleep of exhaustion and felt the spoon of steaming pottage touch his lips. He accepted one wooden spoonful, then another; he could feel the warmth creep through his chilled bones under the pile of sheepskins as the thick meat and vegetable soup filled his empty stomach.

"Good. Eat. 'Twill make you strong." It was an older woman's kindly voice, repeating the same formula with every spoonful, as a mother coaxes a sick child to take food.

Hogar opened his eyes. The woman was elderly and heavy-bosomed; she wore the aproned wadmal smock and iron collar of a thrall. She smiled as she spoonfed him. He closed his eyes; it was an effort to keep them open. He felt weak, drained; his body ached.

"Good. Eat. 'Twill make you strong."

He took another mouthful. With the warmth came

the return of life to his veins; for this he was passively grateful; he sensed he had been close to death, a watery, drowning death. Tortured by memory, he hallucinated, saw the monstrous wave breaking. He cried out as it struck the ship . . .

"There, there," soothed the woman. "It is all right, now. You are safe here. Good. You have eaten it all. I'll get some more."

As he heard her move away from his pallet he was aware of a door opening. The whine of the wind and the chill of the night were shut out as the door closed.

A man spoke. "How is he, old woman?"

"He is awake now. He eats. I am filling the bowl again."

Hogar knew he was at his side bending over him before he opened his eyes to see a man in his middle years studying him with concern. Lines of toil were etched deep in the rugged, weather-beaten face above the graying yellow mustaches. His hair was cropped close; a gray cap streaked with fading yellow. He, too, wore a thrall's collar. His belted smock and leathery skin were all of a color, tanned by the sun and sea wind.

"You will be better now," he said. His kindly blue eyes held a smile.

"Where am I?" Hogar asked, wondering at the rude, unfamiliar surroundings.

"This is Dorn steading. I am Hrapp the reeve," was the friendly reply. "Half-drowned you were, washed up on Loki's Rock, when I found you. The field thralls brought you here to my hut. Mine and my old woman's. She is called Gerda. She made a pallet for you near the hearth, where it is warmer."

Gerda returned with the replenished bowl.

"Eat," she urged.

"Eat," echoed Hrapp. "Her good thick pottage will make you strong." He stood watching. When the bowl was emptied again, he said, "You were bruised and bleeding. We poulticed your wounds with herbs. 'Tis a wonder you were not pounded to pieces by the sea. The surf is brutal cruel in such a storm as we had. You were in Odin's palm, no question, not to be dashed to death against Loki's Rock."

"I thank you both for saving my life and caring for me as you have," said Hogar gratefully. "Who is your lord?"

"Runulf is thane here at Dorn," the reeve replied.

"Have you apprised him of my presence?"

"Aye. Rest now. Sleep, if you can."

"I will be up by the morrow," Hogar assured him. "I must work the soreness out of my body to get back my strength. I will help you in the fields."

"We will see," said Hrapp, "when the thane comes. Now 'twould be good for you to rest."

Hogar closed his eyes and heard the man and woman move away. He courted sleep but his mind was so a-churn, sleep would not come. He tried to relax, and lay on the pallet staring up at the exposed wattling under the thatched roof that formed the hut's ceiling, letting his thoughts tumble as they would. His head throbbed. Gingerly, he touched the lump behind his ear.

That craven dog, Gwern! he thought.

His whole body pained him. Gradually, his thoughts slipped away. He slept . . . and in his troubled dreaming, he felt the blow on the back of his head from the skeeg as the wave struck amidships; then he was being washed over the side and blacking out. The shock of the cold sea revived him. The weight of his weapons and trappings pulled him down. Struggling out of his bearskin, he let it float free. He tore at the buckles of his baldric and harness. With them loosed, his trappings and weapons fell away . . . his chest was bursting. He surfaced on the crest of a wave and filled his tortured lungs with quick gulps of air. He went under. He unstrapped his boots . . . finally, he managed to kick them off. The sea tore away his breeks. His lungs seemed to burst with pain. He was floating downward in a pool of darkness . . . sinking . . . sinking . . . Soft hands took his gently as the Storm Maidens of Ran appeared in a burst of bubbles, dragging him down . . . down . . . to the sound of their eldritch singing. . . .

He cried out and sat up wild-eyed, drenched with sweat. The room was suddenly cold as the door was held open. The chill air awakened him from his nightmare. He shivered, and covered his nakedness with a sheepskin.

In the doorway of the reeve's hut stood a man of gross and wolfish mien, whom Hogar took to be the Thane of Dorn. Behind him, a man-at-arms held a flaming brand against the night.

"Lord," mumbled Hrapp, tugging at his forelock as he held the door; Gerda dropped an awkward curtsy and a spoon at the hearthside where she stood as Runulf the Thane entered. A grumble from the man-at-arms with the torch was barely audible as the reeve shut the door on him in his haste to keep out the cold.

"So this is what the sea has washed up," said the thane sourly. "A young Thor, and naked 'twould seem, save for a sheepskin tucked about his loins. Who are you, Asyr?"

"How know you I am Asyr?" asked Hogar boldly, making no effort to rise.

"*I* lord it here, fellow. I am Runulf of Dorn. You are on my land, fed and sheltered by my reeve, who tells me you talk in your sleep; of Valhelm, of pirates and gold; of a ring, and a sword, and a sinking ship. You have a bold tongue. Answer the question. Who are you?"

Hogar instinctively disliked the man. He was coarse of manner and, judging by the food stains on his fur-lined robe, a glutton as well. There was a sinister glint to his strange yellow eyes.

"I am Asyr. Royal Asyr," was the proud reply. "I am Hogar of Valhelm, the king's thane, rightful-born atheling and someday King of the Asyr."

"Welcome, Hogar of Valhelm," said Runulf, extending his fat, hairy hand a-glitter with rings. "How is it the sea has cast you up on the rugged coast of Utgarth, at Loki's Rock?"

Hogar sensed something in the thane's look and manner that belied the sincerity of words and gesture. What matter? Runulf of Dorn would not have word of his banishment in so short a time. He took the hand proffered in friendship with private reservations, without fear of being held for ransom or sent home in chains.

"I was captured by Fomorian pirates," he recounted, partly in truth. "They stripped me of my weapons, trappings, and purse, and threw me over the side. They believed I had wrought the witch storm that nigh foundered their galley. The sea robbed me of my boots and breeks and tossed me naked on Loki's Rock, where your reeve found and befriended me." He gave Hrapp a dour look. "So I talk in my sleep, do I?"

"My reeve only performed his duty by making known your presence here," said Runulf. "Blame him not; for you did ask him yourself if I was apprised, which is proper. His hospitality, poor though it may be, has been given gladly. I now offer you mine."

"Being for the moment penniless, and without raiment as you see," Hogar replied, "I accept your hospitality gratefully, Runulf of Dorn. My sword would be at your service—at a price—had I a sword."

"Well spoken," said the thane. "Had you said otherwise, I would have thrown you back into the sea." He turned to Hrapp, addressing him sharply. "How is it you have not given him clothing?"

"How could I, lord," the reeve mumbled miserably, "when all I own is on my back?"

"Open the door," Runulf ordered. Hrapp obeyed. The man-at-arms holding the fire brand was waiting there, sword in one hand.

"Nels," Runulf said, "see that this lying rogue is clothed and armed. He is now in my service. You will be quartered with the others in the guardroom," he told Hogar curtly. "Take your sheepskin and go with Nels."

"Stay!" cried Hogar, flushed with anger. "You are quick to name me liar and rogue, it seems. If this be your hospitality, I prefer the sea. I am not yet your hired sword."

"You said yourself your sword was at my service at a price," said Runulf, arrogantly. "We will speak of wages when I send for you." He turned on his heel and was through the door.

Hogar seethed. He had been offered the thane's hospitality, then dismissed like the lowliest mercenary. Rising to follow Nels, he glowered, his thoughts dark.

"Look to yourself, Runulf of Dorn, when you place a sword in my hand, that its price be not your head!"

VIII

Starulf Rides Forth

The icy wind blew through the gutted walls of Skaane, as though heralding the appearance of the shadowy figure standing before the burnt-out ruins of the once-impregnable keep, now slowly falling to rubble.

Here had reigned the King of the Rhens, the dead Ogmund, who lay moldering in his howe; here were born his only issue, the lovely, red-tressed Ermengard and her dwarfed sister, Fjaerlda, with the twisted back; here, too, had come the brothers Helmer and Hothir, younger sons of Thorir Treefoot, King of the Asyr, both bent on winning the hand of Ogmund's fair daughter. Here the ravaging Vandir had laid the torch to the land in their march to conquer the Nord kingdoms vassal to Nordgaard; later to be turned back by the valiant Starulf, who mustered an army of karls and thralls from the surrounding fylkes and steadings, and stood fast against the invaders and their cohorts, the Fire Lords of Thool and their Black Legion. How so few, ill armed at best, put to rout the ruthless and all but invincible horde marshaled under King Hern's war banners and the dragon pennons of Thool, was told afterward by many a tongue. Few thought to credit the Wizard of Lom, once seen walking the battlements and casting spells.

The shadowy figure faded amongst the fallen stones of the outer walls, to appear again within the ruined bailey as a recognizable humanlike form.

A thief, perhaps? So it seemed to the suddenly awakened oldster lying on a pallet of straw, in the shadow of the fallen wall of what had been the mews. In the adjacent stall, a gelding whinnied.

"Stand and be recognized!" came the challenge, with a rattling of arms.

"Be still, stout heart," spoke the intruder softly. "Starulf, you know me well."

"The-Gray-Bearded-One!" was the awed whisper from the shadows.

"Sooth, that is one of my many names," said the Wizard of Lom. For it was he standing there in shadow-wraith form, bathed in an eldritch glow. The moonlit straw pallet revealed Starulf's reclining figure armed with an ancient byrnie, baldric, and sword.

"Passing strange, the dream I was dreaming when thou awakened me," said the Old Warrior. "I saw thee in it, O Wizard."

"Nay, it was no dream. I summoned your shadow self," the sage replied. "And now I appear before you in the same like."

The gelding whinnied again.

"How now!" cried the watchdog of Skaane. "What would thee with me? Forsooth, I am but a poor old karl on whom ill times have fallen."

"Stop mewling. I feared as much, that I would find you lying slug-a-bed, idling over a dream," chided the wizard's wraith form. "Arise, sluggard, and to horse! Ride forth, Starulf, in the service of the fair Ermengard, now Nordgaard's queen."

For two days Ketil the Skald had kept to the road, resting his mount and sleeping when he must; eating when and however he could. On the second day the rains began, coming down in a driving torrent that caused Ketil to take the wrong way at a muddy fork, where the road branched through a forest. He soon found his way blocked by a lone mounted warrior.

"Stand and be recognized!" came the challenge.

"Recognize this, when you feel it in your guts!" cried Ketil the Skald, drawing his sword as he booted his chestnut stallion into a charge. The two armed horsemen met in the driving downpour with a clash of iron on iron. The exchange was short-lived, and Ketil had the better of it; the challenger was forced to give ground in the muddy and uncertain footing, losing his helm in the process. It was the slip of a hoof that saved the challenger's life. Ketil was about to bring his broadsword down in a death-dealing slash when he recognized the old familiar face scowling fiercely at him through the rain.

"Starulf!" he cried joyfully, but natheless keeping up his guard. " 'Tis you, Old Warrior!"

"Who speaks, and calls me such?" came the gruff rejoinder.

CLANG!

Ketil deftly parried the blow.

"Starulf, you old fool! Put up your sword. 'Tis Ketil the Skald."

CLANG!

Again Ketil parried.

"Starulf! Desist, you grumbling old bear! Forgive me, but I would have slain you out of hand had I not recognized that doughty old face."

"Come up, if thee dare, thou baseborn knave!" roared the Old Warrior.

CLANG!

"Baseborn, am I? A fine name for a friend and comrade in-arms from the old days, when Ogmund lived and was King of Rhenish Skaane."

CLANG!

"Come up!" growled Starulf.

CLANG!

"Enough, I say. 'Tis Ketil the Skald I am, as I have told you fair, in all sooth. I have ridden to enlist your aid."

"Is it thee, then? By the gods, I see it is!" cried Starulf. "Well met, Ketil, for I am on my way to Arn in the service of a queen. Thou will ride with me. As a matter of fact, I insist you do. I've already taken the wrong road twice."

"Who is this queen of yours, old friend?"

"Ermengard of Skaane. Now Queen of the Asyr, I'm told."

"By the runes!" cried Ketil. "So she has fled to the Swan Queen for sanctuary?"

"That she has, forsooth," said Starulf. He had dismounted on recognizing the skald at long last, and was busy brushing the mud from his retrieved helm.

"On to Arn with you, then, Starulf, and serve her well. Tell Ermengard that Ketil the Skald rides throughout Nordgaard, fylke by fylke, to rally the jarls of the realm to her cause, and depose the false-king." Without further ado, he kicked his mount's flank and was gone.

IX

Hired Sword

Hogar tested the balance and weight of the blade. The leather-wrapped hilt of the broadsword gripped well in his hand. The feel was right. For a hand-me-down guardroom sword, it was a good weapon. He returned the blade to its scabbard and buckled it onto his mercenary's harness that bore the metal of Dorn; then with a wild cry and a leap, he assumed a swashbuckling stance as the broadsword flashed again in his right hand.

Nels's laugh was deep and guttural as he watched his younger comrade-in-arms draw, slash, and thrust at imaginary antagonists. The ruddy-faced Utgarthian sat at table chawing noisily on a knuckle of venison, with a tankard before him. He wiped his blond beard on the back of his hand, licked his fingers with the sound of popping corks, and drained the tankard.

"More brew, here!" he bellowed to the buxom kitchen wench who stood eyeing Hogar's agility of foot, hand, and sword with unabashed admiration on her pockmarked face. "Sit down and eat, Hogar," he shouted. "Gods, man! You can always sword it; but good deer meat is getting cold on your trencher." He applied himself to the knuckle again. After a long pull at his tankard, he said more quietly, "You'll find Runulf is not always so generous. Many a night it's ragout from leftovers for the guardroom mess. He's a poor hunter. Yet hunting is his passion. 'Tis passing strange, come to think of it, that Runulf hunts only at night. And comes back empty-handed. I can drop a stag at two hundred paces with a crossbow quarrel; farther with a fair shaft." With that proud boast, Nels drained his tankard. "More brew, here!" he called again.

Hogar took his place opposite Nels the Bowman at a long trestled table that could easily seat twenty warriors. Laying his naked sword on the boards beside him, he attacked his victuals with appetite. Washing down a mouthful with small ale, he looked down the table where he and Nels ate alone and curiously eyed the guardroom itself. He knew after spending a night there that the trestles and boards later would be stacked against a wall, and benches spread with sheepskin throws for sleeping. The tower room was without a fire of any sort to take the chill off the damp walls slotted for defending bowmen.

"Your first mercenary post, eh?" said Nels, grinning, wanting friendship.

"I am not yet sworn," Hogar replied. "Runulf mentioned others. Where are they?"

Nels went on eating in his noisy manner, gulping down great drafts of the inferior ale.

"You and I are the only ones left," he said at length, with a loud belch. "Some are dead. The others had no stomach for facing the Fenris-Wolf and fled."

"Come, now," Hogar scoffed. "You scarcely expect me to believe that. Every Nordlander knows the saga of Ragnarok from childhood. The Fenris-Wolf was slain that bloody day. What has that to do with us?"

"Ragnarok was a thousand years ago. 'Tis *now* that has to do with us," said Nels, with a dark look. "We are mercenaries, hired to fend Dorn—"

"Against the Lokian troll-fiends said to haunt it?" asked Hogar with a laugh.

"Thor's hammer!" cried Nels, banging his tankard down hard. "Guard your tongue! 'Tis no wives' tale, I tell you. Have you not noticed how Runulf is forever casting an eye over his shoulder? I tell you, the Fenris-Wolf is risen again—and has whelped in Dorn Woods!"

"How can such a thing be?" Hogar was incredulous.

"How else do you account for the bloody killing of men and beasts in the night?" asked Nels, in a loud whisper that echoed in the empty guardroom. He drained his tankard in one great gulp.

"By Loki's troll-fiends?"

"The Fenris-Wolf!" whispered the bowman hoarsely;

then turning, he shouted, "More brew, here!" When the wench had refilled his tankard and withdrawn, leaning across the boards he whispered intently. "One mercenary after another has disappeared in the night, only to be found on the morrow with his throat torn out—"

"Enough, Nels!"

Runulf of Dorn stood in the guardroom doorway, scowling. "Nels is a gifted liar when his tongue is loosed," the thane told Hogar reassuringly. "Particularly after the third tankard. How many have you had, Nels? Go sleep it off in the byre," he commanded.

The ruddy-faced warrior rose grumbling to his feet. Hogar knew Nels was not drunk. He had been silenced by the Master of Dorn for reasons unknown.

The Fenris-Wolf? Certainly not. The tale was ridiculous.

Hogar watched Nels silently withdraw; nor did he fail to catch the guarded look signed from the doorway: *Have a care!*

Runulf seated himself opposite the Nordsman, next to the place vacated by the bowman. There was an intense look in his strange yellow eyes.

"What nonsense has Nels told you?"

"Something about men and beasts with their throats torn out," said Hogar, feigning drunkenness. "Methinks I am in the need of air, after three tankards of this cheap ale." He rose and sheathed his sword.

"Stay where you are," said Runulf firmly. "You are sober, and I know it. This fool tale of the Fenris-Wolf whelping in Dorn Woods has every harebrained thrall on my land afraid of his shadow. My mercenaries have deserted me one by one because of wild, unfounded rumors; now I have only Nels—and you. Mere wives' tales they are, I tell you! And that settles the matter!" He pounded the boards with a hairy clenched fist.

"So be it," said Hogar. "However, there is another matter yet to be settled between us. The price of my sword in your service. You were to send for me and speak of wages."

"I have yet to know if your sword be worth its

hire," said Runulf. His wolfish mouth twisted in a half sneer.

Hogar had resumed eating while they conversed. At this slur, he put down the joint of venison on which he was chawing, wiped his fingers on his breeks, and half rose to his feet, his sword hand resting on his hilt.

"Try me," he said coolly, staring Runulf down.

The thane's yellow eyes wavered.

"Temper, temper," Runulf chided, feigning good humor. "I seek a boon, not combat."

Hogar reseated himself at his trencher, which he attacked with fingers and dagger.

"Name it," he said, with his mouth full.

"Thrallsfest begins on the morrow," the thane told him. "Nels will convoy me and my household to the village for three days of merrymaking, as is the custom."

"I know it well from my own country," said Hogar. At Thrallsfest even the lowliest serf was granted three days leave to carouse in the village on the largess of his lord. "'Twill take another three days to get your thralls sobered and back to work," he ventured.

"All the more reason why I need you to defend Dorn against reavers and poachers in my absence. You will be cooked for. Hrapp and Gerda will remain to tend the steading. 'Tis not my wont as thane to plead defense of my holding; rather, it is my tenants' bound duty, thrall and karl alike, as well you know, to bear arms when called on. But the unfounded rumor repeated to you by Nels has spread in the village, that the Fenris-Wolf is risen again, and has whelped in Dorn Woods—attacking my men and my livestock at night, and tearing their throats out. None will rally to my call, though I be their lord. I cannot put the whole village of Dorn in chains. That is why it is imperative I be generous with the villagers during the fest. I therefore ask a boon: serve me, Hogar of Valhelm, until Thrallsfest is over and I am returned."

"A boon from a lying rogue?"

"Nay, a slip of the tongue. You'll surely forgive one who once fought under Valhelm's jarl?" An artful smile played on Runulf's lips. Like a cat that has just devoured the dog, thought Hogar. He had disliked the thane on sight; there was about the man a sinister something he could not yet put a finger on.

"In what campaign?" he asked. "I recall no mention of Runulf of Dorn in the battle rolls. My stepsire, Jarl Hothir, did boast much of his prowess in the days when he took the field against the Vandir."

"Before Hothir's time. I was Jarl Helmer's sworn vassal."

"My father? But how can this be? This is Utgarth. No Asyr is liege lord here."

"The oath of blood honor was pledged in secret," said the thane darkly.

He lies, thought Hogar. To what purpose?

"Back to the business at hand," said Runulf abruptly. Hogar sensed that the thane had artfully changed the subject.

"Until wages are offered and accepted, I am not your hired sword, Runulf," he said boldly. "I need a purse. Let us then agree upon a set time that I will give token service for your hospitality. How say you to a sennight?"

"You have a glib tongue," said the thane. "A sennight it shall be, then. One gold ring and found for your sworn oath."

Hogar snorted into his tankard.

"You jest! You threatened to throw me back to the sea, did I choose not to serve you with my sword," he reminded him. "Throw your offer of one gold ring into the sea instead. Do you believe I would sword it for one gold ring and found?"

" 'Tis a fair price for token service."

"You dare mock me because I am here, washed up on your troll rock?" Hogar cried out angrily. His sword hand, now gripping the hilt, was about to draw against the thane.

"Temper, temper," repeated Runulf, with the same artful smile, unruffled by his guest's breach of moral code by threatening to draw against his host. Hogar relaxed his hand, and brought it to rest on the pommel of his sword.

"The pirates who tossed me into your lap robbed

me of ten gold rings and a dozen halves. That is the wage I ask," he said firmly.

"For a twelvemonth, then," countered the thane.

"A sennight, and no more. You think I would give oath to serve you a twelvemonth for such a measly purse?" Hogar demanded.

"No more than I would willingly pay you the same for a sennight," was Runulf's counter. "For the son of an old friend, seven gold rings for seven days and nights. 'Tis a fair offer."

"Ten it is, then."

"Seven, I say."

"I say ten."

"Eight."

"Nine, and—"

"Done!" cried the Thane of Dorn, pounding his fist on the board.

"Not so fast," said Hogar. "Nine gold rings and a harness, unmarked by your badge; armed with sword and dagger. And leave to be on my way with a jangling purse on the eighth day."

"Done, say I," declared Runulf. " 'Tis no bargain. By the gods, I swear it! But if you handle a sword as well as you haggle, 'twill serve my purpose well. The wage is agreed between us. Give me then your oath."

Hogar had misgivings; but there was little choice for him, penniless and outlawed, standing in hand-me-down guardroom boots as he was.

"You willingly offer nine gold rings, trappings, arms, and found for a sennight?" he asked incredulously, for he had won more than a fair wage. "There is something up your sleeve other than your arm, then, say I."

"I need a stalwart sword," said Runulf of Dorn. "Serve me well, by remaining to stand against reavers and poachers, should any such come in my absence, and you shall be rewarded above the sum we have agreed upon."

They stared each other hard in the eye for a long moment; this time the strange yellow eyes did not waver. Hogar soberly formulated the oath, guarding well his own secret.

"Runulf of Dorn, I, Hogar of Valhelm, do swear you true, to defend your lands and your body from danger and hurt, be it by reaver, poacher, werwulf, or troll, for these next seven days and nights as your paid mercenary, for the hire of nine gold rings and found, plus weapons, harness, and free leave. I do this of my own free will, being freeborn, and without coercion on your part, so that you may attend Thrallsfest with your household and thralls for the merrymaking in Dorn village."

"Well spoken," said Runulf. "Ancient custom has it that you offer me your sword hilt first, in token of your good faith and true heart. But no matter." He shrugged indifferently.

"You are not my liege lord, and this is no oath of blood honor between us," Hogar reminded him. "I am your hired sword for a sennight and no more, Runulf. Only because I need a purse to further me on a vowed quest, have I sworn me as I have."

Without a by-your-leave, Hogar rose from the trestled board and strode from the guardroom. He could feel Runulf's glaring eyes on his back. He ground his teeth on the angry thoughts that filled his mind.

"I fear I shall spit me a than before I quit Dorn!" he told himself.

X

"Berserkers!"

On the second day of Thrallsfest, a well-earned appetite found Hogar at table opposite Hrapp in the longhouse kitchen, wolfing down the noonday meal, hovered over by Gerda and her eternal "Eat, eat."

A few miles away in the fishing village of Dorn, Runulf the Thane and a pair of fierce-eyed, runagate berserkers had their heads together over horns of mead in the common room of the inn where much bawdy merriment was astir.

Despite the boisterous talk and laughter, the sinister trio kept their voices low. At an adjacent table, Nels the Bowman nursed a half-emptied tankard, an ever-watchful eye on his lord between long pulls of good ale. He scarcely made out a word between the three, until the runagates were taking their leave. It was then he heard Hogar's name and the word "ransom," causing him to suck in his breath so that a great belch rolled up from his gullet, like the rumbling thunder of Asa-Thor. Runulf looked his way, his yellow eyes narrowed in a scowl.

"Enough, Nels," barked the thane sharply. "Get some air, and blow the stink off you. Look to the thralls while you are about it. Mind you none of them gets his nose too wet. The morrow brings yet another day of festing. Be off with you!"

The burly Nels made his exit with a characteristic grumble. Once beyond eye's reach, the bowman made directly for the deserted mews, left unattended by the stableboys who had joined in the carousing. Nels saddled up unobserved and rode softly at a walk to the road fronting the inn. He had a good hour's ride ahead of him. The runagates' ship could easily outrun him on a favorable wind. Resolutely, he turned the dapple gray in the direction of Dorn Hall at a driving gallop, racing against time.

Meanwhile at the steading, Hogar shoved his trencher aside and emptied his tankard; then he turned again to his self-imposed farmyard chores, stripping himself to his cross-gartered breeks to work out the soreness in tendon and thew. Unencumbered by harness or sword, he was pitching fresh hay into the empty byre with Hrapp, from a hayrack that had fortunately been protected against the storm, when the first of the runagates clambered up over the scarped cliff where it sloped down to the pebbled strand that lay beyond Loki's Rock.

It was in reach of the old launching shed that the runagates had beached their sixern. Bristling with spears, swords, and axes, and clad in ox-hide sarks and heavy shoon, across the field came the fierce-faced nine, trampling down the muddy tillage. Ignoring the sheep and kine at graze, they made straightway for the grange and thrall cots, gnawing their shield rims as they ran.

"Berserkers!" cried Hrapp as he sighted them. "Odin preserve us!"

"See to Gerda," Hogar told him. "Be quick, while I hold them off."

"Fire and iron cannot harm them," the reeve called back over his shoulder as he jumped down from atop the hay wain and bolted for the longhouse kitchen door.

"Arm yourselves!" Hogar shouted. His own harness and sword were hanging on a peg in the byre where he had left them, unmindful of the old Nordlander proverb, "He who walks apace from his sword is a dead man."

With an ancient pitchfork the only weapon to hand, he took his stand against the marauders. The first to charge the byre was upon him with a frenzied yell, swinging a murderous-looking ax gripped in both hands. Feinting the attack, Hogar thrust upward with all his might and sank the bronze tines of the fork full depth in the axman's chest. The ax fell harmlessly as its wielder slumped dead. There was not time to draw forth the pitchfork and defend himself before another of the yelling runagates was at him with a wicked thrust to the throat. Nimbly sidestepping the vicious, curved short-sword, Hogar retrieved the fallen ax. With a backhanded swing just inches above the ground, he caught the second berserker ankle high and toppled him minus both feet across the corpse of his predecessor.

"So much for iron!" cried Hogar with a fighting grin. He brought the ax down on his screaming adversary's skull, splitting it open as he would a melon. He barely had time to retreat into the byre and slip home the bar. Instantly, there was a heavy pounding on the barred door. He cast a searching eye about the interior and the fallen-in roof for some way out, for now the pounding was succeeded by a heavier ramming sound, which could only mean the reavers were battering down the door by running the hayrack against it. He wondered why they had not yet stormed the longhouse. An assault there would have brought a scream from Gerda. It was clear what their purpose was when he heard a voice in command shouting, "Take him alive! He is no good to Runulf dead, you fools! Take him alive!"

So the craven thane is behind this, thought Hogar grimly.

At the same instant, a daring plan for his escape and the entrapment of the reavers came to him as he discovered a tallow lantern and a crude tinderbox. He struck a spark with the flint, ignited the tinder, and lit the wick. The candle guttered in a sudden draft and all but went out. Shielding the feeble flame with his hand, he got it burning brightly none too soon; the runagates were forcing the byre door. In a moment the bar would give. Hogar made his way quickly to the hayloft, lantern in hand. Setting it down, he drew up the ladder after him; he heard the byre door splinter under attack. With the battle cry of the Asyr roaring in his throat, he tossed the lit lantern into the mow. The hay caught, and the flames leaped high as he swung himself out the loft door on the hoist rope, back and forth, timing his drop to the hayrack now pushed halfway through the broken door below. One more backward swing brought Hogar near the fire, now spreading wherever its hungry tongues could lick. With a deft freed hand, he grabbed together a sheaf of burning hay. On the forward swing of the hoist there was no time to twist the hay into a torch; it burned freely and too fast. Swinging one-handed out the loft door, he let go the rope and fell on the half-emptied hayrack jammed in the byre door. Tossing the burning sheaf, he rolled clear and dropped to the ground.

The hay-laden wain caught fire at once. At a glance, he saw the runagates had turned the wain around to batter down the door; the wagon tongue stood free of the entry.

"Here is my weapon!" Hogar cried out to the gods, praying they would grant him strength over his enemies. Avoiding the flames, he detached the tongue from the wagon; with the heavy pole hoisted on his shoulder, he quickly made his way to the rear of the byre, standing ready.

Already half consumed by time and neglect, the byre was now fully ablaze. From within came the terrified shrieks of the entrapped reavers. Axes newly sharpened for bloodletting now chopped at the wooden back wall in desperate, splintering blows. Keen edges cut through; the planking gave. Two fierce-faced berserkers came bursting through with singed hair and smoking beards. Hogar let them step clear of the cloven wall before he swung the wagon tongue and crushed their skulls like eggshells under foot.

"So much for fire!" he cried. "Drop your weapons and come out empty-handed," he shouted to the others still within the flaming byre, "or by the gods, I'll splatter your brains on the ground for the birds to peck at."

"Quarter! Quarter!" the trapped reavers screamed.

"Come out as I have commanded you," shouted Hogar, the wagon tongue held ready to swing from the shoulder.

It was then, as the fire-crazed rogues shoved and fought their way through the chopped out wall and threw down their arms, he heard the clatter of iron-shod hooves on the courtyard flags; a byrnie-clad rider reined back a half-winded steed, coming then into the mews at a clip-clop.

"You had best be come as friend, and not as liege man to Runulf of Dorn," Hogar called grimly over his shoulder, barely taking his eyes off his captives, "for one swing of this pole can both unhorse and unman you."

"In all sooth, I am come as a friend. Do you not know me?" boomed Nels the Bowman; for it was he indeed, as Hogar saw once the subdued runagates were marshaled outside the burning byre. "To what avail have I spent this poor beast at the gallop from the village, to warn you of Runulf's blackhearted treachery? I see you have already dealt with four of his cutthroats. 'Twas that berserker pair there, with their brains bashed in, I saw huddled together with Runulf at the inn. When I heard them speak your name and the word 'ransom' in one breath, I rode here posthaste."

"Well done, friend, and welcome; you come in the nick of time," said Hogar, grinning his relief. "Nock me an arrow in your bow, Nels, and put it through the head of the first rogue who dares move a hair." He shouted toward the longhouse for the reeve to show himself, but Hrapp and Gerda had already seen the blazing byre. They came running from the kitchen even as he called, with a wooden bucket in each hand, and sloshed water from the horse trough on the flaming structure to no avail. The spavined roof fell in completely at last, burning briskly.

" 'Tis beyond saving," Hogar told them. "Have done. The byre is gone like a summer love."

Nels dismounted awkwardly, keeping a bead drawn on the runagates with a nocked shaft. Gerda held the reins for him, then led the lathered gray to the stables. Hogar sent Hrapp to the saddlery for rawhide thongs to bind the five prisoners. Meanwhile, he selected a broadsword from the pile of surrendered shields and weapons, sizing up each knave as the reeve returned and bound their hands behind them, then to a loop drawn about the neck.

"Now, you rogues," said the Nordsman tersely, "you serve a new master. Each of you is my thrall. And so will you remain, until you prove yourselves worthy of being freedmen. Who amongst you would not serve under Hogar Bloodsword, and go a-roving? Let him stand forth and have his say at his own peril."

A grumbling arose amongst the captives; they stared back sullenly at their redheaded conqueror. Surly-eyed, one by one they accepted servitude rather than bow their necks to the sword; all save a great bear of a fellow with huge blond mustaches, who stood forth with swaggering insolence.

"I, Svadi, am already a freedman," he growled, with his heavy jaw thrust out defiantly.

"You were a thrall before this," Hogar taunted, "and a fool then as you are now, Svadi." He turned to Hrapp. "Release him. He has the smell of galley chains about him." When the reeve had cut the fellow loose, Hogar told him, "Go then, an you will not serve me willingly and well."

With a roar of derisive laughter directed at his enslaved comrades-in-arms, the burly Svadi turned and shambled bearlike across the furrowed field, making for the scarped cliff over which they had clambered. Hogar allowed him a good start before he addressed the bowman.

"Nels, you have boasted you can bring down a stag at better than two hundred paces with a fair shaft," he said. "Bring me down yonder bear. But softly does it—let the shot wound, but not kill. I would have Svadi alive. Methinks when I have lessoned him well, he'll make me a doughty bosun."

Nels loosed his arrow. It took the runner in the left calf, and brought him to earth with a cry of pain. Fitting a second shaft, Nels strode across the field. The wounded runagate, aware the big Utgarthian approached him with nocked bow, made no attempt to rise, but lay where he had fallen, alternately cursing his useless leg and the ill wind that brought him to Loki's Rock.

On reaching him, Nels pulled Svadi halfway to his feet and put an abrupt end to his cursing with a clout to the jaw; then as if shouldering the carcass of a kill, the big bowman carried the senseless runagate back to the mews. There Hrapp drew the arrow, and Gerda cleansed and bound the wound. This done, Nels propped Svadi against the horse trough and sloshed a bucket of water over his head to bring him around. Svadi shook himself like a wet dog and sat there stunned as a duck in thunder, unable to believe his senses.

"Do you swear me true, now that you've had the time to reconsider?" asked Hogar with a wry smile.

"I so swear, lord," said Svadi. "I will serve you with my life, if need be."

"Well spoken."

"And I can tell you, lord, that my four brothers, Frodi, Haaki, Hromund, and Finnur, here, will serve you likewise well. They answer to me, now, with our berserker leaders and two others dead from the blows you dealt them."

"If this be so, I would hear it from them," said Hogar.

"Speak, then, my mother's sons!" Svadi demanded. "He will be a fair lord, will Hogar Bloodsword, say I. Swear him true, my brothers."

The sworn oath of fealty was given sullenly by all but Finnur, who boldly refused.

"I will be thrall to no man," said he, left fist clenched.

"Bite your tongue, Finnur!" cried Svadi. "Give oath, or by Thor's death, I'll whip you standing on one leg!" He tried to rise, but Hogar placed a firm hand on his shoulder.

"Nay, Svadi," he said coolly. "Finnur is like a stubborn ox. He'll do what he is told, right enough." He strode over to the dissenting brother and struck him a blow between the eyes with his fist. "But first, I must get his attention." It was a blow to fell an ox. "Leave him lie," he told the three brothers who would have helped the fallen Finnur to his feet, since Svadi could not.

"It will lesson him to bite his tongue," said Svadi in his deep bearlike growl.

Hogar eyed each of the rogues sternly. "The five of you are under the sword until you can be trusted. To the guardroom with them, Nels, and slay the first who makes a false move." To Hrapp he said, "Gather up the weapons and shields in oilskins, and take them to whatever ship these paltry knaves have beached."

On his return presently, Hrapp reported, "By your leave, lord, it was but a fishing sixern they came in. The surf was dragging it out to sea when I got there. So I let it go and loaded the weapons in Runulf's old longship—left lying in its launching shed since his roving days. She'll be fair seaworthy again, lord, when her seams are caulked anew."

"A longship, you say? By the gods!" swore Hogar with a grin. "How many oars?"

"There are holes for twenty."

"You did well, Hrapp. Twenty oars, eh? That means forty karls rowing in two shifts. A ship, by Odin! An omen from the gods! Tell me, is there a sail?"

"Aye, lord. Blood red it is. Stored with the oars in safekeeping."

"Get them," said Hogar, his eyes bright at this stroke of good fortune. To Gerda he said, "Cut me three ravens out of black cloth, and sew them to the sail. Outlawed I am; by the gods, an outlaw will I be! I shall fare forth under the raven banner of my pirate grandsire, Thorir Treefoot, on my quest for the treasure of Nardath-Thool. Aye, and there's a full share of the booty for any man who goes a-faring with Hogar Bloodsword."

XI

Half Beast, Half Human

A warming longfire crackled in Dorn Hall where Hogar sat at meat in Runulf's high seat, served by a beaming Gerda and Hrapp, who gratefully thanked their new lord for striking off their thrall collars and heard out the strange tale of Hogar's fey dream and the sinistrous city of his quest.

The old longship had been run out of its launching shed and put to sea with Nels seated in the bow, arrow nocked and ready against any untoward move by the five rogues manning her oars and tiller, there being no wind up to fill her raven sail. The big bowman had his orders; he meant to carry them out to the letter and beach the ship on a wooded holm he had spoken of down coast of Dorn village. Free of pounding surf, with stands of oak and ash suitable for needed ship repairs, the small islet therefore had been agreed upon as a trysting place, once Hogar had settled his score with Runulf the Thane.

Over a horn of ale while the reeve and his woman took their supper, the Nordsman spun out his tale of the Volva's prophecy and his sworn vow to seek out and win the Ravensword and Odin's rune-ring. Not till the tale was told and Hrapp and Gerda had cleaned up their trenchers did Hogar say a word about the basehearted thane's perfidy.

"Runulf will expect to find me held captive and no doubt the pair of you slain in the bargain," he said, "with his hired minions carousing here against his return on the morrow. But his pan of milk has soured.

The craven dog shall answer for his treachery. You have nothing to fear. Let us to bed, then, for a good night's rest."

Hrapp banked the longfire, and Gerda brought sheepskins and sleeping furs. The three of them were soon stretched out on benches, snoring. Outside on the flagstoned mews, a grisly greeting lay awaiting the thane's arrival.

At cockcrow, Gerda was up bustling in the longhouse kitchen. The appetizing sizzle of deer meat brought Hogar and the reeve to table, eager to break their fast. The Nordsman had rearmed himself with sword and baldric. He ate hungrily, yet was ever alert for the clatter of iron-shod hooves announcing Runulf's return.

"Can you not defend yourself?" he asked Hrapp, seeing the reeve wore neither sword nor dagger at his belt.

"I am not thrall-born, lord," said the freedman with pride. "Once I was a bowman. The old cunning is still in my arm."

Hogar replied with a sound clap on the shoulder and lapsed into silence over his meat, his mind churning with a plan.

It was high noon when Runulf rode into Dorn, herding before him a clutch of pot-valiant thralls reluctant to resume their miserable existence after three days of bousing. The thane brought his horse up sharply on entering the mews; the unexpected sight of both berserker leaders amongst the four lying slain unsettled him. The stink of death in the midday sun smote his nostrils hard and sent the thralls scattering.

"How now!" Runulf cried out, wheeling his mount. "What is amiss here?" The gutted byre told him his treachery had gone awry. He looked about him, instinctively fearing for his life.

"Nels! Nels! To me, to me!" shouted the thane as Hogar showed himself and strode from the opened kitchen door in baldric and breeks, sword drawn. Runulf reared his steed with flailing hooves poised to trample the Nordsman who came at him with deadly resolve.

"Draw, you basehearted swine!" Hogar cried. The

craven thane blanched; putting his horse to the whip, he fled the courtyard and broke for the woods. At the forest edge, he looked back. From a slotted window high in the tower, a bronze-tipped arrow caught the sun.

"No!" Runulf shrilled. He wheeled.

Too late.

The bow twanged. The loosed shaft whirred and buried itself deep in the horse's breast. A second arrow took the thane between the shoulder and the neck, unhorsing him. He rolled clear of the screaming animal as it went down, striking wildly. Bubbling red froth bearded its muzzle.

"Nels, you traitor!" Runulf shrieked at the tower. "I'll have your head for this!"

Hogar came running, sword in hand.

"Nay," he called out, " 'tis Hrapp the reeve who strikes his first blow as freedman against the coward of Dorn." The flailing hooves did not keep Hogar from moving in quickly to slash the horse's throat, ending its agony.

"Murderers!" screamed Runulf. Beside himself with fear and pain, he rose clutching at his wound as though to draw the shaft, and fled afoot into the woods.

"Follow me!" Hogar shouted to the tower, and gave pursuit. From behind him as he reached the forest edge, came a sharp warning. In the courtyard entry stood Hrapp, down from the tower, with an arrow nocked in his bow.

"Stay, lord!" he cried. "You know not the dread peril of Dorn Woods."

Even as he spoke, from the depths of the forest gloom there came a high, ululating cry that was half beast, half human.

Dorn Woods was a tanglement of thorns and clawing withes, except where a deer path ran through the dense undergrowth of brushwood and small trees. It was this path that Nels the Bowman took in hunting game for the thane's table; it was along this same path the wounded Runulf had fled, leaving a blood spoor splashed red and wet upon living and fallen leaves alike. It was here that Hogar followed, sword in hand, now and then chopping the way clear of tangle vines and bramble. Hrapp stalked close behind, an arrow nocked and ready for any appearance of the unknown denizen whose eerie cry had chilled his spine. The sun had long since dropped behind the World's Edge when the thicket began to thin out amongst the murky shadows that loomed ominously ahead of the two.

Behind them were Gerda's tearful pleas not to enter the dread woods, where (she insisted, as had Nels) the reborn Fenris-Wolf had whelped the fiendish brood that preyed upon Dorn steading, tearing out the throats of livestock and men alike.

"You'll not be coming out alive, once gone in," was her calamitous and weepy admonition.

"I follow my lord," Hrapp told her resolutely, but not without misgivings of his own; for he, too, believed the spreading rumor of werebeasts inhabiting Dorn Woods, which Runulf the Thane adamantly dismissed as an old wives' tale. Hogar refused a flagon of courage to fortify himself against whatever peril lurked beyond the forest edge. He gave orders for the unceremonious disposal of the four slain berserkers in the lime pit, for the flaying and tanning of the slaughtered horse's hide for shoe and harness leather, and for the roasting of its carcass to feed the returning thralls, many of whom were still too drunk to cook for themselves; then, still clad only in baldric, breeks, and boots, he entered Dorn Woods shadowed by the doughty reeve.

Before them now, where pale shafts of twilight pierced the murk, the blood-marked trail ended at a meadowlike clearing. In its midst rose a grass-grown mound from which came the weird glow of witching lights, like foraging tongues of bluish flame thrust out of a hundred hungry mouths. Before the mound there bubbled a spring of limpid waters. Beside this there stood a womanly figure mantled in white and girded with a great sword, a woman of unearthly beauty, with long flowing raven tresses. She beckoned to Hogar as he stepped clear of the tanglewood and trees.

"Stay your shaft, Hrapp, till I give the word," he cautioned the reeve, who remained hidden in the bramble. To the figure in the white mantle, Hogar said nothing; he wondered that no horse was tethered nearby where she stood, for the smell of horse sweat was strong in his nostrils downwind of her, now that he had entered the meadow. Her answer to his unspoken thoughts was a peal of mocking laughter.

"So the stallion scents the mare!" she cried in the Old Tongue. "Come to the arms of Huldren, and I will make love to thee. Thou art a man, and I am a woman. Lie with me, my king, and I shall give thee not only a throne to sit and riches unbounded, but a wondrous sword out of yonder howe, and bear thee a brood of wolves."

Dropping her mantle, she whirled in a wild, sensuous dance of utter abandon, showing him her nakedness. Maddening to behold at first sight, with each pivoting step her unearthly beauty faded, to reveal at last a disgusting troll wife with a loathsome and terrifying face, the wild hair of a hag, the burning eyes and fearful jaws of a she-wolf, the hands, arms, and breasts of a woman, a hooved werebeast with the rump of a rutting mare.

"Get you gone, monster!" cried Hogar, shielding his eyes from the horror of her. For a moment, he stood immobile as stone. Huldren lifted her tail and neighed, flaunting her desire.

"Take me to wife, thou very stud of a man, I beseech thee. Great is my longing for thee, as the mare longs for the stallion to cover her." She came toward him, arms open for his embrace.

"Begone, foul hag!"

Hrapp stepped from the tanglewood, bowstring drawn back to his ear as he spoke. "Begone! Or I shall put out both your fiendish eyes, quick as I can nock an arrow."

Huldren let out a high, ululating scream, half raging woman, half maddened mare. Her eyes glowed with fire as she cast a troll-spell with runes on the hapless reeve.

"Be thou become an ash, like thy bow!"

The rigidity of revulsion left Hogar with the binding of the rune spell on the faithful Hrapp.

"You shall do him no scathe!" the Nordsman cried out, advancing against the monster with drawn sword.

Too late. The spell was cast.

Where Hrapp had been a moment before stood a sturdy ash tree; one limb bent like a drawn bow.

"Have at thee, thou witch hag!" Hogar yelled, lapsing into the Old Tongue spoken by the monster; he thrust at the foul heart that beat beneath the troll wife's womanly breasts.

Deftly sidestepping his sword point, Huldren sought to cajole him, saying, "I would lie with thee and love thee, not fight thee, my chieftain."

"I lie not in the arms of trolls," Hogar retorted, again seeking to spit her on his sword. She was too quick for him. He recovered and stood facing her, wiping his brow with his arm.

"The smell of thy sweat is sweet to me," said Huldren. She felt the mare blood rising in her. "Come, thou stallion, I long for thee!" She gave forth with a fierce neigh. "Lie with me, my king, in rut as stallion to mare, and I will give thee not only unbounded riches and the sword I have offered thee, but knowledge of all things."

"Get thee gone, thou hag spawn!" cried Hogar. "The stench of thee is foul beyond belief."

Huldren's gorge rose.

"Spurn not my love, mortal; for then shall thee have my hatred and enmity. Thou had best not be in bad odor with Huldren."

"Ha! 'Tis thee who art in bad odor, thou hag!" laughed the Nordsman, deriding her.

"Thou art a fool!"

Spelling out runes, Huldren cast a glamour on the grass-grown mound, causing the blue witch-fire to leap higher. Drawing the great sword girded at her waist, she ran upon Hogar, crying, "Die, then, an thou will have me not!"

The moon rose high as they met head-on in fierce swordplay, till the meadow rang with the sound. They fought long and hard, and bloody was the battle they waged one against the other, until both being spent, they drew apart to drink of the healing waters and rest themselves, to bind their wounds with wild herbs and stanch the blood flow with willow bark. And as they leaned on their swords, breathing heavily to renew their strength, they fought with words in the Old Tongue of the skalds, hurling invectives and abuse on each other.

"O Huldren, thou witch!" Hogar jibed. "Loveliest of troll wives! Thou hell hag! Most desirable of horrible fiends, thy beauty blinds mine eyes. My lust for thee rises in my bowels. I defecate on thee!"

"Put up thy sword, O warrior," cried Huldren. Changing shape, she lumbered toward him in the form of a great troll bear. "Come to my arms, that I may crush thy ribs!"

With a deft thrust, Hogar pierced the bear's gleaming right eye. The werebeast roared in anguished pain and vanished. In its stead stood Huldren, one eye blinded and running blood.

"O mistress of shape-shifting," the Nordsman jeered, "turn thee to a serpent, that I may trod thy head beneath my heel."

Instantly at his feet there coiled a deadly reptile, fanged and horrible to behold. As it struck he slashed down with his sword to sever the hideous head. The viper was no longer there. In its place, Huldren, again mantled, stood taunting him a few feet apace.

"Go lie with Loki!" Hogar shouted.

"Then die, mortal, since thou will not bed me!" cried the she-troll. Raising the great sword, she advanced. Hogar came to meet her; they fought furiously, and with every sword stroke Huldren bound him with runes, so that his strength began to wane. The great sword came down about his head in a rain of deadly blows. He parried the strokes well, and again the meadow resounded with the clang of blade on blade, as he went to one knee under the press of the monster's assault. Again he saw the great sword lifted to strike, saw it descending. He parried weakly, driven to both knees by the force of the blow. Huldren, a triumphant cry welling in her werebeast throat, towered over Hogar with sword raised to deliver his death.

And from Dorn steading at that fatal moment there came the crowing of a cock to herald the break of day.

"Look to the east!" cried Hogar, rolling clear of the great sword. "The dawn is upon thee, thou foulest of trolls!"

The blow never fell. Like all trolls who remain overlong aboveground and behold the light of early morn, Huldren and her upraised sword stood turned into a pillar of gray stone.

"Be thou stone forever!" cried Hogar. He lay on the dewy meadow grass exhausted from his close brush with death at the hands of the loathsome troll of Dorn Woods. Too weak to rise, he slept; and in his sleep he dreamed of enchanted trees that turned to hideous trolls. Armed with great swords, they closed in on him with mocking laughter, in an ever-diminishing circle. From afar came the crowing of a cock, and as the swords descended upon his head a great heaviness came into his arms, into his legs, so that he could no longer move to defend himself; his eyes were blinded by an awful grayness in the early light of day. He heard himself crying out in the stony silence that embraced him, was now his forever. But no words came. He knew then, in the dreadful silence of his mind, there was nothing but the awful grayness of stone.

Hogar awakened from his horrible dream drenched in clammy sweat, to find his strength renewed and his mind jubilant, as it came to him that Huldren's binding powers had ceased with her destruction. Hrapp, he saw, was no longer spellbound; the doughty reeve knelt beside him, poulticing his wounds with wild herb leaves dipped in the rejuvenating spring waters. The witching lights no longer burned on the grassy mound. Yet, like an ominous shadow fallen across the meadow, the feeling of ensorcelment remained.

"Your wounds are healed, lord," said Hrapp in wonderment.

"Well done, good reeve," Hogar answered gratefully.

"There is magic in yonder spring," said Hrapp. "The herbs soothed, the willow bark stanched the bleeding, but look at you. The wounds are closed as though never opened by the troll sword. 'Tis the water, by the gods! Let us drink of it, lord, for protection against whatever ill may befall us ere we quit these foul woods."

XII

The Sword from the Howe

When they had drunk their fill of the healing waters, Hogar cast a wary glance toward the pillar of stone, then about the meadow.

"Whose howe would be raised in this eldritch place?" he asked the reeve.

"I know not, lord."

The answer was carved on the lintel stone set above the cairnlike entrance to the mound, beyond which stood a wooden door.

"Mark you," Hogar warned Hrapp, "keep a sharp eye out." Scraping away the lichen from the runic inscription on the stone, he made it out to read: HORD THE OLD.

The Nordsman stepped under the lintel. The weathered, metal-bound oak door gave, creaking open an inch to the touch of his sword point. The rune lock had been released by the last one to enter the howe. The sight of a bloodstain on the threshold quickened his pulse. Had Runulf taken refuge here?

"Give me cover!" he said quietly to Hrapp. Kicking the door open wide, Hogar burst through the doorposts to find himself in an antechamber of sorts. The room was empty, dark, and forbidding. The only illumination came from the light let in through the opened outer door. Opposite this a second door, with a heavy iron rune lock like the first, stood ajar; beyond that, the flickering light of a low-burning lamp was agitated by the incoming breath of air.

With Hrapp close at his heels, Hogar shouldered

open the second door. They entered a dank, partially excavated tomb dimly lit by a lone tallow lamp. A veritable cave, stacked with mildewed sea chests spilling over with treasure, had been hollowed out of the earth-filled mound, revealing one side of a funerary longship, its once-tar-blackened hull now green with mould and grave rot. Part of the deck had been dug clear to expose an ancient skeleton in ring mail and horned helm, and provided a burial niche for the miraculously preserved body of a yellow-haired and -bearded Asyr noble. A jarl, judging from his trappings and tarnished metal. Beside the body lay a broadsword cased in a shagreen-wrapped scabbard. At the warrior's feet—for such he surely had been—a round, iron-rimmed wooden shield still retained its original blazon of a red lion.

The face he looked upon was his own death mask!

Instinctively, Hogar knew he was gazing on the long-dead face of his father, Helmer Bloodsword. The Volva had spoken true. He drew a deep breath and sheathed his guardroom sword. Recalling all the Weird of the Gods had revealed to him in the sea cave, for a moment his memory rang with the Volva's words: *"Vengeance shall be thine against the false-king Hothir, who slew thy father and took his bride."*

Hothir!

For twenty years walking in the jarl boots of Helmer Bloodsword, the brother he had slain; Hothir, who had lusted after the Rhenish bride Helmer had got with child; Hothir, who had usurped both the jarl's bed and jarldom by sorcery and murder; who later slew his royal brother, Thorodd Fairhair; who at long last proclaimed himself King of the Asyr and banished the true heir to the Raven Throne from the Nordland forever.

It was not by chance, his being here; it was the will of the gods that the witch storm of the Volva's prophecy had cast him up on Loki's Rock!

Deeply moved, Hogar reached over the gunwale and lifted the sword from his dead father's side. Drawing the two-edged blade from its scabbard, he found each side was inlaid with a striking crimson serpent, fangs spread wide at the sword point. He read aloud the runes rist on the cross guard, spelling out the name of Helmer Bloodsword's battle blade.

Skull Breaker, his father had named it.

Raising *Skull Breaker* aloft, Hogar cried out his solemn vow: "I, Hogar Bloodsword, son of Bloodsword, true Jarl of Valhelm, First Jarl of the Realm, and true King of the Asyr by rightful succession had he but lived, do swear by the gods who brought me here, as my witness, by my dead father's body and by *Skull Breaker,* his sword, that his murderer, Hothir Longtooth, shall one day pay me back in the coin of his own blood, for the wrongs wrought and the evil done."

"You swear it well, Hogar." The panted laugh that followed the words came from a dark recess of the tomb, barely touched by the frail tallow light.

Hogar recognized the voice from the shadows as Runulf's, and knew that in the darkness lay the Thane of Dorn, dying of his wound. Or had Runulf, too, drunk of the rejuvenating waters?

"You broke your sworn oath to serve me true," the panting voice accused from the shadows. "But I forgive you that. Let the sword you now hold in your hand be the sword I promised you. The nine rings of gold in wages due, take from yonder chests, with the harness and trappings you bargained for; and whatever else you may need or desire. I leave my treasure to you. Take the sword I give you out of the howe, and with it put an end to my suffering."

"I broke no sworn oath," said Hogar grimly. "You betrayed me."

"Ever greedy was I." Runulf sighed in the darkness. "Nor could I close my purse to the ransom you would bring alive. In all sooth, it was to Hothir and not Helmer that I swore blood oath, as you surmise, that day twenty years long gone, when Hothir slew his brother from ambush. Look behind the right ear. The crossbow bolt is still bedded there. We brought the body here from Skaane and laid it in this old howe I had partly hollowed out for my treasury. I was pirating in those days in the Orkna Ey. The runic inscription on the lintel stone is a kenning on the word 'hoard,' which I found amusing.

"Why did Hothir not slay me out of hand to still my tongue? Because he knew full well that one day he might need my services again in disposing of his nephew, the king's true heir. Aye, it was a strange twisting of your destiny threads that washed you up on Loki's Rock, Hogar Helmer's son!

"You have come to slay me, Asyr. Have done, then. She will not come now."

"She?"

"Huldren of the White Mantle," said Runulf with a reverence in his voice. "It was to her I came at night, in this howe. Foolish Nels thought I hunted. She was the only woman I ever loved. We shared the ecstasy of blood orgy."

"Huldren was no woman," cried Hogar with revulsion. "A foul witch hag is what she was. A troll wife, with the rump of a rutting mare."

"Was? Was? You have slain her!"

"She begged me to lie with her, you fool," replied Hogar with disgust. "I told her to lie with Loki, that I slept not with trolls. We fought till cockcrow."

"You have slain her!"

"Nay, she is turned to stone."

"Give me a hand up, murderer," Runulf demanded from the shadows, "that I may rise and die on my feet as befits a thane, with my sword raised against mine enemy." He was panting heavily now, with a strange low growl in his throat.

Hrapp lifted the tallow lamp to dispel the shadows from the dark corner where Runulf of Dorn lay breathing hard. The reeve's sharp eyes caught the glint of a dagger in a hairy hand poised to strike—nay, not a dagger, but—

"Talons!" cried out the reeve. The lamplight glow caught Runulf's features. For a shuddering moment, both lord and karl saw a hairy and inhuman face snarling savagely at them out of the half-lit shadows. The heavy breathing was not that of one dying.

It was like an animal panting.

"Beware the fangs!" shouted the reeve as the thing on the floor of the tomb gave a bestial cry and sprang.

Hogar's slashing sword took the taloned hand off at the wrist; with a step into the shadowy darkness, he drove the blade of *Skull Breaker* through the foul heart of the half-human, half-beast thing that strove for his throat and looked away from what had been Runulf of Dorn, spitted on his sword.

"Werwulf!" whispered Hrapp, in dreadful awe of what he beheld. "You must cut off his head, lord. Else he will rise from the dead each night to tear out our gullets, as he did the mercenaries and the sheep."

"I know the tale," said Hogar grimly. "In Nordgaard we, too, tell of werbeasts." Dragging the corpse by the hair, he struck off the wolf head. Holding the grisly trophy high, he strode to the funerary ship's gunwale. There, with his eyes again upon the face of his dead father, he cried out fiercely, "Vengeance, sire, begins with Hothir's cur turned werwulf!" He placed the dripping head below the shield and turned to the reeve. "Let the dog lie at Helmer Bloodsword's feet, as is the custom amongst the Asyr. When you have done, good Hrapp, count out nine gold rings from Runulf's hoard for wages due, and find me trappings befitting the new Thane of Dorn. For such am I become by the will of the gods!"

Later, with *Skull Breaker* swinging from his baldric, Hogar strode from his new-won treasury in fine leather and metal to his liking. Nine gold rings jingled in his pouch. The reeve followed, with his bow slung over his shoulder, a small cask tucked under one arm.

"No key in the lock, and the door left unguarded, what then becomes of your treasury, lord?" asked Hrapp, hesitant to cross the threshold.

" 'Tis a rune lock," Hogar informed him with a smile. "Closing the door seals it. When the runes graven on the iron plate are rightly touched, it will open again." He pulled the door shut. "So shall it remain till my return. Come, then; let us be off for a trencher of meat and a horn of the mead you have plundered."

XIII

Ragnahild

Hogar Bloodsword rode out of Dorn steading the next morning on Nels's dapple gray with his helmet hung from his saddle horn. The wooded road would bring him down coast to his trysting place with the burly bowman and the five rogues left in Nels's charge. It was toward midday when he drew reins beside an old woman in a tattered shawl, where she stood in the roadway weeping.

" 'Tis me old man them bloody wood thieves has done in, lord. Pray, give me what help you can. Come this way, lord, an it please your worship. He's lyin' just inside them trees over yonder."

"Well, Mother," said Hogar kindly, "let us see if I can give you heart's ease." Muttering her thanks, the old woman took hold of the bridle, leading the gray forward a dozen yards into the thicket of hazel and oak.

"Here we be!" she shouted of a sudden, giving the bridle a sharp yank that pulled the snaffle hard against the gray's mouth. It reared high with a frightened whinny, as four wood thieves fell upon horse and rider with oak staves and fierce cries.

"Mind the horse!" cried the old woman, pushing aside her shawl to reveal a ruffian's face, as Hogar was pulled from the saddle and clubbed down in a babble of shouted oaths.

"Don't let him draw!"

"Whack the bugger again!"

"Cut his pouch!"

"It's the horse we want, you fools! Leave the jonker his fancy trappings. Do you want to dance on a gibbet? We can sell the horse."

A clout on the head stunned the Nordsman momentarily. He rallied in a blood-red haze; rising unsteadily, he somehow managed to free his blade. With both hands overlapping on the hilt, he swung the serpent sword every which way, not seeing; a sharp outcry told him *Skull Breaker* had cut deep. A second blow on the head brought a flash of blinding pain. Stars exploded behind his eyes. And then there was nothing but darkness.

Hogar's head pounded; his body ached. A raucous cry smote his eardrums. His vision blurred when he opened his eyes. Something sharp jabbed at his cheek, drawing a trickle of blood. He rolled away and sat up, fighting off his attacker, a huge raven that came at him again with its beak spread. Protecting himself with one arm as best he could, Hogar felt beside him for *Skull Breaker*. Finding the blood-caked sword, he struck out futilely at his tormentor. The raven croaked and flailed him with its wings. Rising, the better to defend himself, Hogar for the first time was aware of the shawl-clad wood thief lying dead near by, cloven through the side, with both eyes pecked out. It was the spurious old woman who had decoyed him from the road to be robbed of his horse and pouch.

From the slant of the sun through the trees, he knew it to be late afternoon. He had been lying unconscious long enough for the predaceous bird to mistake him for a second corpse on which to feed. Still woozy from the clubbing, he barely managed to keep clear of the raven's talons and rapacious beak. His sword, he knew, was useless against it; in his weakened state, the bird was too quick for him. It came at him again and again, determined to rake him and peck out his eyes. In desperation, he grabbed at the raven with his free hand, protecting his face with the other as he did, and caught it by the ruffed neck. The bird beat its great wings frantically. Hogar repressed his urge to wring its neck, knowing the raven was sacred to Odin, that it gave its name to the throne to which he was the rightful heir, and that he had adopted the shield marking of his grandsire— Thorir Treefoot's three ravens—as his personal blazon. He flung the bird away from him unharmed. Flapping its wings to right itself, the raven took sanctuary in the nearest oak, from where it gave him a raucous scolding.

Hogar's only reply was to put as much distance between him and the voracious carrion eater as he could, unwittingly wandering deeper into the forest until he could walk no longer. His body heavy with fatigue, his head pounding, he crawled under a welcoming oak to rest. He was asleep the moment his head touched the pillow of fallen leaves.

He awakened hours later, strangely refreshed; he had somehow slept off the aches of his beating. True, a thew here and there still gave him a twinge of pain, but for the most part he no longer hurt; the pounding in his head and the fatigue were gone. His pecked cheek no longer bled. He looked about him, sleepily appraising his whereabouts. Enjoying the touch of the afternoon sun on his skin, he lay basking in its golden warmth awhile before stirring himself. He bounded up suddenly, with the realization that he had slept the sun around, that he had been beaten and robbed. The wood thieves had stolen his horse and his pouch, jingling with nine gold rings. He reached for his sword, relaxing as he touched the familiar shagreen scabbard, and found he still wore the trappings he had taken from the howe in Dorn Woods. He was out of one woods into another. Only this, he mused, was no dread place of ensorcelment. Surveying the expanse of oaks and their great overhanging branches heavy with foliage, he remembered the raven attacking him. This brought to mind again the slain wood thief, the loss of his mount, and the brutal truth of his present situation. He was afoot.

It was then he heard a sound that set his heart to leaping. From close at hand came the unmistakable whinny of a horse. Moving quickly in the direction of the sound, he soon found to his disappointment it was not the stolen gray returning, as he had hoped. Tethered to a great oak in the center of a grove on a small rise just ahead, a saddled but riderless white mare stood restlessly pawing the mulch about the tree's exposed roots. Beneath the hospitable shelter of the big tree, safe from the mare's tether range and set out invitingly on the leaves, a round loaf of brown-crusted bread, a small cheese, and a leathern bottle whetted Hogar's appetite.

Approaching hungrily, he kept a wary hand upon his sword. The mare whinnied as he passed her. He spoke softly to her, and let her nuzzle his free hand a moment; then he lifted the loaf on sword point. Cradling it in one arm, he sheathed the blade and cut himself a crust of the good-smelling bread with his dagger. He tore at it with strong white teeth, glancing around for the provider of this welcome repast. Seeing no one, he squatted on his haunches and carved himself a morsel of cheese to complement the tasty bread crust. His hand was arrested in its reach for the leathern bottle by a loud splashing of water from nearby, followed by a peal of girlish laughter.

The sounds came from below the grove, behind a low bed of rushes that grew in profusion out of the rocks screening a small forest tarn. Fed by a warm spring, it lay not a stone's throw from the great oak. Putting down the loaf, Hogar sheathed his dagger and strode down to the pool's edge, still munching on a mouthful of stolen bread and cheese, his hand on the pommel of his sword.

The cause of the splashing was a comely blond girl bathing nude. She was about Hogar's age; her provocative curves and luscious bosom caught him in the throat and loins. The small red swan-shaped scar above her left breast he took for a birthmark. His unexpected appearance brought an anguished cry to the girl's lips. Slipping quickly below the water's surface to conceal her nakedness, she regarded him fiercely as he stood mocking her modesty and embarrassment. At the tarn's edge, a short spear had been thrust in the wet earth. On the butt end of its shaft was hung a winged helmet; a warrior maid's trappings were piled upon a sword that lay close by.

"Turn your back!" the girl cried indignantly. "Could I but step from my bath and arm myself without being ogled, thou knave, I would answer your gaping with my spear. If you be other than a peeping churl who spies on a woman in her bath, then turn aside your eyes and give me a hand out," she commanded, "that I may afford you a lesson in manners."

Hogar smilingly did as he was bid. Leaning forward in a crouch, he offered his hand to pull her out of the tarn. The girl swam to the water's edge and accepted his hand. It was then, with a firm grip, that she taught Hogar a lesson: never trust a woman intruded upon in her bath. When he would have pulled her out of the tarn, with his eyes averted as demanded, she pulled him in!

As he floundered and spluttered, at first in outraged surprise, then with a slow, bubbling burst of hearty, good-natured laughter, the girl climbed nimbly out of the water. Hastily buckling on the warrior maid's girdle that supported a scant skirt to drape her loins, she clapped the winged helmet over her braids and pulled the spear from the muddy edge of the pool. Thus armed, with her breasts still bare, she turned the spear point against him.

The water struck Hogar midriff high as he stood up and waded toward her, shaking the water from the rusty mop that fell about his neck like a drenched red lion's mane.

"Well done," he said, still laughing.

"Stay!" she warned. "One step closer and I will spit you like a hare."

"So, warrior maid," said Hogar with a sudden scowl, " 'tis combat you crave." His sword described a wide arc, flashing out of the water in his hand. The girl faced him, momentarily unaware she held a headless spear. "Spit me like a hare, will you?" he cried. "Let us see now how you handle a sword."

Discarding the useless shaft, she took up the sword that lay beneath the rest of her trappings beside the tarn. Sword on sword, she met his slashing blade in a brilliant attack that forced him back a pace as he waded knee-deep to the water's edge.

Slash! Parry! Counter!

The warrior maid held her ground.

Odin's beard! She is magnificent, thought Hogar.

She swords it like a man. Beware! The maid fights to the death!

He attacked. The girl returned blow for blow; they stood a sword length apart, blade to blade, in a wild fury of master strokes that echoed throughout the grove. Slowly, Hogar gained the advantage. Forcing her back, he won the tarn's edge. Stepping across the wet earth in a bold stride, he met each slash and thrust of her sword; the girl attacked even as she retreated before his onslaught. And then, like the master swordsman he was, Hogar found the opening for the kill. But it was ever so gently that he placed his point against the red swan above her heart, knowing that if she had been a man he would have thrust the blade home; for her sword was upraised for a slashing parry. The blow never fell. Her sword arm wilted.

"Have done!" said Hogar, breathing hard; for the warrior maid had winded him. The knowledge sent a crimson flood from his neck to the rusty locks hanging wet on his brow.

For a moment he feared she was about to fall upon his sword. Instead, as he withdrew his blade and stood back a pace, she lowered her point, then drove it into the earth.

"Take me, or slay me," she cried, still proud in defeat.

When Hogar did not reply at once, she misread his silence and dropped to her knees with head lowered for the death blow. He stepped forward then and, lifting her cleft chin, looked deep into her tear-brimmed eyes.

"Why should I slay a warrior maid whose heart I have won by her own code in fair combat?" he asked gently. Sheathing his sword, he raised the girl to her feet and kissed her on the mouth. She clung to him, willingly returning his kiss. For a long moment they held each other close, tenderly, in their first embrace.

"How are you called, girl?"

"Ragnahild," she told him.

"It is meet that you be named 'battle maid of the gods,'" said Hogar with a nod of approval. She saw he was pleased with her and her name, that he found its meaning suited her well.

"You fought me like a true Asyr," he said. "As for myself, a few yesterdays ago I was Hogar of Valhelm, the king's thane. Today I am called Hogar Bloodsword, a hunted outlaw with a price on my head."

That he wanted her, she knew; but what she must say, must now be said. With that resolve, she cast her Weird to the winds as she spoke.

"I am Vandir born, not Asyr."

"By Odin, you do cruelly jest!"

"By Weor, and all the Vandir gods, I am proud of my birthright!" Ragnahild retorted hotly. "Take back your kiss, Hogar Bloodsword, if you will. Though we be sworn blood enemies by the fickle whim of the Norns, I take not back mine. Slay me, then, and be done quickly, I pray you, if one of us must die by the other's hand; for I will not draw sword against the man who has won me fair."

"By the gods, sweet enemy, you are more desirable than any Asyr maid who stirred my loins with a longing to bed her. Vandir or nay, you shall live, for I have chosen to have you."

He took her in his arms.

"Here is my kiss again in the bargain." When he released her, Ragnahild took up her cloak from beside the tarn and drew it about her shoulders, but when she would have gathered the rest of her trappings and sheathed the sword she had thrust in the earth, he took her by the arm.

"Leave them for now. Come," he urged her.

Ragnahild allowed him to lead her up the rise, trembling at his apparent eagerness to claim lord's right as conqueror, for she was a virgin. Hogar's next words brought a ripple of golden laughter to her lips.

"There is bread, cheese, and wine under yonder oak, near where you tethered your mare. I have ridden long, fought with wood thieves, slain one, lost my horse, my helmet, and my pouch, won me a warrior maid of rare beauty, and my stomach grumbles for want of food."

She no longer feared what was to come. Still laughing lightly, she said, "It is but poor, simple fare from my saddlebag that I have to share with you, my lord."

Under the oak tree he spread her cloak. Lying thereon, they broke bread together. The wine warmed them. Later, when she was ready to receive him, she came into his arms. When they had ungirded their loins, he knew her; and she knew for the first time of love's fierce sweetness. The mare whinnied once, when she cried out; then all was still but for the pounding of two young hearts.

XIV

"Valkyrie!"

When they had taken their fill of love, Hogar and Ragnahild walked naked to the tarn, where they bathed themselves and splashed each other playfully. It was then he asked her concerning the mark above her left breast.

"It is not a birthmark, if that be what you surmise," she told him. "It is my swan-mark."

"A swan maiden," Hogar half whispered, as though to himself.

"I am but a novice of the order," said Ragnahild, indicating her unfeathered initiate's cloak. "This was my first combat with a man. A swan maiden may take a husband or a lover, but she must accept the first man who bests her in battle, or be slain. Either by him or by her own hand. I am glad thou were the one, Hogar Bloodsword, for I love thee." For a moment she lapsed into the Old Tongue of the skalds. "I carry thy seed in my womb. I shall bear thee a son, and he shall be called Hukert, one day King of the Asyr and the Vandir; and there shall be peace at last between our peoples."

"The name Hukert has a good ring to it," was the best reply Hogar could muster. Her directness staggered him. Asyr women did not presume so. Yet her frankness in speaking her mind brought them closer together. She wanted him for her mate. His heart warmed to the thought of Ragnahild bearing his sons. Words came easier for them. They spoke of many things, wanting to know each other better. She told him then how she had come to enter the Order of the Red Swan.

"My mother remarried," she began. "But first, I

must tell you my father was Chieftain-of-a-Hundred-Swords to the Vandir king, and died bravely in defense of his liege against the Asyr. My mother was King Hern's ward. Left with us children—there were three of us; I had two brothers, both now dead of Asyr arrows—and without my father, she grew lonely. Being approached one day by the king to do so, my mother remarried. But the king's choice was a rake. It was because of my stepsire and his ill treatment of my mother—who died of a broken heart—that I left Wulfstane, my father's steading, and sought refuge in the Swan Queen's order. Thus did I escape the evil shadow of Lord Drakko."

"Drakko!" cried Hogar, taken aback. "The Vandir king's emissary?"

"You know him, then?" Ragnahild asked.

"It is he who threw down his sword, the craven, when I would have run him through the throat for daring to lay a hand on my lady mother; he whose left ear I notched, as a reminder that when next we meet I shall kill him. This man—this dog, Drakko—is your father?"

"My stepsire," she corrected him quietly.

"Even so," said Hogar, "by Odin, I have sworn to kill him." He recounted for her the events of that night at Grimmswold keep, which now seemed so long ago for all that had happened since, of the duel with Drakko, of the circumstance that led afterward to the brawl with Blund, and how, in need of a weapon, he had drawn the spurious king's falchion from the oak.

"For which I was banished. Outlawed by my father's brother—nay, my father's slayer he is," he said bitterly. "Jarl Hothir, who now calls himself King of the Asyr, is both my stepsire and uncle. I have sworn a vengeance on his head." He told her of the Volva's revelation in the sea cave, and of Runulf of Dorn's confession. "Therefore my solemn vow to the gods to quest for the sword and the ring I must win to wreak my vengeance."

Ragnahild fitted on her breastplates of silver and bronze as he spoke. These she had left beside the tarn with her high-strapped sandals, which she now stepped into and buckled on.

"Come, my lord husband," she said, taking her sword from where she had driven it in the earth. "It grows late. We must be on our way if we would find an inn before nightfall."

"Husband, is it?" he mocked her with a grin. "One kiss, and she has a ring through my nose!"

"Lover, then, my lord, an it please you more," said Ragnahild, knowing she would eventually have her way. Without waiting for him, she strode briskly up the rise to the great oak. Buckling on her warrior maid's girdle, she hung her sword at her side and threw her cloak about her shoulders. "We will share the mare," she told Hogar as he dressed and armed himself.

" 'Tis just past sundown and dusk comes quickly. The dark brings out the trolls, as well you know." With that, Ragnahild took the saddle, leaving Hogar no choice but to mount behind and ride pillion.

Coming out of the grove, they regained the road, which they followed down coast without incident until they sighted a detachment of Utgarthian lancers seated about a roadside fire not far ahead. Ragnahild reined up quickly. In the twilight darkness, the lancers were not yet aware of their approach. They were too busy passing a wineskin back and forth amongst themselves. It was evident as the riders drew closer that the wine had made the rounds once too often for some, if not for all.

"Five of them," Ragnahild whispered over her shoulder. "They are drunk," she said, keeping her voice down. From nearby a horse whinnied.

"Yonder is where their mounts are tethered," Hogar told her softly. "I'll steal one." He slid down from behind the saddle.

"You must not be recognized. Have you forgotten there is a price on your head?"

"Who in Utgarth would have such tidings?" he asked. "I must tempt my Norns, it seems, for a much-needed horse. The two of us are more than enough for your mare." He started off, but she called him back with a whisper.

"Stay, Hogar, I have a more daring plan." She quickly told him what she proposed.

" 'Tis a bold stroke," he agreed, with a grin. "They are drunk enough to believe what they think they see."

So it was that with Hogar lying across her saddle horn like a slain warrior, Ragnahild kicked the mare to a gallop. With a wild Valkyrie cry, she hurdled the center of the fire. Scattering the startled patrol like frightened rabbits, she vanished into the gathering dusk.

The drunken Utgarthians collected themselves slowly.

"Valkyrie!" exclaimed the first to recover his wits.

"You're in your cups," said the one who staggered most.

"By the gods!" bellowed another. "There's been no Valkyrie in a thousand years. Not since Ragnarok. The wine has rotted your brain, Brugar."

"I saw it with mine own eyes!" insisted the one thus addressed. "It was a Valkyrie, I tell you. She was carrying a slain warrior across her saddle horn."

"I saw it, too, Brugar. Just like you," swore a fourth lancer.

"You're both drunk," said a fifth.

"Listen!" cried Brugar. "Do you hear that? Here comes another one!"

Ragnahild meanwhile had circled wide, taking care not to be visible in the firelight. Now, coming at full gallop, she jumped the mare once more over the center of the blaze, with Hogar still draped across her saddle horn, playing dead.

"Valkyrie!" cried the befuddled patrol as one, seeking cover from the pounding hooves that hurdled their heads by a hairsbreadth miss.

The third time, Ragnahild made the jump alone; the next moment brought Hogar in her wake, a great roan gelding between his thighs, taking the leap with ease.

"That was a man!" cried one of the lancers as the last of the two riders vanished in the gloaming.

"Have you no eyes?" demanded another. "Brugar is right. They were Valkyrie."

"You're in your cups," repeated the one who staggered most.

"The last was a warrior riding alone."

"You lie!"

"Who are you calling a liar?"

Hot words led to cold iron. There was a clash of swords, and blood flowed. The three who escaped a thrust in the gut were trampled by their own steeds. Cut free, the horses thundered over them, eager to follow the big roan into the darkening dusk.

XV

The Rallying of the Jarls

Of the three jarls called to council in the cause of Nordgaard's queen, only two graced the high table boards before the crackling longfire in the great hall of Skona. A third was proxied by his nephew. Absent from the Council of Jarls were Orlaf of Thone, who marched in the van of the Usurper, and the spurious King of the Asyr, Hothir Longtooth, himself.

Crowding the high seat with his mighty bulk sat Lothbrok Forkbeard, Jarl of Skona; to his right was seated burly Jarl Urik of Ardvarth; on his left, Ingvar, Jonker of Svend, deputized by his uncle and overlord, Mulik the Unsteady, Jarl of Grundergaard, who remained at his garth incapacitated by an attack of gout.

Present also, and seated according to rank, were the vassal lords, jonkers, and their retainers from every steading and garth of the three jarldoms expected to swear fealty to the queen. Grizzled, hawk-nosed Ketil the Skald faced the assembled lords and their sworn karls, from where he stood toasting his back before the longfire trench. The mead flowed freely.

"Lords, and stalwart karls," began Ketil, speaking for all to hear, "ease up on your quaffing, I pray you, ere reason takes leave of you. We are called together for a purpose more noble than bousing ourselves into a stupor, and our neighbor under the table. We are called in the queen's cause. All of you are come of your own accord at my behest. To each jarl present have I spoken privately; thereby have I spoken to every liege man and sworn karl in this hall by proxy, save one. There sits amongst us one with whom I have not spoken—Ingvar of Svend—who sits for his uncle, Jarl Mulik. Conveniently indisposed with the gout, Mulik remains at Grundergaard. I have broken bread at his board, and it doubts me the fare was so rich."

Ingvar flushed to the roots of his long yellow hair that fell in greasy strands about his narrow shoulders. Tall and bony, with the face of a knave, he stood towering in his anger at the skald's bold innuendo about his liege. His drinking horn overturned as he lurched unsteadily against the high table boards.

"Dare you question Jarl Mulik's loyalty or intent?" he snarled. "If this were not in council, skald, I would silence your impertinence with my sword."

"If it's satisfaction you seek, Ingvar, step out to the courtyard, and I will be pleased to oblige you," Ketil returned hotly. None of the council was armed; the custom at Skona was to disarm before entering the great hall.

"Thor's balls!" bellowed Lothbrok Forkbeard. "No brawling in my hall. Sit down, Ingvar, you bloody drunken fool! The skald speaks boldly enough, forsooth, but with good provocation. We all know what keeps Jarl Mulik at home. The craven is hiding under his bed. I have sat at meat at Grundergaard, and it is even as the skald says. Thin fare it was, by the gods! Gout, my arse! Mulik is waiting to see which way the wind blows."

"Hear! Hear!" shouted those at the lower tables not wearing the badge of Grundergaard. Those who wore the Blue Fox glowered, casting black looks about them. A fist flew at an offending nose. A drinking horn smashed down on a partisan pate. Soon all at the lower tables were at each other's throats, overturning the boards and benches; grappling, biting, gouging, like baited animals on the rushes in Skona's great hall, while Lothbrok Forkbeard stood roaring from the high seat, "Thor's balls! No brawling in my hall!"

Ketil the Skald, chanting staves at the top of his voice, egged the brawlers on until, in the thick of it all, Lothbrok brought a drinking horn down on his head, with sufficient force to put an end to his improvised lines about a gutless tub of lard, rhyming with Grundergaard.

When he finally came around, urged back to consciousness by a bucket of cold water sloshed in his face, Ketil found himself wet and shivering on a bench before the longfire amongst Lothbrok's snoring berserker guard, with a sleeping fur thrown over him. Urik and Lothbrok were again seated at the high table, drinking beaker for beaker. The great hall had been set to rights. Ingvar of Svend and his brawling henchmen were long on the road back to Grundergaard. Those of Urik's underlings not billeted in the guardroom and barracks for the most part, were likewise snoring on fireside benches. Some, more amorous than boused, were bedded with fair-braided wenches of their choosing. Any that needed patching up were nursing their hurts and bruises in the infirmary, such as it was. Lothbrok Forkbeard was not one to pamper the wounded. If they can walk, they can fight, were his sentiments.

"So I didn't break your skull after all," he bellowed jovially to Ketil, seeing the skald rouse himself. "Come, join us in a horn, while we knock our heads together over the problem that springs not only from the queen's cause, but from your quarrel with the Jonker of Svend and the ensuing brawl."

When the skald was seated at the high board, Lothbrok toned down his voice to a mere shout, his normal manner of speech.

"From where I sit, Ketil," said the Jarl of Skona, "it looks like two against three."

The skald poured himself a horn of mead from a flagon brought by a sleepy pot boy. As he ruminated over Lothbrok's premise, Urik growled, "The Blue Fox will march on the side that affords him the advantage." Refilling his tankard to overbrimming, the burly Jarl of Ardvarth downed half of it in one continuous swallow, before he resumed speaking. "Mulik covets Skaane."

"Skaane!" cried Ketil the Skald. "With its burnt-out hall and crumbling walls?"

"He would rebuild Skaane, were it his."

Lothbrok nodded in agreement with Urik.

"Ermengard would never give him fief. Are you forgetting the queen is Ogmund's daughter?" Ketil asked. "And how would Mulik defend Skaane if he did rebuild it? 'Tis a long, hard ride to Grundergaard, with the holdings of inconsonant lords lying betwixt them."

"Mulik is nothing if not ambitious," said Lothbrok.

"Not to mention greedy," put in Urik.

"Are you saying Hothir would fief Skaane to Mulik by royal grant, if the fat swine supports the false-king's cause—even though it be the queen's heritage?" Ketil shook his head at his own question.

"Not so," argued Lothbrok. "Skaane was part of the queen's dowry, true; but it is now a crown fylke lying dormant. No claim put forward by the scattered Rhens, even by the queen herself—for all know she is royal Rhenish—would deter Hothir from his purpose."

Ketil looked hard at Lothbrok.

"So then, 'tis two against three, as you say," he agreed. "Mulik marches against the queen, and wins Skaane as reward for his loyalty to Hothir, and becomes scot-king. Is that it?"

Lothbrok nodded and emptied his tankard.

"If that is the way the wind blows," said burly Jarl Urik.

"By Odin's beard!" cried Ketil the Skald. "It will blow that way only if our heads are hung from Hothir's saddle horn!"

"Aye!" The two jarls spoke as one. A determined look passed between the three men.

"We march, then?" asked Ketil jubilantly.

"On the morrow," said Urik, banging his tankard down.

"T'morrow is already come," shouted Lothbrok Forkbeard. "Ho, there, pot boy!" The greasy lad who leaned against the kitchen door frame half asleep, came running forward, rubbing his eyes open.

"Yes, lord?"

"Wake Oleg, my captain of warriors," Lothbrok shouted. Roused from his mead-heavy slumber, Oleg rolled off his bench and stumbled to his feet. He faced the high table with a surly countenance.

"What would you, Forkbeard?"

"Wake the lords and their karls wherever they are; if bedded too snugly, kick their arses out!" shouted the Jarl of Skona. "Tell every man jack to arm himself, that we march at once in the service of Nordgaard's queen."

"Aye!" cried Oleg. Kicking over the benches where Lothbrok's berserkers lay snoring, he yelled, "Get your arses out of there!" With his men muttering and cursing at his heels, he led them out of the hall to rouse the others.

Ketil the Skald rose and begged leave of his host.

"But you ride with us to Arn," Lothbrok boomed.

"Nay, lord," said Ketil. "It is my intention to skirt Grundergaard, keeping my eyes peeled for signs of treachery. Ingvar of Svend is the fox in the henhouse. I doubt me not that Mulik is but clay in the hands of that sculptor of lies. Already, methinks, the barefaced Ingvar has Mulik a-horse, and the Blue Fox rides to join Hothir's van. We three will meet at Arn, or on the field of the queen's choosing. Meanwhile, may Odin ride with you—and me!" With that he struck hands with the two jarls and strode from the great hall, making his way quickly to the stables.

XVI

Tidings and Good Counsel

At the crest of turf above the dunes that swept down to the sea's edge, Hogar and Ragnahild reined up facing choppy waters and an angry sky. On the beach below stood a fisherman's hovel, with nets draped about the door and hung out to dry on nearby clumps of reeds. Caulking the fishing skiff beached below the hut was a red-bearded giant of a man. He was no longer young, but his physical build and bearing was that of a mighty warrior, though his humble fisherman's garb denied this.

With the approach of the two riders, he looked up over his shoulder in a startled way. Reaching into the skiff, he brought forth a battle-ax and stood glowering at them as they nosed their horses down over the dunes.

"No need for arms, friend," said Hogar reassuringly as he and Ragnahild rode up. "We are not enemies; we have ridden all night and half the day, and we have gold to pay for the night's lodging, and to ferry us across to yonder isle."

"She leaks," grumbled the red-bearded man, with a jerk of his head toward the skiff, "and a storm is brewing, by the looks of the sky and the smell of the wind." His belligerence tempered by the promise of gold, he put back the ax.

"How are you called, fellow?" Hogar asked.

"Lif," was the laconic reply.

"When you have done with your work, Lif," Hogar told him, "you may give us supper." He drew open the pouch he had plundered from the dead Utgarthian patrol. Breaking a gold ring, he tossed half on the sand at the fisherman's bare feet, then he prodded the gelding over amongst the taller reeds to be tethered. Dismounting, he tied up Ragnahild's mare as well and gave her a hand out of the saddle. They turned to see Lif biting hard on the half-ring with strong white teeth; satisfied it was gold, he gave forth a burst of good-natured laughter.

"You would be Hogar Bloodsword." He grinned. "It looks like the sky is clearing after all. A good supper it shall be, lord." He stared then at Ragnahild. "A battle maid. So." He looked away sheepishly. "Nels said nothing of a maid." He cleared his throat, plainly embarrassed, and added lamely, "There is but one bed."

"That need be no concern of yours, Lif," said Hogar.

The red-bearded giant shrugged. "I will sleep in the skiff," he grumbled. "My stomach growls for food. We'll have supper now. Fish stew. Come along and wash up."

That night Hogar stirred in his sleep, half aware of a third presence within the hovel. He fought the irresistible force that lifted his eyelids and brought him half awake.

He sat bolt upright at the sight of the wraithlike figure standing before him, and sleep fell from his eyes and mind like a discarded garment. Ragnahild slept on undisturbed. Hogar's hand instinctively sought his hilt; the blade was half drawn as he spoke, full drawn ere his feet touched the earthen floor.

"Speak out, specter! Who and what are you?"

"Sheath thy sword, Hogar. I bring down no evil upon thee. It is I, the Seer-of-All."

"Long dead, from the look of you," said Hogar. He swung his sword at the wraith form in a vicious slash. "I would shorten your ghost by a head!" The blade sliced through the shadowy neck, but the head did not fall; unsevered, it spoke out as before.

"Again I say, sheathe thy sword, Hogar. I am come to give thee good counsel, and tidings of thy lady mother, now queen."

"Wherefore do you speak in the Old Tongue," returned the Nordsman, "if this be not ensorcelment, and you are not a troll fiend?" He slashed again at the wraith form, and as before, his sword slew naught but empty space.

"Peace, Hogar. Let there be plain speech between us, then. Your sword swings at my shadow self, cutting thin air. I am the Wizard of Lom, once court magician to Ermengard's sire, the dead Ogmund, King of Rhenish Skaane."

Hogar put up his sword.

"Peace, O Wizard. What tidings bring you of my mother the queen?"

"She has taken sanctuary with Queen Astrith of the Swans at Arn. Ari Oxmain, that sturdy one-eye at Grimmswold, has declared for Queen Ermengard; a stout fellow, and loyal to the death. With him ride a score and ten handpicked stalwarts newly sworn in the queen's service, having renounced shield oath to the false-king Hothir. For they know now the cruel truth of how and why Helmer, first, then Thorodd, his royal brothers, both died by his bloody hand. Your mother the queen is well, and sits in safety at Arn," said the wizard, "while Ogmund's old commander Starulf busies himself levying an army to field under her war banner against the usurper."

"Good tidings, indeed," replied Hogar. "What counsel bring you?"

" 'Follow thy Weird.' So said the Volva, speaking for the silent gods. Heed you well their counsel. For your Norns have tied the threads. The runes are cast."

"You know, then, of the vision that came upon me in the sea cave, of the quest I am sworn to achieve?" Hogar asked.

"In sooth, I am the Seer-of-All, as I did attest," replied the wizard. "You seek the rune-ring of Odin and the Ravensword."

"Tell me more of the Ravensword, and how I may find it."

"Legend would have it the lost sword of the god Frey," said the Wizard of Lom. "Dwarf-forged, elf-fashioned, and graven with elfin runes the length of the broad blade from cross guard to point. Once lost, it is said to have passed from hand to hand down through the years before and since Ragnarok, where Frey fell for want of his sword. Through how many hands it has passed remains unsung. One thing is known: Thorir Treefoot won the famed runesword from the pirates of Thairm, in the Orkna Ey. It was he who struck his raven mark on the wondrous blade. Thus did the lost sword of Frey come to be called 'Ravensword.' With it Thorir Treefoot swung his last sword stroke against the Vandir and the Fire Lords, ere he fell on the field of Skaane.

"Whoever pried the sword from Thorir's dead fingers remains nameless; it is said the Ravensword was not found on the field, when those who came to bury the Rhenish dead drove off the gray wolves and ravens, red in claw and tooth from ravening the windrowed corpses of the slain that bloody day. Much was the wonder at the tale told by some, that out of the sky there came a darkness of whirring wings; of gryffonlike talon tracks on the heath where the battle was waged.

"The skalds chant of the sword's disappearance," the wizard's wraith went on. "How the Ravensword fell from Thorir Treefoot's hand and vanished into the earth where eerie wraiths rose up to receive it. Another tale is told, too: how the Ravensword fell into the hands of the Fire Lords, how they sent their Black Legion of Skulthurs in support of the hard-pressed Vandir that day, and how they descended upon the field of Skaane to claim the sword for Nardath-Thool."

"The Volva spoke of such a city, rune built with the ring Odin lost on the battleground at Ragnarok," said Hogar. "She spoke also of the ring being hidden there with my grandsire's sword. Tell me, O Wizard, how do I best find my way to Nardath-Thool?"

The wizard's wraith form glowed as the reply came from shadow lips.

"In the Cold Waste of the Sorcerers, which lies beyond the Finnamark, there the Nemedian city of your quest rises upon the rubble where once stood Asgarth, the home of the gods. Here, with Odin's ring, Nemed First built white-walled Nardath in a verdancy begot of sorcery. All else about this ensorceled place is utter desolation, vast and perilous. In sooth, death awaits the unwary traveler who would venture to Nardath of the White Walls, that fey city ruled by the sorceress queen Tha. Nol Dragir, the dragon-spawned Archon of the Thalmanda Fire Lords, is her half brother. His domain is the Black Citadel of Thool, which rises towering from the very heart of this warlocks' nest you must seek out to win your quest.

"Attend, Hogar. The way to Nardath-Thool is fraught with great danger," said the shadow wraith.

"I am oath sworn to make the quest," said the Nordsman.

"Fare north, Hogar," said the wizard, "as the lodestone guides your ship, as far as sail and oar can take you, beyond the perilous bergs and the Frozen Sea; there, the ice-troll caves through which you must pass are yet more hazardous. Find your way safely through these caves, and your ship will enter the harbor of your quest. Beside the witchcrafted Sea of Nemed, there will you find the rune-built and sinistrous city you seek, rising from the mists. Fare north, then, Hogar; and tarry not. 'Follow thy Weird.' The gods give you godspeed!"

Hogar furrowed his brow. "But what of my mother the queen? Quest or nay, is not my place in her service until Hothir is laid by the heels?"

"You have my counsel," said the wizard. "Queen Ermengard sits safely at Arn, as I have told you, while you seek out the sword and the ring. Starulf will not take the field without his queen's command. Meantime, Hothir waits at Nordgaard. It is the will of the gods that he be brought down by your hand. Go then, on your quest. Recover the rune-ring. Win the Ravensword. And with it wreak your vengeance. Send word of your faring by Ragnahild to Arn. There shall she have your child, attended by two queens.

"Now listen well. A word of Ketil," the wizard's wraith continued. "The hawk-nosed skald rides the fylkes of the realm to rally the jarls. Skona and Ardvarth are loyal to the queen. Orlaf of Thone rides in Hothir's van. Mulik of Grundergaard is a straw in the wind. His nephew Ingvar, Jonker of Svend, is the fish to fry," said the sage. "When he is caught," he added, using his hands as though he were playing a trout.

"What then, if Hothir does not wait at Nordgaard?" Hogar asked. "What if he marches on Arn through Lom Woods?"

The wizard's shadow wraith gave a chuckle.

"I would make things appear as though a wise old fox had pulled his hole in after him. And all the while I would sit there unseen, silently laughing up my sleeve."

"Sooth, have you not more up your sleeve than laughter?" In spite of the wizard's disapproving scowl at this impertinence, Hogar chose to go on. "What of your magic?"

"Question not my powers, O Hogar," chided the wizard. "Rather, question your own endurance and might; for Hothir's sorcerer will soon work dark spells to thwart your purpose. When it is known to him of your quest, Hothir will march quickly on Nardath-Thool. For he must win the true king's falchion to secure his kingship; and Odin's ring to bring down the walls of that warlocks' nest on those who hold the two treasures you must win for yourself.

"Therefore, set forth before him, pitting yourself against spellcraft greater than ever you would dare imagine, that of the sorceress Tha, Queen of Nardath, and the dragon magic of her half brother, Nol Dragir, the Archon of Thool."

The shadow wraith was gone then, like a puff of wind. Hogar lay down on the pallet where Ragnahild dreamed undisturbed, his mind a-churn through the sleepless night.

XVII

Death Stalks the Marriage-Fest

Red-bearded Lif broke a frugal fast alone and had finished caulking the skiff before the Nordsman appeared in the hovel doorway, haggard from loss of sleep. Lif served up a skillet of fried herring, which Hogar and Ragnahild attacked with good appetite, dipping chunks of quick bread in the hot fat and washing it all down with cooling quaffs of surprisingly good ale.

It was late in the afternoon before Lif ferried them across to a white-beached holm. They were met by Nels at the agreed upon trysting place in answer to Lif's halloo. The burly bowman boomed a welcome to his lord with privileged familiarity, and greeted Lif as an old friend.

"So it's a warrior maid you have won to wife, Hogar. Thor's hammer! With those golden braids and those breasts, she is the spit and image of Frigga herself. There'll be merry talk at your marriage-fest. I will pour the bridal cups myself, by Thor!"

The shadow of a smile lurked at the corners of Hogar's mouth.

"Ragnahild, this loudmouth rogue is Nels the Bowman, who'll fill our pledge cups this night."

"Come see your ship," Nels urged proudly later, when Lif had returned to the mainland to dispose of the horses. He then led the pair to where the longship lay, with its mast unstepped in a crude launching shed concealed by scrub pine.

Svadi came from the grove to join his brothers on

seeing Hogar approach the shed. Tools and buckets of wild sheep tallow used for greasing the ways were set aside, as they came forward with grins of welcome for their lord and sheep eyes for the armored maid at his side. All touched their forelocks respectfully but Finnur. His eyes were bold and daring.

"She is a braw lass we have here," said Finnur bluntly. Hogar's brow darkened in a scowl.

"Bite your tongue, brother!" growled Svadi, making a fist. "She is the lord's lady."

"I speak only of the ship," retorted Finnur slyly.

" 'Tis well you do," said Hogar. Clearing his brow, he appraised the longship from upflung stern to stem post, both carved with grotesque, fierce-fanged sea-serpent heads. "She shall be called *Sea Raven*, this braw ship. Tonight her name will be amongst the toasts at the marriage-fest. We shall ask an omen of the gods that she sails on the winds of good fortune. You have done well, Svadi. You and your brothers have earned your meed. Tonight you shall sit at meat as freed men and skoal the bridal cup."

While the wooded islet had rung with the sound of sword on sword during many a duel to the death in years gone by, never had there been heard the stroke of an ax felling trees to build a longhouse. Nels and his charges had erected lean-to shelters of greenwood boughs for sleeping quarters. They chose a small clearing, an old dueling ground, amidst a fragrant pine grove to serve as their hall, pillared by lofty trees reaching up to support a roof of open sky. Here they dug a longfire trench and hewed planks from felled logs for benches, trestles, and boards. To Svadi, who still limped from his half-healed arrow wound, had fallen the lot of steward, in charge of provisions and the kitchen. The big fellow fortunately had a way with herbs which abounded in wild profusion. Nels brought meat to the table with his bow. Svadi and his brothers had proved themselves trustworthy, else the longship would not have been readied for sea as Hogar now found it.

Evenfall, with its pleasant scent of pine needles and

the succulent aroma of roast wild pig rising from the spit over the glowing coals, brought all hands to table with good appetite and cheerful mien. A bridal bower had been built. Lif, whom Hogar had accepted as a member of his company, had returned with a hogshead of ale. As Svadi served the roast pig Lif filled the cups Frodi had fashioned from gourds found dried on the vine.

It was a merry company assembled under the greenwood shaws. Many a bellow of laughter resounded over a ribald lay or tale as roast pig filled contented stomachs and the level of the ale in the cask went down and down.

Ragnahild was radiant, and when her turn came proved herself entertaining as the next in reciting some Vandir story, or singing a stave, and the telling of her first quest as a warrior maid.

Hogar related his adventures after the longship had sailed from Dorn beach, of his battle with the troll witch Huldren and how he slew the werwulf Thane of Dorn, of Hrapp the reeve's bravery; but not a word of the treasure buried deep in Dorn Woods did he mention, and for good reason. He told of being waylaid, beaten, and robbed by wood thieves, of how he escaped, and of his meeting with Ragnahild over crossed swords at the edge of a forest tarn.

Nels fell off his bench with laughter at Ragnahild's telling of her Valkyrie ride with Hogar draped across her saddle horn, playing the slain warrior to the confusion of the drunken Utgarthian patrol.

All eyes were bright and warm with good fellowship, save two; what thoughts Finnur kept hidden behind the rim of his cup none of the others guessed. But in his drunken mind, Finnur repeated again and again to himself, "I shall have that Vandir wench!"

As the longfire coals burned low the time came for toasts. The *Sea Raven* was skoaled, and Hogar promised each karl who served him well a full share of the spoils when he went a-roving. Many a toast was raised, and many a cup was downed. At last, Nels filled the bridal cups as his privilege. Hogar rose then from the bench where he and Ragnahild sat in lieu of a high seat.

"With this cup do I take thee, Ragnahild, to wife," he pledged. Ragnahild then rose, cup in hand.

"With this cup do I take thee, Hogar, to husband." Having exchanged their vows and kissed, the bridal pair drank their cups to a resounding "Skoal! Skoal!"

"May Frigga give you many sons!" boomed Nels. Draining his own cup, he herded the others from the grove, saying in a loud whisper, "We have no further business here." To Finnur, seeing he would linger over his cup, he growled, "Come along, tosspot."

Ragnahild awakened as the questing hand violated the privacy of the bridal bower. Her flesh crawled, but she did not cry out. A glance told her Hogar was gone to relieve himself. Whoever was outside the bower had waited patiently for such a chance. With battle-maid instinct, she rose naked from her bridal bed and struck out with the drawn sword she was wont to keep at her side through the night. There was a sharp hissing gasp outside the bower as the descending blade severed the intruding hand at the wrist, and the bloody stump was withdrawn. Before the dastard could flee the moon-lit grove, Ragnahild, like a blond goddess of war, her blue eyes flashing with fury, stood parting the bower entry half naked, half robed, reddened sword gleaming in one hand. In the other, she held up the gory severed member.

"Stand, churl!" she cried out fiercely. "It is not thy hand I would take, Finnur—but thy head!" She hurled the grisly trophy at the feet of her pain-sobered attacker, who knelt unarmed four paces distant, binding the bloody stump of his right arm with a garter. "Thou would-be spoiler of women, I challenge thee to the death!"

A cornered rat's fear shone in the wretched Finnur's eyes. She whose naked body he had sought in lust stood there no longer half robed, but armor-clad now, in swiftly buckled-on breastplates and war girdle glowing with moonfire, a smear of his own villainous blood soiling her bare midriff. Beside her stood Hogar, just returned from the latrine, naked as the unsheathed sword in his hand. Ragnahild held him back when he would have donned his harness.

"This is my battle," she told him firmly, but he natheless busked on his byrnie.

Rushing from their shelters came Nels and Lif, weapons drawn to defend their lord's lady, followed by the unarmed Svadi and his other brothers. Finnur made no resistance. He was quickly seized and roughly held by the bearlike Svadi, whose tears of anger and shame ran down his cheeks unheeded as he sobbed, "Finnur, Finnur. You bloody fool!"

The wands were cut and staked out to mark the combat square. The rules of combat were Ragnahild's to declare: a duel to the death with broadswords, without shields, customary exchange of shield blows waived; with no daggers concealed.

One lone protest was loudly voiced by Finnur.

"I have lost my sword hand." He held up the bound stump like a whining mendicant.

"Then fight with the other," growled Nels. "I have seen you work tools with either hand. You swing an ax with your left hand, Finnur, not your right. Thor's hammer!" shouted the bowman, suddenly remembering. "You fought left-handed with a sword at Dorn steading, you bloody son-of-a-troll! It would be natural to part the bower with your right hand, before reaching in with your left."

Hogar searched his memory of that fray. Satisfied that Nels had seen right as he rode into the mews at Dorn, the Nordsman turned to his fair-braided bride, proud approval in his fire-blue eyes. With a nod, he ordered the duel to begin.

"Bring the knave a sword," ordered Ragnahild, stepping into the marked-off square. "Defend thyself, Finnur, thou troll-spawned cur!" she cried as he faced her armed and snarling, his lust transmuted to hate.

She attacked at once, bringing the fight to Finnur with lightning-quick slashes, driving him from one corner to another. Finnur had not lost his sword hand. He fought back left-handed, but with the heart gone out of him. He parried badly, and Ragnahild's blade opened his cheek to the bone. As his brothers grimly looked on Finnur howled like a wounded beast and fled the square. Lif's lusty voice rose over the hubbub.

"To the landing! He's making for the skiff!"

But Finnur abruptly changed his course of flight to the far side of the island. Fleet of foot, he was soon lost to view amongst the moon-lit trees.

"A boon, lord!" Svadi petitioned. "I am fast for my bulk, and I know this holm. Let brother bring brother to justice."

"Aye, lord," cried Frodi. "We are four to his one. Give us leave to bring you Finnur."

Hogar was about to consent when Nels the Bowman's voice exploded with sudden truth.

"Thor's hammer! He means to scuttle the *Sea Raven*!"

Once out of sight, a bloody-cheeked and vengeful Finnur headed for the launching shed, as Nels had surmised. He had reached the longship and struck the first left-handed blow against the overlapping strakes at the waterline, the ax cutting deep into the bow with a vengeance, when he heard his name shouted from the woods. He drove the ax again and again into the sturdy oak hull, as though possessed of troll strength. Ever nearer came the shouts. Finnur paused in his mad destruction, ax held ready to sell his life dearly against the first karl to appear; then desperately, he turned back to the ship, striking away chocks and supports in a crazed fury of pain and hatred born of his frustrated lust. The longship strained to break free. Finnur leapt across the greased ways as the first of his pursuers broke from the woods. It was Nels, nocking an arrow as he ran. The loosed shaft took Finnur in the throat as the underpinning gave. He fell across the ways, gurgling a wordless cry, as the *Sea Raven* slid down serpent prow first over his spread-eagled body, crotch to head, and out into the waiting sea with her launching lines flying.

All hands stood stunned, some turning away from the grisly sight, although human sacrifice at a launching was common practice in the Nordland. Nels the Bowman's booming voice broke the shocked hush.

"An omen! Her keel is bloodied!"

"Good fortune is Norn-woven in her sails!" cried Ragnahild.

"Grab her lines!" shouted Hogar, wading knee-deep before he remembered he was armored. Lif was first to swim out and take hold of a line. The labor of hauling on the lines and pulling on the oars to beach the *Sea Raven* began. While the mast was stepped and sail-rigged, Svadi and his remaining brothers buried Finnur's crushed and bloody corpse in the woods, alone and unnoticed in their grief and the shame he had brought upon them.

XVIII

Trouble with Hromund

Finnur's ax had done the *Sea Raven* little harm. The deep bites it made in the bow strakes were soon caulked with animal hair and pitch. Readied for sea, she was off the beach in shoal water with a lusty heave-ho, her sparse company wading out to board. With her oars shipped and her heavy square sail filling, she ran before a light breeze with the gods smiling down.

Hogar stood at the stern eyeing the heavens with Ragnahild at his side. To steerboard, Nels held a steady hand on the helm.

"I need men!" cried Hogar to the skies. "Gods! Give me a fighting crew of stouthearted karls to fare me on my quest."

"Cutthroats, I ween," put in Ragnahild, laughing.

"Aye," Hogar agreed, turning to her with a grin. "Cutthroats and gallows birds, to storm the gates of Nardath-Thool. A runagate crew, handpicked from the sea scum that hang about the jetties and pot houses of Thairm, in the Orkna Ey. Seafaring rogues who can handle an oar and sail as well as sword and ax. But first we put in at Dorn for ship stores."

The wind held. He beached his ship on the pebbled strand beyond Loki's Rock and hauled her into the old launching shed—from which Runulf of Dorn once had gone a-roving—safe from the vehement surf.

It was from here, Svadi and his brothers remembered, they had come up over the scarped cliff to plunder the steading and take the Nordsman alive, only to win a thrall's collar apiece for their pains.

Hrapp and Gerda welcomed their lord and his warrior maid with open arms. During the three-day stay, Svadi was charged with vittling the ship for the run to the pirate-infested seal islands; Frodi, Haaki, and Hromund with breaking out cloaks and furs against the cold weather to come; and Nels with mustering arms and armor from the guardroom and armory, and choosing hands from amongst the hardiest thralls eager to pull an oar for a purse of gold.

Hogar and Hrapp, the while, had their own labors to perform. Of these they spoke naught to the others. Gerda alone knew what errand took them deep into Dorn Woods. On their return, three tasks had been accomplished. Hogar's murdered sire, the rightful Jarl of Valhelm, had been given decent burial; Runulf's grisly corpse and severed head were hung from a sturdy tree limb for the ravens to feed upon. Enough gold for the ship's treasury was carried by the reeve in a sea chest. Both lord and karl alike had looked but once upon the large gray stone standing in the meadow near the grass-grown mound.

A bountiful board was spread on the eve of departure. Gerda insisted on calling it a faring-fest, although the *Sea Raven* was yet to be refitted in Thairm for the perilous voyage that lay ahead. Hogar's quest for the Ravensword and Odin's ring was natheless skoaled in faring toasts. The brave adventure intrigued the doughty Hrapp. He begged to be amongst its crew when the *Sea Raven* sailed, but Hogar would have it otherwise.

"Nay, good Hrapp," he told him kindly. "There is that which needs your attention here. When I have sailed, you must see to it Ragnahild has safe passage to Aals. From there she will ride to Arn."

"You would sail without her, lord?" asked the incredulous reeve. "And let her journey to Arn alone?"

"Nels will convoy her," said Hogar, "never fear. Ragnahild shall carry word of my faring to my mother the queen, and await me there till I have won the Raven Throne as king in my own right, for the while I am meant to rule in Nordgaard. I would protect my queen-to-be, whose Weird it is to bear me a son who shall sit the Raven Throne in my stead. For so have the Norns woven my threads of destiny."

With that he beckoned Nels to him and took them both aside to instruct them. When he had done, he told them, "Speak naught of this to Ragnahild. I have not yet divulged to her my intent."

The evening went well thereafter, but for a pair of untoward incidents. The first sprang from Hromund's disposition to sullenness. His morose demeanor had heightened since Finnur's death. He soon guzzled himself into drunken belligerence. At first gloomily silent during the faring toasts, he became loud and truculent the more he drank. Rising at length from the side benches, he advanced with an unsteady gait upon the high seat, tankard raised in a toast.

"Skoal!" he shouted, roaring drunk. "To my dead brother, Finnur—"

Svadi's big fist silenced Hromund with one mighty blow.

"By your leave, lord," said the still-limping Svadi. Taking hold of his brother's collapsed form, he dragged him from the hall.

So began the trouble with Hromund.

The second incident came about later that night, when on retiring Hogar told Ragnahild she would not sail with him on the morrow, that she and Nels were to take passage for Aals and ride from there to Arn with a message for Queen Ermengard.

Ragnahild's blue eyes blazed with anger on hearing Hogar would fare alone.

"Then shall you bed alone, my lord husband!" was her heated reply.

XIX

A Long Black Galley

Next day when the tide was high, the *Sea Raven* was run down greased blocks into the surf and boarded, with her sail billowing in a brisk blow. Hrapp and Gerda with the household karls, and all the field thralls and their broods, were on hand to bid their lord safe faring. Nels was amongst those who cheered, but of Ragnahild there was no sign. Seeing this, Hogar turned his face from the shore. Pursing his lips in a grim line, he held the steer oar firm. He would miss her laughter and her lovemaking. But a longship was no place for a woman to birth a royal child. Not that she was due; it would be many a month before he returned from his questing. By then Ragnahild would have been delivered of a son safely at Arn, with two queens in attendance.

He turned the helm over to Lif.

"If the wind and the weather hold fair," ventured the red-bearded giant, "we will make landfall by the seventh day."

"May the gods will it," Hogar answered. "There are scarcely enough hands between us to man the oars in shifts, should we lose the wind."

He looked uncertainly at the twelve field thralls Nels had chosen with care. Landlubbers, every one! None had ever pulled an oar in his miserable soil-bound life, let alone swung a sword or ax in combat. By the gods, he would teach them!

The wind held, but Hogar struck the sail and drilled his thralls in handling the oars, with Lif at the steer oar. Svadi the while, as bosun, attempted to instruct those not rowing in the use of arms, hoping his clumsy charges would not kill each other in their ineptitude.

In this he had the help of Haaki and Frodi, but Hromund sat idle when not taking his turn at the oars, his hatred for Hogar mounting.

By the second day at sea, the thralls managed to stroke the *Sea Raven* smoothly through fair-weather waters at times; but they were landlubbers at best, and mostly their efforts had the oars in a tangle like jackstraws. Svadi found them equally hopeless in the use of weapons.

On the sixth day, a scudding mist arose. Hogar hoisted sail to spell the oar-weary thralls.

Svadi kept a keen stem watch from then on, straining to see through the enveloping fog, with a great cloak pulled about himself against the wet cold. The ship's lur bellowed mournfully.

Overhead, the flapping sail spoke with the wind that sped the *Sea Raven* on her course. The mist thickened, rolling in on the scud. On deck, both freedmen and thralls lay weather-fended in great cloaks. Lif kept a steady hand on the steer oar, his eyes searching out the sun that of a sudden had gone blind. Hogar stood by, frowning his displeasure at fickle Tyr's inconstancy. And presently from the bow came Svadi's loud cry of "Sail ho, dead ahead!"

A long black galley bore down on them as it hove through the mist, oars out and dipping in rhythm, pulling hard against the wind, sail hauled down to give her headway. All hands on the longship saw the black wolf flag break from her masthead.

"A Fomorian pirate, and she means to board us!" Hogar shouted, exultant at the prospect of his first engagement at sea. "Strike the sail! Sound the lur! We'll board her first if we can, as she comes alongside. Shields! Spears! Grapples ready!"

The two ships came together, bow to stern. With a shout, both crews cast grappling irons; when the ships locked board and board, the melee began. Spears flew thick and fast. Blood flowed, and men fell dead and dying on both decks as the woad-tattooed Fomors came scrambling over the side in great numbers, where they were met with sword, ax, and spear by the *Sea Raven*'s stalwart few. Hogar leapt to his ship's waist, fighting off the boarders and fleshing his sword in throat and gut, to meet the attack of a huge, black-bearded rogue with but one eye. As their swords crossed he recognized Lon Thoddrach.

"Well met, Fomor!" he cried, slashing hard at the scarred and blue-tattooed face he had good cause to remember. "We have a bone to pick between us."

"Damn my eyes!" bellowed the Fomor chieftain. He parried the blow deftly. "Stab me if it's not Hogar Bloodsword back from a watery grave." Countering with admirable skill the while he spoke, Lon Thoddrach roared his pleasure at seeing the Nordsman alive; then came fierce words. "Lay down your arms, and I call off my wolves. Resist, and you die!"

Hogar knew he had no move but surrender. It was that, or death; for himself, and for Svadi, Frodi, and Lif, still fighting valiantly in defense of their ship against unconquerable odds. Still meeting the Fomor's blade, he looked about him as they fought. Hromund and Haaki lay still on the bloody deck. All twelve thralls lay slain, cut down like mown hay before the scythelike onslaught. It was then Hogar saw Hromund move, and sensed he had feigned death to save his skin, that he had raised neither sword, nor spear, nor ax against the boarders. Haaki lay where he had fallen, his sword wetted with Fomor blood, his skull cloven.

"Throw down your arms!" Hogar commanded, disarming himself as he spoke the bitter words. "Tie that craven to the mast and flog him!" He looked Svadi, Frodi, and Lif squarely in the eye as he ordered Hromund put to the lash. The two brothers reluctantly dropped their blooded blades; Lif tossed his gory ax to the deck. Without a word, they dragged Hromund to his punishment. He screamed as the cat cut his back.

Lon Thoddrach stepped over the *Sea Raven*'s gunwale, sheathing his sword.

"Wisely done," he said, giving Hogar a bluff clip about the shoulders. "I am fain not to have slain you for playing the fool, Nordsman." His fierce black beard split in a white-toothed grin. "A bone to pick, say you? As I recall, it was your Nordland gods who washed you over the side that stormy-weather day, and none of my doing. I recall more. There's a gold hoard you spoke of. With no map other than the one in your head to lead a body to it. And I mean to have the share you promised me. Gwern!" he shouted to his evil-miened oarmaster without turning his head. "Throw these corpses to Ran, and cut the grapples. Look alive, damn your eyes!" To Hogar he said, "You and I have faring plans to make over a friendly bousing bowl, mate."

"Not so fast, Fomor." Hogar bridled. "Where else I may fare, I mean to captain my ship."

Lon Thoddrach bellowed his laughter.

"Brave words for one with but two swords, an ax, and a craven dunghill cock left to back him," he roared. "You've lost your ship. She's my prize, fair won. Look about you." He aimed a thumb at his cutthroat crew. "I'm fifty strong to a handful. Your lives are forfeit, Hogar Bloodsword, an I so choose. But nay, I offer you my hand. With you as mate, and me as chieftain of the *Black Wolf*, we'll share your hoard of gold and plenty more plunder to boot, between us. Now there's a bone to pick! Come, we'll drink on it ashore, with a wench on each knee, by bloody Cromm Cruaich!" Sensing the turmoil in the Nordsman's mind, he laid an encouraging hand on Hogar's arm. "Take your helm, mate," he said; then he bellowed, "Gwern! Twenty rowers to man these sweeps!" The order complied with, he shouted, "Cast free both craft! Oars out! Pull, you bastards, pull! Put the *Wolf* about, Gwern, you scurvy dog! I'll follow you in to Thairm."

XX

The Road to Arn

Meanwhile at Norgaard, when the word was brought to Hothir by his spies that Ragnahild was with child in the stronghold of the Swan Queen, the False-King of the Asyr was wroth. For word was abroad that Hogar was the sire. Since a bairn so sired would someday be the rightful heir to the Raven Throne, Hothir Longtooth assembled his warriors to march on Arn and throw grit in the oil of succession. A sword thrust through both mother and bairn, should Ragnahild be delivered of a son; otherwise her own instant dispatch would resolve the dilemma.

So it was that Hothir sat at meat on the roadside the eve of his first day's march on Arn, mulling the matter over a horn of mead, when a horseman was heard approaching camp at a good clip. It proved to be a rider from Grundergaard. He was past the sentry and out of the saddle on bended knee before the false-king in a trice.

"Welcome, Ingvar of Svend," Hothir gave him greeting. "What tidings bring you me? Is Jarl Mulik weary of straddling the fence? Does the Blue Fox march with his king? A cup for my guest!"

The tall and bony jonker drank greedily to wet his dust-dry gullet before answering.

"A Vandir war party is moving this way, my king," said Ingvar. "That is the most urgent of the tidings I bear you. I circled the Vandir unseen, but saw for myself they were led by Lord Drakko. Break camp, my king, and begone from here at once. The Vandir outnumber you five to one."

"I am at meat, as you can see," said Hothir imperiously. "Vandir or nay, I have a duty to my stomach to give it dinner, not butterflies. Drakko, you say? Let him come. I can deal with that craven. Does Grundergaard march in my van, or not? Speak up."

"My king, I have ridden a stout horse to death to gain your side. Be sure Ingvar, Jonker of Svend, is loyal, even to the point of—of—" He let his voice drop, and sought to cover his stammer with a long pull on his beaker.

"Out with it, man! You hide something in your cup," snapped Hothir. "How is it you ride alone?"

"My uncle and I had a falling out, my king." Ingvar's knave face was pale with fatigue and dust, but there was fear gnawing at the back of his eyes. "Jarl Mulik marches with no one. Being loyal even to the point of murder, sire, I—I slew him. For his treason." The word seemed to give him courage. "Yea, for his treason—against you, my king."

"So that's why you ride alone!" said Hothir, his voice cold as a serpent. "You bloody fool! By murdering their jarl, you have driven the men of Grundergaard over to the queen, and the men of Svend with them!"

Enraged, he struck the Jonker of Svend across the mouth, bringing blood. Ingvar's hand instinctively went to his hilt. The naked sword was in his grip before he could check his temper.

A dozen spears were on him at once.

"Hang the dog!" Hothir roared. "So will I measure out justice to any man who draws upon his king. Up with the varlet on yonder oak, and let the ravens pick his lank bones clean." He washed down his anger with a long draft from his tankard. "Fetch the shaman to read the stars."

Hours later, Drakko reined his horse as he and his Vandir host rode up alongside the gibbet tree. Ravens were already greedily tearing at the yellow-haired corpse twisting on its rope.

"Shall I cut the poor bastard down, lord?" asked the shield karl riding at Drakko's side.

"Nay, let the ravens feed. Ingvar of Svend is of no further use to me. The false-king liked not the message the jonker bore him, I see. Hothir's train is before us—ride on! I have a juicy bone to toss the Asyr dog."

In a wayside inn not far from Grundergaard, Ketil the Skald sat savoring a shoulder of lamb and cabbage, downed with a beaker of ale. His fine appetite paled with the advent of the night watch, who searched the premises as a possible hiding place for the craven slayer of Mulik the Unsteady, whose body had been discovered at table, where the jarl spent much of his time, with his eating dagger driven through his heart. On hearing those tidings, Ketil pushed his unfinished trencher from him, drained his tankard, and, having satisfied the watch of his presence at the inn all of that evening, was soon heard galloping hard on the road to Arn.

XXI

Street of the Wind Sellers

From the rugged, red sandstone cliffs that rose steep and uneven to giddy heights above the indented shore, came the raucous cry of wheeling seabirds. Below on their breeding rocks, washed by the fast-running roost of the tide, a seal herd barked its presence to the pair of galleys passing between the barren and treeless banks, stroking smoothly dipped oars up the low-lying firth of Thairm.

Salty language was loudly exchanged by the Fomor pirate chieftain and the rat-faced wharfmaster over moorage fees as the two galleys tied up alongside others of their ilk at the sunset-gilded jetty that had seen many a sea wolf come and go. The squalid, iniquitous port flourished as a haven for pirates of every breed; and so it had, long before the saga-sung days of Thorir Treefoot and the faring that won him the Ravensword, and earned him his fanciful sobriquet by the loss of a leg.

Once ashore, the crew of the *Black Wolf* and the rowers of its prize headed for the brothels and pot houses huddled cheek and jowl along the waterfront stew. Lon Thoddrach steered Hogar into the Shark's Bight, a dingy shebeen where carnal pleasures were as accessible as grog, for the price. Entering on their heels, Lif and Svadi chose a nearby table where they could keep an eye out should the Fomor chief rescind their liberty, and where they could have their backs to a protective wall in the bargain. Since Hogar had insisted they sailed wherever he fared, they were free to roam the port. They were forbidden arms, being crew members of a captured prize; a wooden bench leg or a table plank would serve in a tavern brawl. Frodi had set forth likewise unarmed on his own mischief. Hogar alone had been privileged by rank with the return of his sword.

Close by and already well into the tankard before him, sat Gwern the oarmaster, drinking morosely alone, rankled over his chief's intent that Hogar sail as the *Black Wolf*'s mate—a berth he long had coveted.

As the evening wore on, Gwern rose grumbling to go check on the hired watch on both galleys. The two wharf rats he had chosen at random were at their stations, tallow lanterns lit against the creeping darkness. Stealthy of foot, Gwern boarded each ship in turn, and slipping up behind the watch, he had a dagger between their ribs before either could cry out. He robbed both corpses of the gold paid in hand and tossed the burning lanterns amongst the *Black Wolf*'s underdeck stores, where the flaming wicks would quickly take hold. This done, he released Hromund. Merciful slumber had come to obliterate the coward's pain. Gwern shook him awake and cut him free from the mast.

"Come with me," he muttered. "Your back needs looking to. Tuck this dirk in your belt." Hromund obeyed silently. Once off the dock, they turned down a series of dark and uninviting alleys. The last of these, befouled with the stench of human filth, led them none too soon into the Street of the Wind Sellers.

"Keep close, dagger in hand," cautioned Gwern. Presently he stopped at a doorway. Telling Hromund to put up his dirk, he sheathed his own and knocked heavily three times, then twice more. In a moment the door was unbolted and swung inward. An ancient crone reeked garlic and tooth decay on them as she cackled a welcome.

"Come in, come in, lords," she said, fawning. "Is it a spell-wind yez seek, or a wench to bed? I've both to sell, an it please yez, at a discreet price."

"A bit of doctoring first, Granny," Gwern grumbled, pushing past her into a squalid rookery that stank like an uncleaned hawk mew. "This way," he told his companion.

When the old hag had nursed Hromund's lacerated back with hot water and unguents, she left it unbound so it would not fester and brought three cups of sour wine. Sipping noisily from one, she simpered coyly. "A bag of wind yez be wanting to buy, eh?" She dispensed with the earlier nicety of address, knowing all along they were not lords, but seadog scum, and got down to the business at hand. "This one's back is too sore to hump a wench, and I'll take oath yez're not a woman's man." She leered up into Gwern's evil, tattooed face. "I don't keep fancy boys," she snapped. "How many knots?"

"Three knots, Granny," said Gwern. "A wild, wailing three-knot wind. A wizard wind, and be quick. I have other business."

"An ill wind yez'll need to blow the likes of yez any good," said the crone. She blew her foul breath three times into a soiled rag, then tied it up with three knots; and lo, her hand held a small inflated bag over which she mumbled eldritch words of witchery.

Gwern paid her, and they stepped into the street.

"Here, tuck this into your belt," he told Hromund, handing him the wind seller's spell charm.

"I saw you pay the old crone in gold," said Hromund. "For what, I ask you? All she sold you was this knotted rag." He began to laugh uneasily. Gwern took hold of his arm roughly.

"Do not laugh, fool. Within these knots is tied the spellwind of misfortune and sorrow. In sooth, with each knot loosed the wind blows stronger. Within this knotted rag, as ye stupidly call it, lies the power to wreak vengeance on whomever ye will. Think on it, Hromund. I leave ye here. I have other business." With that, Gwern turned away and was gone.

Hromund called after him, being uncertain of the way they had come. There was no answer. From the distance came the sound of running feet. Left alone, he was obliged to retrace his steps as best he could. When at last he came within sight of the jetty, after a wrong turn or two, he found the darkened sky lit with flames. He moved closer in awe, slowly, like a dream walker on leaden feet, and saw one of the galleys was afire. A crowd had gathered and was milling about with much shouting and confusion. A few steps nearer, and he knew the ship. It was the *Black Wolf* that was burning!

Fear tore at Hromund's guts. He would be found missing, charged with escaping, and blamed for firing the galley. Panicked, he turned to flee. As he did, a tall figure stepped out of the crowd, pointed in his direction, shouting, "There he is! There's the murdering rat! Stop him! Don't let him get away!"

Hromund saw his accuser was none other than Gwern.

The crowd became an angry mob, closing in on him with drawn knives catching the fireglow. Amongst the hate-filled faces were those of his two brothers and Lif. Each held a bludgeon.

"Svadi! Frodi!" he shouted, terror shrilling his voice. The three moved toward him, a determined pace or two ahead of the yelling mob, their faces dark. Were they coming to help him, or kill him? His question became a scream. He dropped to his knees, pleading.

"Don't kill me! Don't kill me! I swear I didn't do it!"

Brandishing their tavern bench-leg bludgeons, Svadi, Frodi, and Lif stepped to the cringing coward's side, holding the motley crowd at bay.

"Justice!" they cried as one.

Hogar and Lon Thoddrach came pushing their way through the crowd, with Gwern at their heels, his voice raised in accusation. In the background, alongside the flame-brightened jetty, the *Black Wolf* burned at the waterline. Billowing clouds of smoke smudged the starry skies.

"Damn me, if he won't swing from a gibbet for this!" bellowed Lon Thoddrach, in a rage. "Burn me, will he? Damn his eyes!"

Hogar gripped the Fomor's arm.

"I smell the head of a dead fish here. Patience! Hear him out. Lay aside your bludgeons and your knives," he told his three stalwarts and the ugly mob. "Let Hromund speak out in his own defense."

"Look in his belt!" shouted Gwern, stepping forward. "Ye'll find the dirk he slew the watch with." He seized Hromund, quick hands probing the coward's belt. "Look! Look! What did I tell ye?" He pulled out the dirk and held it high. Unnoticed, he palmed an object in the other hand. "Look again in his belt, sez I, and see what else he has tucked away there." He brought away his hand and held it open. In the palm lay two gold bits. "Now will ye believe me? Here in his belt I find the same gold bits I paid the watch. See for y'selves."

"It's a lie! It's a lie!" Hromund screamed.

Shouts arose from the mob.

"Hang the blighter!"

"Cut the bugger's heart out!"

"Burn him!"

Lon Thoddrach raised a hand for silence. "Avast!" he roared. "I'll hear the craven out. Belay there, damn your eyes!" He was a power in Thairm, and got what he demanded. The unruly crowd settled down to a low grumbling, then angry silence.

Justice was swift, if not just. Hromund told his story. Gwern was believed. So was the incriminating evidence of the forbidden dirk and the two bits of gold. Nothing was seen of a wind seller's spell rag tied with three ominous knots. It was not found in Hromund's belt. No one thought of looking in Gwern's, for no one had seen him palm it and tuck it there.

And so ended the trouble with Hromund.

He was hanged on a gibbet for a crime he had not committed.

And the head of the fish still stinks, thought Hogar, as he stood on the stern of the *Sea Raven* watching Gwern bully the crew. The longship was being readied for faring, to seek the gold hoard Lon Thoddrach had come to believe in. And well it was that he had. Hogar told him naught of the Ravensword; nay, nor the rune-ring of Odin that lay hidden within the sinistrous city of Nardath-Thool. Now bounden by shield oath to the one-eyed Fomor chieftain, he would sail as mate on the ship he had captained and lost.

XXII

Siren Song

The *Sea Raven* coursed through thrashing gray seas and blinding mist, whipped by the wind that howled in the bellying raven sail like the fettered Fenris-Wolf. Overhead, the fog-veiled sun hung like an unlit lantern in the salted sky.

Lon Thoddrach strode the stern with Hogar standing fast at the steer oar, the wetness clinging to their great cloaks. Underfoot, the stout oaken timbers shuddered with the relentless pounding of the sea. From the bow came the forlorn lowing of the ship's lur.

Hogar's eyes fell on Lif as the big Utgarthian moved along the ship's side, bailing. Every longship leaked. He prayed that the gods still smiled on his quest, that whoever's hands had built the *Sea Raven* had built her well. The newly caulked seams and retarred hull would hold against the surging sea. It was inherent in the sleek lines and clinker-laid strakes of Nordland-built sea steeds that they drink from Ran's cup below the waterline, but with little thirst.

When the *Black Wolf* burned, Lon Thoddrach had manned the *Sea Raven* with a cutthroat crew of seafaring rogues, rowing them in three shifts. Of the three score and ten pirates who lay about the deck bundled in great cloaks and furs, all but three were woad-tattooed Fomors. Svadi and Frodi, seated in the ship's bow beside a charcoal brazier, kept their own counsel and a sharp weather eye on Gwern the oarmaster, whom they blamed for their brother Hromund's hanging. That the evil-miened Gwern had killed the watch and burned the *Black Wolf* still stood unproved, except in their hearts. They had spoken to no one of this—not even to Lif, whom they trusted, nor Hogar, their lord, whom they served. But the latter, they knew, was the motivating reason for the watch murders and the burned galley. Why Gwern hated Hogar or how Hromund's hanging fit into the oarmaster's machinations was not clear to either of the surviving brothers; but the answer would come with watching and waiting. So they waited, and watched.

With the oars shipped in the foul weather that blew them before the wind, and no rowers to bully with his knotted skeeg, Gwern stood the stem watch. Furtively, he fingered the spell-wind charm he kept tucked in his belt. He felt the two knots that remained to be untied. He had loosed the first knot on heading out of Thairm, as the *Sea Raven* held to the northerly course set by the hated Nordsman who had robbed him of the mate's berth he so long had coveted. With the untying of the knot, he had loosed the spell-wind's first mighty gust. With it had come the witch weather that blinded the ship he was determined to destroy, and with it the hated Hogar. What cared he for his chieftain, or his shipmates? What cared he, for that matter, for his own life now, were it to be the price of vengeance?

Loose the second knot! whispered his evil genius.

He brought the talisman from his belt; with trembling fingers, he untied the second knot . . . and with the untying, a mighty rush of wind swept the ship's bow with a wizard blast that tore Gwern from the stem post and hurled him backward to the deck, the spell-wind rag still clutched in his hand for all to see.

The waters rose up in great swells till the ship was at the mercy of the heaving deep, as the spell-wind of misfortune and sorrow the old crone had conjured was further unleashed. With the loosening of the knot came the wailing gust that ripped away the raven sail and snapped the mast in two. One man was washed over the side as the surging waters swept the longship at the beam. Svadi and Frodi saw the wind seller's charm clutched in Gwern's hand; crawling to where the oarmaster lay stunned by the force of the wizard wind, Svadi threw the knotted rag on the brazier. It smoldered on the hot charcoal a moment before it went up like tinder. The evil wind spell was consumed by small, angry flames; the weather calmed, so that the blinding mist dissolved and the sky was sunlit again.

So it was that Gwern's vengeance went awry; but Svadi and Frodi were avenged because of it. Gwern confessed under torture at their hands. They broke his thumbs.

"Damn your eyes, Gwern, for burning my ship!" the Fomor chieftain roared. "Blast you, for letting me gibbet the wrong rogue, for setting a witch wind in my sail. Break his legs!" he bellowed.

Svadi was bearlike in his strength. Gwern swooned as the leg bone gave. Frodi brought him around with a bucket of water dipped from the sea. Svadi lifted Gwern in a crippling bear hug. The oarmaster screamed once. Svadi broke his neck, and threw his corpse over the side.

A cask was broached, and Lon Thoddrach and his cutthroat crew got roaring drunk. Not so Hogar, who maintained his post at the steer oar; nor Lif, who kept bailing; nor Svadi and Frodi, who stood the stem watch keeping a lookout for floating sea ice. Drunk as they got, the Fomors continued rowing, and sped the *Sea Raven* ever northward as they dipped and stroked her twenty oars. The lur sounded mournfully from the bow.

The first iceberg was sighted early that evening. The gathering mist brought the wet cold down upon them, steaming the breath and riming beards. More and more bergs were encountered; with nightfall came eldritch lights, illuminating the sky and sea with awesome arcing colors. Pulsing flashes of white light revealed grotesque troll shapes sculpted by the wash of the sea on the glacial mass looming weirdly ahead, amidst an ice floe that now half encompassed the ship.

Instinctively, Hogar knew the gaping gargoyle mouths in the ice mass would be the troll caves he sought. Beyond them lay the wasteland wrought by Ragnarok a thousand years ago. There, beside the inland Sea of Nemed, he would soon see rise the alban walls and ebon towers of rune-built Nardath-Thool. With a steady hand on the helm, he guided the longship between the treacherous bergs and the broken field of sea ice, toward the eerie caves. At the stem post, Svadi and Frodi stood awestruck at the wondrous sight. Lif pointed in disbelief, forgetting for the moment to bail.

And then—but a ship length away, out of the largest cave's mouth, breaking through the ice floe, there arose the loathsome and hideous head of a monstrous denizen of the deep, its horns trailing sea wrack and slime, its horrible jaws extended wide to engulf both ship and crew.

"The Kraken!" The frightened cry went up from the stem watch, and men fell screaming into the sea.

"Back oars!" Hogar shouted. "Stem fighters forward! Cast spears!"

Oars broke; spears shattered impotently against the foul Midgarthsorm-like head. Sobered by impending peril, Lon Thoddrach roared orders from the ship's waist.

"Swords and axes forward, damn your eyes!"

His Fomors sprang to the attack. Svadi and Frodi hurled their spears, and drew. Lif swung his ax. Hogar held on desperately to the steer oar as the galley's carved stern rose skyward. For a long moment he clung there; then he fell, to land on a bobbing fragment of sheet ice soon awash under his weight. Before his horrified eyes, the *Sea Raven* disappeared into the gaping maw that snapped shut over man and ship alike, and the terrifying sea beast sank beneath the icy waters to its lair.

Bobbing in the wake of the sounding behemoth, the ice floe on which Hogar found himself marooned was tossed like flotsam in the turbulent swell, washed toward another of the caves. A spear floated near enough to be retrieved; he drove the spear into the wall of ice just below the cave opening with all the might he could muster, bounced about as he was by the sea. The spear held until he attempted to draw himself up onto the lip of the yawning cavern.

It was then he heard the seductive and wondrous singing, and beheld a golden-haired siren seated within the mouth of the cave. Her alluring arms reached down to him. Hogar took a proffered hand in his. As he did so, the siren's arms writhed; arms no longer, but two hideous coiling tentacles, they seized him before he was aware of his momentary delusion. A third tentacle snaked around his body. The singing that had ensnared him ended abruptly. Hogar struggled to free himself and bring spear, sword, or dagger into play as the sea troll shape-shifted into a slimy horror. He was drawn up onto the ice shelf and dragged into the sea troll's cave to be devoured. In his struggle to survive, Hogar somehow freed his throwing arm and drove the spear through the writhing, tentacled spawn of the deep that sought to drain him of life. The sea troll recoiled; emitting a womanly scream, it shape-shifted again. Once more he heard the seductive and wondrous singing; again there appeared before him a half-woman creature with flowing golden hair that fell in long strands over her voluptuous breasts and about her hips, below which coiled the unspeakably foul tail of a sea troll. From her graceful shoulders, two frightful serpents undulated in gestures of obscene desire.

"Come to Thylla's arms," sang the siren. "I would devour thee with kisses, thou very gift of Ran."

Hogar wrested the spear from the ice where he had thrust it through the vanished tentacled horror. With both hands he drove it deep between the voluptuous siren breasts that would tempt and delude him, until but half the shaft protruded. With a high, piercing scream, the sea troll shape-shifted again. A white seal transfixed by a spear drew itself away from him, out of the cave and to the ice-shelf edge, oozing an inky black trail in its wake. Turning once to cast him a baneful eye, it dove into the sea.

Breathing hard, Hogar stood at the mouth of the troll cave in disbelief of what had happened.

A sea serpent had swallowed the longship and its crew.

A sea troll had ensnared him; else he would have perished.

The gods showed themselves in mysterious ways, he

mused. Or had all this been sorcery—a rune-spell illusion cast by a sorceress queen, or whoever held the sword and ring he sought?

He looked about him. He had survived, had found shelter, albeit the barest kind, from wind and sea, in a fouled troll cave that gave onto a passage—leading where?

XXIII

The Cold Waste of the Sorcerers

The sea troll's lair opened onto a large cavern. Hogar searched for any possible way out other than the sea at his back, all the while concerned with the problem of how to keep warm and find food. He soon stumbled upon a half-hidden passage, where he came face-to-face with two hideous troglodyte males covered with shaggy white body hair. They crouched half erect, leaning on the knuckles of one hand. A firebrand was held in the other. Brutish eyes glared at him from under low, beetled brows; fangs were bared in a savage snarl born of both surprise and fear. Throwing sticks hung from crude belts encircling the waist of each frightful creature.

Ketil the Skald had told tales of the snow beasts said to inhabit the ice-troll caves since the extinction of the Ice Age race. Hogar found them harder to believe real on seeing them than on hearing them described. In the torch-lit passage, he and the brutes stood appraising one another. With a low guttural growl, one of the he's raised his throwing stick. Hogar's dagger was drawn, thrown, and deep in the aggressor's heart before the creature could hurl his weapon. The other shaggy beast, seeing his comrade struck down, emitted a cry of alarm and fled whence he had come.

Hogar retrieved his dagger from the carcass, wiped the blade on his breeks, and picked up the fallen firebrand. For a moment he pondered on the only egress that lay open to him, long enough for a number of torch-bearing snow beasts to appear at various levels of the cavern, in openings heretofore undiscernible because of the fantastic formations that dripped and rose from ceiling and floor.

A wild cry went up amongst the creatures as they discovered one of their kind lying in a pool of blood.

"You kill Yukha!" screamed a great brute in pidgin Old Tongue. Hogar took him to be the leader of the angry pack. Hairy hands went to throwing sticks.

"Kill! Kill!" the pack chorused. Ten or more snarling snow beasts had assembled. Hogar's pulse quickened. One sword and dagger were no match for a dozen deadly throwing sticks. Ketil the Skald's counsel again came to mind: retreat is sometimes the better part of valor. He made an expedient exit. Holding the firebrand high to light the only means of escape, he disappeared into the passage, which led he knew not where.

It branched off in two directions not far ahead. The first way brought him to another cavern. This he did not explore for a way out; instead he retraced his steps rather than risk being cornered by his pursuers, whose wild cries he could hear echoing behind him. The other way turned abruptly not far ahead, ending in a patch of daylight. He ran to meet it.

What Hogar's eyes beheld at the end of the passage brought an astonished cry to his lips.

Before him lay the desolation wrought by Ragnarok—it could be nothing else, he told himself—in frightening evidence of world upheaval, of earthquake, and heaven-rending fire and destruction long past. Myriad fragments of marble, beryl, and porphyry stretched across the trackless waste, like a rainbow fallen in ruins. With a twist of pain in his vitals, Hogar knew that he looked upon the very field where, a thousand years before his time, the gods lay slain. What once had been Bifrost Bridge arching in glorious rainbow splendor, over which Odin and Thor and all the gods rode to many-mansioned Asgarth, now lay broken in shards, on the ancient battleground once stained with the god-blood of those who fell at Ragnarok.

Hogar carefully picked his way down the icy bank. Shading his eyes with one hand against the haze, the other resting on his sword hilt, he peered across the rubbled Cold Waste for some sign of a living thing in this gloomy desert of death. Strangely, the barren landscape belied its name; the air was not cold. In the distance, he could make out a shimmer of dark waters; beyond that, what appeared to be towered walls of white and black rising specterlike out of a dense thermal mist.

Far ahead, a large vulture swooped low in the gray, sunless sky; or so the black form winging its way toward him appeared. From somewhere in the trackless desolation before him, there rose the eerie howl of a cruel denizen of the Cold Waste known to roam far afield for meat when hungry, the great white wolf of the Frozen Lands. A second ululating wolf cry went up, this time closer at hand. Hogar remembered the wild dog pack and felt the cold sweat break. There was no defensible position against a skulk of wolves but the caves behind him. He well knew the danger that lurked there.

The wolves now showed themselves. Giving tongue as they converged in a pair and broke into a fast lope, they quickly narrowed the distance between them and their quarry. Hogar could barely make the shelter of the caves before the wolves would be upon him. The vulture thing had closed the gap with the beat of its enormous wings. As it swooped low over the loping wolves Hogar saw the grotesque being was clad in black plate armor. A short sword hung at its side; its grotesque helm left the terrifying gryffon beak bare. Vulture it was not, nor gryffon, yet somewhat of both. Something less than human, this frightful winged creature certainly was. And he was intended for its prey, should it reach him before the wolves did.

Hogar broke and ran. Up the icy bank, he slipped and stumbled toward the caves. Halfway he turned, sword drawn, to defend himself, only to find his stalkers attacking each other. As the gryffon-like wings cast a foreboding shadow upon the loping wolves, one of the pair leapt high to snatch the black-armored vulture thing from the air. Two fierce green eyes blazed behind the half visor of the grotesque creature's grilled helm. Swooping low with raking talons, it laid its savage attacker's belly open. The surviving wolf fled. Not soon enough. The winged monster caught it up in a sweep of gryffon claws and tore out its heart. Turning to face the caves, the frightful creature folded its wings and preened its talons. In a rasping croak, it addressed Hogar in the Old Tongue.

"Go back, O Mortal! Return whence thou came. 'Tis well that thou stand within reach of yonder caves. There my kind venture not. Enemy though thou are, a boon is granted thee without thy asking. I have saved thy life. Be grateful I do not take it. Go back!"

"Who and what are thou?" Hogar managed at last to ask in the ancient vernacular, curiosity conquering revulsion at the sight of so terrifying a being.

"I am a guardian of the ring."

The ring!

Hogar's heartbeat quickened.

Was this awesome creature, then, a guardian of the ring of Odin?

"Are you man or monster?" he asked, masking his emotions.

"Neither. I am a Skulthur. A captain of the Black Legion. Go back!"

"I seek Nardath-Thool," said Hogar, thinking it best not to divulge his knowledge of the rune-ring. "Is it not beyond this wasteland?"

With the sweep of one great wing, the grotesque warrior indicated the misted and towered horizon.

"Yonder lies the realm of the Fire Lords. For the last time I warn thee, O foolish mortal. Go back! Remember thou are one, and we are legion. Begone! Come not again the way of Nardath-Thool."

With that gruff admonition, its gryffon wings spread for flight and the Skulthur rose airborne. Hovering a long moment in silent warning, the hideous creature wheeled like a great bird of prey and sped across the gray, sunless sky.

A guttural cry behind him turned Hogar's eyes toward the caves. In the mouth of each cave stood an angry snow beast, throwing stick in hand. It was the pack he had eluded. The leader pointed a massive arm toward the interior of the caves and bared his fangs in ugly accusation.

"You kill Yukha." With a sweep of his arm, he pointed down the icy bank. "You kill chuga."

"Wolves," said Hogar.

The leader shook his massive head. "Chuga," he repeated in pidgin Old Tongue and hand signs. He threw back his head as far as his short neck would allow and emitted a fair imitation of the cry of the great white wolf.

"You kill Yukha, you kill chuga." He struck his breast with a great fist. "Yog," he grunted, indicating himself.

The Nordsman made the same gesture in return.

"Hogar," he said.

Yog nodded. "Ho-Gar," he repeated. "Ho-Gar kill Yukha. Ho-Gar kill chuga. Yog kill Ho-Gar," he announced for all to hear.

"Kill! Kill!" chorused the pack.

Hogar tightened his grip on the hilt of *Skull Breaker*, waiting for the first snow beast to make a move. He barely saw the throwing stick that struck him in the forehead. The white world of ice caves before him went black.

XXIV

Glikka

Hogar came to his senses aware of two things. His head throbbed with a dull ache. He was lying prone, tethered to a short stake driven into the earthen floor of an immense limestone cavern. It was damp, but not cold; nor was he uncomfortable. It was some while before his eyes could compensate for the dim light or his nose could ignore the disgusting smells that hung heavily in the close air of the cave.

He knew from the touch that he was lying on the soft pelt of some sea mammal. Possibly a sealskin. His weapons and baldric had been confiscated. He was clad only in his breeks and boots. The first thing he remembered as the headache subsided was the throwing stick in Yog's hairy fist, raised to hurl. With that memory came the realization where he was, and how he came to be there.

From where he lay, Hogar could see several small fires burning on the different cave levels grotesquely sculpted by erosion. Around each fire pot squatted a group of snow beasts. In each squatting place there was but one male. The males were feeding. The females squatted beside their communal mate, with their hairy dugs drooping to their bellies, patiently waiting for him to toss them his leavings of the raw flesh on which he was gnawing.

From the litter of fish heads, shells, and small bones about the cavern floor, it was apparent the hideous beasts sustained themselves on fish, mollusks, and seabirds, or fed where they felled their larger kills, such as the seal from which the pelt beneath him had come. Remnants brought to the squatting place accounted for the scattering of sizable bones. Numerous large tusks suggested the whale horse was a favored choice of menu.

The skinned carcasses of the wolves lay near their bloody pelts on the filth-covered cavern floor. From time to time, one of the he's would waddle over to cut a strip of raw flesh with a sharpened flint stone. The portion was toted back to his squatting place to gnaw on, in chunks sawed off just beyond his mouth with the crude stone knife. His leavings he tossed to his she's for the pot.

They were having a feast. Hogar was glad it was wolf flesh and not his own on which the snow beasts were dining in their best style. He wondered why Yog had decided not to kill him. He did not know it yet, but the answer to that was stirring a large earthen pot over the fire within reach of his tether. It was an old she. Were it possible to be more hideous than her kind, she succeeded. She obviously had the squatting place to herself. She bared her yellowed fangs at him in a pleased way, as though she owned him. She did; but this, too, Hogar did not know then.

Rising from her pot, the old she came over to him, ambulating in a low crouch. The knuckles of one hand touched the cavern floor, balancing herself as she moved. With the other she scratched herself where she itched.

"Glikka cook for Ho-Gar," she announced loudly, looking around the cavern at each of the squatting places, to be certain she was heard. She tugged at his tether.

"Come," she urged him.

"No," said Hogar. He got to his feet, pulling away from the revolting creature.

"Ho-Gar come," the old she insisted. "Glikka cook. Ho-Gar eat. Yog say. Glikka tell Yog. No kill Ho-Gar. Give to Glikka. Yog give. Yog Yukha chief. Ho-Gar squat with Glikka."

It was probably the longest single speech Glikka or any other Yukha had ever made.

"Odin's blood!" cried Hogar. How much plainer could she spell it out? Glikka owned him. Yog had spoken.

"No!" he shouted. "Get away from me!" He pushed the old she from him, keeping her at arm's length. "Go squat by yourself," he told her. Glikka, sentimental old Yukha female that she was, pushed him back, thinking it was a love game Ho-Gar played.

"Glikka like," she said, giving him a hideous grin.

It was then the idea occurred to him. His weapons had been taken from him. He could not go far without them. Here was the only way to get them back. Be friends with Glikka.

"Odin!" he muttered with revulsion. "Let friendship be all the old she wants!"

He patted her flabby arm.

There never was a happier or more hideous grin than the exposure of fangs that came straight from the delighted old she-Yukha's infrahuman heart. Glikka had found herself a he. And Hogar, he hoped, had found himself a means of escape.

He soon observed that only the she's savored cooked meat. The he's were the hunters and fishermen. Each male preferred his food blood raw. The leavings he tossed to his she's for the cooking pot. To the marrow bones, fish heads, and scraps of meat set to boil in melted ice, the she's added bits of sea wrack.

Glikka returned to her cooking pot. Being long unattached, she was the only female in the pack allowed to cut strips of flesh from the communal kill. This she had done when the slain wolves were dragged into the cavern, while Hogar lay unconscious on her squatting place. She stirred and tasted, and stirred in a bit more sea wrack. Generations upon generations of Yukha she's had handed down the recipe. Stirred with a bone or a stick and seasoned with the blood of the catch or kill to taste, it was stew in its most primitive sense.

Hogar sniffed squeamishly at the lump of stewed wolf meat Glikka skewered on a sharp stick and poked under his nose. Strangely enough, it smelled good. He was famished. He tasted it. It tasted good. He told her so. Glikka bared her fangs in a smile and began feeding him stickful by stickful. His empty stomach accepted the boiled meat. Soon, to his own utter disbelief, he was eating from the pot.

"Glikka cook for Ho-Gar." She chortled loudly, looking around from fire to fire. Like many old females, Glikka was garrulous, given the opportunity. Having a male to share her cooking pot and squatting place afforded her just that. To Hogar's dismay when they had fed, the old she insisted on squatting beside him on the sealskin. Distasteful as he found this to be, he had no alternative but to play along, if his plan for escape was to work out as he hoped. He put up with her poking and sniffing about his armpits and elsewhere within the limits of patience, and discovered by poking her in the ribs in return, that Glikka was ticklish. This she interpreted as love play; indeed, it kept the amorous old she at a distance, baring her fangs and gurgling with pleasure at least part of the time.

The language of the Yukhas comprised a few debased words in Old Tongue, but for the most part was grunts and hand signs. Conversation did not flow. The attention span of the species was short. There were many sustained silences between grunts, with a spoken word or gesture here and there. It was with considerable difficulty that Hogar managed to communicate his plan and engage Glikka's aid, let alone gain her undivided attention. Scratching was one of her major interests. Hogar at last was obliged to help her pick fleas from her shaggy coat to win her reflection on the problem of rearming himself.

"Yog Yukha chief," he said quietly, not wishing to be overheard. Glikka nodded without interest. Everyone in the pack knew that.

Hogar tried again.

"Hogar kill Yog," he whispered. "Hogar be Yukha king."

"King?" asked Glikka blankly. The word was meaningless.

"Chief," he translated.

"Huh!" She understood.

"Glikka be queen. Female chief," he told her. The old eyes glittered.

"Ho-Gar kill Yog. Glikka be queen. Make Ho-Gar king."

The old matriarch! he thought with a grin.

"Hogar need sword," he said. "Harness. Dagger." He gesticulated. Glikka nodded.

"Glikka get."

"When?"

"When go see Goom."

"Go now," Hogar urged.

"Wait," said Glikka with finality.

There was nothing to do but wait. And pick fleas. While he waited, Hogar wondered what or who Goom might be. At length, having gorged themselves, the snow beasts one by one settled down for the night around the low-burning fires. Hogar lay on his sealskin, listening to the cavern fill with heavy, even breathing. Glikka bedded herself down beside him and soon was snoring like an old sea cow.

Finally, Hogar slept.

XXV

The Chamber of Goom

With the coming of morning, Yog roused each male at his squatting place. Grumbling themselves awake, the he's reached for firebrands and throwing sticks. Yog hefted a bundle wrapped in sealskin for all to see. Grunting their approval, the he's followed Yog out of the cavern.

Glikka awakened Hogar and untied his tether. He yawned and stretched sleepily, watching the last of the departing males with little interest, dismissing them as a sealing party. The she's at the other squatting places began to file out, once the males were gone. Some of them turned to titter at Glikka and Hogar. One made an obscene gesture.

"Where go?" Hogar asked idly above a yawn. Glikka fanned the fire to a blaze, adding dried sea wrack as needed.

"Go see Goom," she answered at last.

Hogar was on his feet at the name.

"Glikka go see Goom," he said. "Hogar need sword. Glikka get." The old she curled back her lips in a hideous smile.

"Glikka get," she said. Cunning lit her brutish eyes. "Ho-Gar kill Yog."

"Hogar kill."

"Glikka queen." She was triumphant in her imagined power over the females who taunted her.

"Go now," Hogar urged, taking hold of her arm.

"Ho-Gar need sword," said Glikka. She ambled off, to return shortly with a sharpened whale-horse tusk.

"Take," she told him, shoving the crude weapon into his hand. "Come. Get sword." She selected a firebrand and led him by another way out of the cavern. Hogar followed her down a descending and tortuous passage pillared by eerie, yet beautiful water-dripped limestone formations. Eventually the labyrinthine tunnel gave onto as eldritch a sight as ever seen by man or snow beast.

The lofty chamber into which the Nordsman followed the old she seemed smaller than the cavern they had just quitted; it was dwarfed only by the immensity of the glacier-entrapped hairy mammoth with its trunk curled upward to trumpet, like a huge serpent coiling over two incredible tusks. With these it had gored its attackers, a pair of great, white saber-toothed tigers, still splashed with their own blood. The splendid beasts were lifelike, as on that warmer day ages past when the moving ice cap had caught the last moment of their struggle for survival, in a sudden glacial avalanche encasing them forever in a transparent, calcareous mass.

Water erosion had drip-sculpted both ceiling and floor of the cavern with weird formations resembling gigantic troll teeth in an enormous mouth.

Hogar stood on the upper level to which Glikka had brought him, looking down from his vantage point upon the death drama perpetually enacted below. From a floor level opening to one side of the stark figures, there proceeded a single file of snow beasts, male and female alike, lighted by firebrands. Each bore bits of sea wrack, a mollusk shell, or a fish bone, cupped as though in solemn offering. Their voices lifted in an eerie atonal chanting of one word, repeated over and over.

"Goom . . . Goom . . . Goom . . . Goom . . ."

The last to enter from the passage was Yog. He still bore the sealskin-wrapped bundle. Hogar realized he was witnessing a votive ritual. Unlike the others, Yog did not drop his offering on the growing trash heap before the sacred grouping and find a place to squat. He stood facing the strange sanctuary until the chant subsided. Only then did he unwrap the sealskin. And solemnly he lifted in both his hands what had been thus concealed.

Hogar stood fascinated. Yog was offering up the confiscated baldric and weapons to his god!

But stay!

Yog dropped the empty sealskin atop the votive heap as his offering. With an obeisance to Goom, he proceeded to arm himself with sword and dagger.

It was a ludicrous sight. Yog had no notion of how to don the baldric. He finally managed to get it over one shoulder upside down; with sheathed sword and dagger in hand, he turned to face his pack. Beating his breast with the weapons held in both hands, he cried out triumphantly, "Yog!"

"Yog! Yog! Yog!" chorused the pack.

On the upper level, Glikka rasped in Hogar's ear, "Kill now!" Her harsh whisper echoed through the chamber and became a shout. Yog looked up. Seeing Hogar and Glikka, he sensed betrayal and screamed his hatred.

"Kill! Kill!"

Clutching the unfamiliar weapons and harness awkwardly to himself, Yog hurled his throwing stick with his free hand. Hogar carefully had gauged his timing, knowing now what to expect. At precisely the same instant, holding the whale-horse tusk by its sharpened tip as he would a dagger, he threw it with great force. And quickly stepped aside. The snow beast's lethal stick sped past him off target. On the cavern floor, Yog clutched at his shaggy breast, now running red with blood. From it protruded the butt end of the long-knife carved from a walrus tusk. With a bestial scream, Yog fell dead; the sheathed sword and dagger he had coveted slipped from his lifeless fingers.

A stunned silence filled the chamber; then a vengeful cry rose in the throat of each Yukha male.

"Kill! Kill!"

With the cry, a volley of throwing sticks clattered harmlessly against the upper-level area that now stood empty. Hogar had pulled Glikka safely aside with split-second timing. Now he leapt from one mushrooming stalagmite to another, using them as steps in his lightning-quick descent to the cavern floor, where the leaderless Yukhas milled about in confusion. He gained the spot where Yog's carcass lay and stood sword in hand before the first snow-beast male charged.

"Kill! Kill!" they screamed.

Much happened at the same time. On the cavern floor, Hogar met the savage attack of gnashing Yukha fangs. On the upper level, old Glikka again showed herself. Not to be denied her great moment, her voice was raised in a triumphant scream.

"Ho-Gar kill Yog. Ho-Gar chief. Glikka queen!"

And at the same moment, dramatically framed in the opening of a hidden panel stood a short, cruel-faced man mantled in motley, a coiled black whip held in one scarred hand. His shoulders were oversized for his body; the muscles of his chest strained against the plain leather harness he wore. It was only when he cracked the whip that Hogar saw his back was crooked and that he dragged his left leg. Behind him crowded a knot of archers in scale leather hauberks and copper sallets. Their bows bristled with evil-looking arrows. The snow beasts fell back before the whip and drawn bows in abject surrender.

"To the cages! Move!" came the barked command.

From the upper level, Glikka screamed, "Ho-Gar kill!" The mantled man looked up, then signed to an archer. A lone arrow flew to its mark, feathering Glikka's shaggy white breast. The old she slumped dead.

The whip cracked!

"Move along, there!" shouted the mantled man. "You too!" The whip cracked at Hogar's feet. "Down the passage and into the slave cage with you, outlander. No labor camp for your kind. Borbas Crookback knows better than that," he said, indicating himself. "With your warrior's thews and that red lion's mane, you will bring a handsome price in Nardath-Thool for the Queen's Pleasure. Take his weapons!"

Hogar's pulse quickened. He was being taken to the city of his quest. What mattered it that he would enter the realm of the Fire Lords and the white-walled city of the sorceress Queen Tha as a captive slave? He would achieve his quest and fight his way out when the chance came. He offered no resistance as he was disarmed and herded into the passageway with the snow beasts chosen for the slave block.

The hidden panel closed after them. The remaining Yukhas turned back as they had come, leaving the cavern empty, with old Glikka's dead eyes staring sightlessly down on the trumpeting image of Goom.

XXVI

Nardath-Thool

The hidden passageway along which Borbas herded his captives funneled them into a stone-walled corral and through a narrow loading run. Beyond this stood three large-wheeled wagons of bizarre design, each a barred cage for the transport of slaves and animals. On the rutted wagon tracks, a string of horned and bell-hung sumpter beasts waited to haul their cruel cargo.

The cage into which Hogar was prodded with the butt end of a spear was strong with an acrid great-cat stench. It afforded no headroom for a man his height, barely enough for the Yukhas herded in after him, before the door of his wretched prison was bolted shut.

The snow beasts crouched together, silently sharing their fear. Hogar squatted on his haunches, grasping the bars for support, and looked out over the hazy Cold Waste. No other traffic moved across the vast desolation. Presently, with the slaver's harsh cry and the crack of his whip, the strange wagon train drew away, bumping along over the rutted and rubbled terrain at a plodding pace, bells ringing.

The day wore on; shortly before the sunless sky gave way to the darkling dusk, out of a threadbare mantle of mist there loomed a shadowy city, mysterious and wondrous to behold. As the slave train approached the stronghold of Queen Tha and the dread Fire Lords, its white walls, tiered blue-tiled roofs, and black towers crowned by an eerie crimson glow, rose before Hogar's eyes like an enchanted oasis, miraculously flowering beside blue-black waters, in the trackless waste of Ragnarok.

Nardath-Thool!

He had reached the sinistrous city of his quest. Somewhere within that chimerical pile lay the sword and the ring he sought. And win them both he would, or die!

Borbas urged his dray beasts on with a cruel whip. The wagons, now hung with night lanterns, bumped along the final stretch of the long journey on shard-crunching wheels. Soon thereafter, they pulled up at the freight dock before the Gate of Thieves. The slave market that throve just within the gate was deserted at that hour. Borbas set a guard over his cargo, took a numbered tile token in receipt of his chattel from the freight master's scribe, and ordered his weary sumpters watered and fed, and his slaves vittled in their cages. This done, he shackled Hogar by the wrists and, flanked by twelve archers against the dangers of the coming night, marched him past the keeper of the gate into the city where he had business.

Nathas Klar, the Queen's Procurer of Man and Beast, poured Borbas a cup of honeyed wine and regarded him with hooded eyes.

"To seal the bargain," he murmured over the rim of his cup.

"A fair price," replied Borbas. They drank; when the cups were emptied, Nathas Klar dismissed the motley clad slaver, who left dragging one foot and greedily fingering the fat pouch tucked in his belt.

Gold had exchanged hands. Twice the worth of a common slave. But this one was a strapping young stallion. The queen would be well pleasured. Nathas Klar chuckled lasciviously and clapped his hands. To the slave who appeared he said, "Bring me the barbarian who calls himself Hogar Bloodsword."

When the Nordsman stood before him unfettered and naked but for breeks and boots, Nathas Klar smiled his satisfaction. A magnificent specimen; a veritable young lion, and red-maned to boot! He opened the sealskin-wrapped bundle Borbas had brought with him.

"Well, well! What have we here?" exclaimed the roly-poly Nemedian. "A baldric, a sword, and a dagger. So it is a swordsman I have bought. Well, well, now. This may change my mind for me." He gave Hogar a shrewd, hooded look. "Here," he said, tossing the sword for him to catch. "Let me see how you handle a sword, if swordsman indeed you be."

Without a word, Hogar caught hold of *Skull Breaker*. But even as he grasped the hilt, the Queen's Procurer cried out, "Ho, a guard! This slave has drawn on me!"

Hogar wheeled to face the scowling pikeman who came at him through the open doorway. Sidestepping the pike thrust, he brought the two-edged serpent blade across the pikeman's neck with a backhanded slash that swept his head from his shoulders in a gush of blood. Standing free of the falling body, he gave a quick look into the hall. Seeing no other guards, Hogar faced Nathas Klar with the crimsoned sword leveled at his treacherous heart.

"Any more base tricks up your sleeve, Nemedian?" he demanded.

"By Tha!" cried the Queen's Procurer, well pleased. "You are swift of hand and foot, and spirited to the point of brashness, Hogar. This indeed makes up my mind. You shall fight under my colors against the queen's champion. Gods! How Tha will wheedle me when she sees you wearing the Orange. She will want you for the Queen's Pleasure, as the games are known. Here, don this baldric and dagger, and sheathe your blade. You will be billeted with the kerns, as we call our warrior-slaves, and trained to fight man and beasts in the arena, as we do in Nardath-Thool. Come. If you wonder that I do not fear your sword, wonder not. You will not slay me, that I know. For I am your open door to whatever it is you seek of Tha, the queen."

Hogar wiped the bloody blade on his breeks and returned it to the shagreen leather scabbard now hanging once again at his side.

"When that door is opened, then will I no longer be your slave, Nathas Klar, but your debtor," he answered boldly.

The Hall of Kerns to which the Queen's Procurer brought him was a spacious wing comprising an armory, a mess hall, and living quarters built around an exercise court equipped for the training of gladiators. Here Hogar was unceremoniously dismissed to fend for himself, while Nathas Klar spoke privately with the master of arms, a pockmarked rogue he had saved from the gibbet. For this mercy, he continued to exact favors as the occasion demanded.

In the warrior's mess, Hogar found a number of tables at which twenty-odd kerns were seated at meat. Every other warrior-slave, it seemed, had a naked wench on his lap. The wine flowed freely. Their trappings were of an ornate fashion strange to his eyes, each bearing a house badge that designated for whom he fought. They were men of different breeds and color, some of whom gave him pause to stare. He had never before seen a yellow or a black man. He was the lone Nordlander amongst the lot.

For all his staring, Hogar managed to seat himself at an empty place, unnoticed by the kerns. A naked wench brought him food and wine, then plopped herself meaningfully in his lap. Her breath stank. Hogar dumped her onto the flagged floor and applied himself to his hot supper with appetite. A second wench offered herself for his pleasure. He waved her away.

"Mayhap you prefer a fancy boy," gibed the black-bearded Nemedian seated across from him. Roaring with ugly laughter, the kern slapped his wench on the buttocks and gave her a knowing wink.

"Eat this with your words!" Hogar snarled as he pushed the steaming trencher in his tormentor's face and rose to find another table.

"You have made yourself a formidable enemy in Nars Anthor," said the older warrior at whose side he now sat. "I counsel you: keep your eyes open, and a drawn sword on the board beside you, friend."

"You say 'friend' when we are yet strangers."

"He is my friend who stands up to an insult as you have," said the other, keeping his words low. "I am Thaul of Tarthiz." Hogar appraised the bronze-skinned Tarthizian with the white mane. He liked him. He gave his own name, and they struck hands.

There was no laughter at the Nordsman's rashness or the ludicrous plight of his howling victim, who stood clawing hot food from his eyes. With a loud oath, Nars Anthor drew and rushed upon Hogar, his anger-darkened bearded face and harness befouled with food and dripping gravy.

Hogar met him swords on. They fought furiously between the tables, working their way to the center of the room. All eyes were upon them. It was blow for blow, neither yielding, both pressing the attack. At length the opening the Nordsman sought came. Nars Anthor faltered in parrying a deft thrust. Hogar drove his serpent blade through the breach, deliberately fleshing it deep in his opponent's thigh, severing the tendons.

"That will lesson you to keep a civil tongue in your head, knave," he said, stepping back to wipe his blade on his breeks.

It was at that moment Nathas Klar returned with trappings for his new kern. The clash of arms had brought him and the master of arms hurrying into the mess hall to see Nars Anthor topple before Hogar's sword. The Queen's Procurer bent swiftly to the wounded kern.

"Hogar, you fool!" he shrilled. "You have crippled the queen's champion. The door I would have opened for you is closed by your own rashness. What a waste of gold. Guards!" he shouted. Four pikemen came on the run. "Disarm this alien dog and deliver him to the Temple of Tha." He turned back to Hogar. "The queen is worshiped daily at this hour by her eunuch priests as the White Goddess of the Oirrin-Yess. Pity the poor bastard who disturbs Tha at her devotional. Take him to her!"

Hogar weighed his chances against four pikes and a dozen drawn glaives. If he was to face the sorceress queen adversely in her own temple, better to be taken before her in chains. Her wrath would not then fall upon his head, but on the sender's. He held out his wrists for the shackles, noting that Thaul of Tarthiz had drawn in his defense.

XXVII

Tha

Following a Daedelian maze of corridors, the last of which gave onto a perfume-laden garden, a circular pebbled path brought Hogar and his escort at length to the narthex of the Temple of Tha. Before immense carved doors of cast orichalch aglow like fire, stood two temple guards. They crossed halberds in formal challenge. Nathas Klar's pikemen pounded the butt of their staves upon the stone-laid portico, delivered their prisoner in chains, and withdrew.

The great doors slowly opened outward to reveal a roofless, white-walled fane, dim-lit by the starless night sky. Seven jade oil lamps sculpted in the terrifying likeness of coiled serpents with darting tongues of flame were set between twelve stone columns forming the nave. From the prayer stalls came the mumbled drone of animal-masked priests in scarlet robes, repeating over and over the Nemedian Mantra of the White Runes: *"Y'a El-hi'u ma r'hl y'a . . ."* the meaning of which was lost in antiquity.

An archpriest in yellow offered up incense to Tha of the Green Eyes. The White Goddess of Unspeakable Beauty sat exalted under an opulently embroidered baldachin, her breathtaking nakedness veiled by a gossamer web of silver threads. A jeweled saber-toothed tigress skull crowned the raven tresses that fell from her ivory shoulders like a loosed mantle, to reveal her scarlet-nippled breasts and alluring thighs. Two white marble tigers, fierce of jaw and long of tooth, arched their backs to make a throne, beside which flamed a caldron cast of orichalch. From its black tripod was hung a chalice of gold. Behind the tiger throne, seven gem-studded steps ascended to the high place. There a lavishly splendored, crescent-shaped ark awaited the pleasuring of its goddess. In this holy of holies the nuptial couch was housed, whereon the sorceress Queen of Nardath-Thool played goddess, and received her random lovers.

Tha parted the Veil and stood forth statuesque in anger at the unwonted intrusion.

"Who enters here unbidden?" she cried out imperiously in the universal Old Tongue. "What do thou here? Profane not the holy rites of Tha. Begone!"

The two temple guards backed away, and the heavy doors closed to leave their charge at the mercy of the enraged goddess-queen. Abandoned to his own devices, Hogar stood entranced a long moment; involuntarily drawn by the witchery and fascination for the most provocative woman on whom he had ever set eyes, he moved toward the veiled sanctuary, dragging his chains between the stalls of mumbling priests.

"Who dares intrude upon the worship of Tha?" demanded the green-eyed goddess.

"I, Hogar Bloodsword, beseech thee, O Mighty Tha, hear my prayer." With those ironic words, the Nordsman strode boldly forward, his chains clanking on the temple stones.

"Prostrate thyself, alien dog!" shrieked the archpriest as the tall, virile figure clad only in breeks and boots stepped brashly out of the dim-lit nave into the flaming caldron's glow.

"Hear me, O Goddess!" said Hogar, standing before her unbowed.

Tha took a step backward at his brazenness, letting the Veil fall between them. Silently she appraised the broad shoulders, the mighty thews, the virile chest, and the noble head of this barbarian who dared intrude upon her, standing unbowed and defiant in her presence, with his unruly rusty locks falling about his neck like a red lion's mane. She felt a catch in her throat. Her loins ached for this magnificent young lion of a man. She moistened her lips with the scarlet tip of her tongue, catlike. No matter what pursuit brought him to Nardath-Thool, no matter that he mocked her divinity with tongue in cheek, he was hers to command. And she would bed him!

"So thou hath come at last at my bidding, Hogar Bloodsword." Her voice was a sultry purr.

"At thy bidding?"

"Remember thee not the Volva?"

"Nay, thou art not the Volva. Her hair was flowing gold."

"Remember thee not the sea cave, and my prophecy of thy future? Remember thee not the quest pledged, for the sword and the ring thou dost seek?"

Have a care! he told himself. She is a Nemedian witch, empowered to read one's thoughts and twist them to serve her own ends.

"Doubt not, O Hogar, that I know thy most secret heart," said Tha. "I am She-Who-Walks-the-Night. Come!" She stretched forth her jeweled hands. "Lo, I cast off thy chains."

The fetters fell from him as Tha beckoned.

"Come to me! To me, to me! I am the purple-lidded Daughter of Nemed, the Incarnate White Goddess, Tha, the Giver of Life." She had resumed her litany. From the dim-lit nave came the responses of the scarlet robed shaved-pate priests.

"Hail, Tha, O White Moon of Nardath."

The archpriest prostrated himself. Hogar fought off the clutch of ensorcelment.

"Wear to me jewels!" cried Tha, pressing her scarlet-nippled breasts seductively upward with glittering ringed fingers. Her mouth pouted. Hogar wavered under her spell. The musky scent of her filled his nostrils, firing his brain with hot desire. He felt his manhood rise. Tha smiled. Her green eyes shone. Bewitched, Hogar took a step closer.

"I am Tha, the Red Goddess of Love and Battle," she cried.

"Hail, Tha, O Red Moon of love's delight," droned the eunuch priests.

"Burn to me incense of spices and musk!" commanded Tha. Hogar took another step toward her outstretched and waiting arms. "Behold!" she cried out. "I am She-Who-Walks-the-Night, the Black Goddess of Doom, who taketh away the Light!"

"Hail, Tha, O Black Moon that bringeth down the Darkness," came the response.

Tha held the golden chalice high; then dipping it in the flaming caldron, she said, "Drink to me wine of molten pearls!" Hogar parted the Veil and took the proffered cup, draining the frothing draft greedily. All else but his lust for Tha fell away like scales from his eyes. His mind held but one conscious thought. She was his for the taking. He reached out for her. Staying him, Tha mounted the first gem-studded step. Facing the nave, she threw back her head and from her lovely throat there came a deep, feline cry as she shape-shifted.

On the step where Tha had stood, a snowy sabertoothed tigress snarled.

"O She-Who-Walks-the-Night, have mercy on us!" intoned the prostrate archpriest.

"Return in thy beauty, O Tha," came the response from the prayerstalls.

And on the step where the white carnivore had been, again stood the incomparable Tha, crying out:

"Behold the Tigress made Woman!"

Mounting the second step, Tha said:

"Where my foot doth tread, there shall thou follow, knowing it is my voice that calls thy name."

Tha held forth a jeweled hand. Bewitched, Hogar followed step by step as she ascended. His loins ached, his hands reached out to know the touch of her wondrous flesh. His mouth longed to know the taste of those provocative lips.

On the seventh step, Tha turned. Stretching out her arms to him, she whispered, "Thou wilt pleasure Tha."

Gaining her side, Hogar pulled her to him, his mouth covering hers hungrily. Tha clung to him, grinding her loins against his. He would have taken her then, but that she stayed him.

"Not here, my impetuous one," she told him breathlessly.

Hogar lifted her in his arms and carried her aboard the ark. At the golden deck rail, Tha dispersed her priests with the sign of the Oirrin-Yess, saying:

"Tha is housed. Her ark, the glorious Moonrath, shall rise as doth the moon. Go with the blessings of Tha."

The scarlet-robed eunuch priests chanted the Mantra of the White Runes over and over . . . *"Y'a El-hi'u ma r'hl y'a . . ."* as they filed out of the temple, leaving it in darkness save for the seven serpent lamps of jade and the glowing caldron cast of fiery orichalch. As the Ark of Tha rose like a horned moon in the starless sky, there came from within the splendored Moonrath the passionate, womanlike cry of a she-tiger rutting with her mate.

XXVIII

"This Is Treason!"

Nol Dragir, Archon of the Fire Lords, scowled darkly under horned reptilian brows upon the saffron-robed informer louting before him.

"Of what treason or blasphemy against the gods do you accuse your queen?" demanded the Archon. Folding his dragonwings, he seated himself on an enormous throne of stone.

"My eyes and ears that serve you well are witness to the iniquities of this false goddess, O Most Worthy Lord," said the Archpriest of the Temple of Tha, for it was indeed he who groveled before the queen's monstrous half brother. "Though my tongue exalts the Oirrin-Yess, in my heart of hearts I worship only the Khthon. She-Who-Walks-the-Night defiles the temple with her fornications. Even now, the Whore of Nardath lies day and night in the arms of the alien slave she has taken for her lover."

"What treason is this, to bed or be bedded?" Nol Dragir asked. " 'Love is the Law.' Were you still a man, you would be in rut for her yourself. Secret devotion to the Black Gods cannot give you back what Tha has taken from you, eunuch. Your accusation smacks of sour wine, pressed from the grapes of your own wrath against the goddess who had you unmanned to serve her as archpriest. Tell me of this alien."

"He is a barbarian from beyond the Frozen Sea, who styles himself Hogar Bloodsword."

"A meaningless conceit, that," snapped Nol Dragir. "How came this barbarian to Nardath-Thool?"

"The Queen's Procurer paid a wily slaver a purse of gold for him, as a gift for Tha; a young stallion to service the queen. Then Nathas Klar put a sword in the fellow's hand to test him and found a worthy prospect for the games. Nathas Klar is no man's fool. Nor is he above turning a profit, even be it at the queen's expense. He thought to fight the barbarian under his own badge, knowing Tha would bargain with him for this Hogar the moment she saw him in the arena. But the barbarian ruined the scheme by putting a sword through the thigh of the queen's champion in a brawl. Fearing the wrath of Tha, Nathas Klar has told me since, he sent Hogar to her temple for punishment at her hands. What happened there I saw with my own eyes, O Most Worthy Lord. Tha delivered the barbarian of his chains and seduced him with sorcery, so that he went randy with lust and would have taken her on the sacred steps had she not stayed him—"

"Enough!" said Nol Dragir impatiently, the sharpness of his voice flicking away the subject as he would a bothersome gnat. "You have the eunuch's taste for the vicarious; but it profits you nothing. What seeks this Hogar Bloodsword here?"

"Tha probed his mind and his heart," replied the archpriest glibly. "She spoke to him of the Ravensword and the rune-ring of Odin, saying she had summoned him."

"By the Khthon!" cried the Archon angrily, his wings spreading in agitation. "This is treason indeed!"

"Yea, O Most Worthy Lord," said the other. "Together they bring down the Darkness!"

"Are you saying Tha invokes the power of the Black Runes that summons the Khthon?" shouted Nol Dragir, rising. For a moment he stood fullspread like an angry winged dragon, awesome to behold. The archpriest louted low to avert his eyes.

"Yea, lord. She invokes herself as the Black Goddess. Her scarlet-robed ones give the response, 'Hail, Tha—' "

"I know the response, fool!" snapped Nol Dragir, meaning to silence his prattle. Priestlike, the other mumbled on, intoning the fateful invocation feared by all who dwelled in Nardath-Thool. " 'O Black Moon that bringeth down the Darkness—' "

"Enough! My sister goes too far. Leave me, priest."

When the saffron-robed informer had withdrawn, Nol Dragir shouted, "Skulthurs!"

Five of the winged creatures stood forward from their secret posts and raised their claws in salute. The dreadful gryffon beaks nodded their obeisance.

"Summon the accused before me. Tha and her paramour shall stand in the Doom Ring!"

XXIX

The Moonrath

Hogar awakened in the arms of Tha. The musky fragrance of her warm naked body brought the heady memory of their lovemaking fresh to mind.

She sleeps peacefully as a kitten, my Tha, but claws like a tigress when aroused, he mused.

He remembered the happenings of the night now past: how the Moonrath was skyborne seemingly at Tha's utterance of a Nemedian rune, the upward lift of the ark beneath his feet, and the sinking sensation in the pit of his stomach, how he dropped to his knees, clawing at the thick-woven carpet to keep from falling out of the sky.

A flying ark!

Could such a wonder be? Mighty Thor, who rumbled across the heavens in his goat-drawn cart, perhaps could devise such a miracle. But for man to ride a horned moon ark through the skies . . . *What sorcery was this?* he had asked himself.

The Moonrath soared five hundred feet above the earth. Surely Asa-Thor rode his chariot no higher than this! Steeling his nerves against fear, Hogar wondered at the smooth, silent flight of this strange craft, floating on air as though borne by a harnessed breeze, with barely more sound than the soft rustle of leaves.

Tha had laughed at his trepidation. She kissed him and led him to the waiting couch.

Later, standing beside her at the golden deck rail, Hogar's eyes drank in the wonders of Nemedian sorcery that lay below the circling ark. In the distance, where the starless sky was probed by weird lights, rose the ice-troll caves, and beyond them the Frozen Sea, whose berg-filled waters met and chilled the Nord Sea of his own sane world. He gazed down in disbelief on fabulous palaces and temples set within a pattern of perfume-laden gardens such as he had earlier entered; wide, tree-lined avenues and malls, spacious parks, and cobbled squares. Out of the midst of the garden-hung walls of Nardath rose the tiered citadel of Thool in a sinistrous cluster of grotesquely carved black towers, like ebony stamens erect in the heart of an exotic lotus sculpted of ivory. All this was beyond his Nordlander comprehension.

Hogar's half-smothered yawn awakened Tha. She regarded him with green cat eyes, pleased with both what she saw and remembered.

"Thou art strong, my lion," she whispered. "Last night thou didst lie with thy tigress and pleasure her much. Thou art my true mate. I shall whelp mighty sons of thy loins, my Hogar, and bring forth a get of indomitable warriors, both lionhearted and tiger-fierce in battle. Together we shall sit the throne of Nardath-Thool and share between us the rune-power thou dost seek."

Then her mouth was on his, hungrily, demanding fulfillment. For Hogar all else but Tha remained forgotten; entrapped in her arms, he lay with her under an enchantment, thinking of naught but pleasuring her and himself.

So passed their days and nights of love, in silkiness and sumptuous comfort. Tha clothed Hogar in splendored trappings, and hung a broadsword in a jeweled scabbard at his side. At a word from the sorceress queen, food and drink appeared out of thin air, served on golden chargers and in ruby-studded cups by unseen perfumed hands. Meanwhile nightly, the ark rode the sky like a silver crescent moon, circling the walled twin cities and passing over a vast hunting preserve. When they stood at the golden deck rail, looking down upon this marvel of Nemedian wizardry, Tha would point out the rune-spelled beasts that roamed the forest or grazed on the grassland scattered with trees and undergrowth, and tell him of the Queen's Hunt: how one day he would ride the savanna below beside her, how bestride snowy saber-toothed tigers and armed with spears, they would track the spoor of their quarry to the beat of drums, and the belling of great white wolves held at leash by the queen's huntsmen. So vast a wild game preserve amidst the trackless wasteland of Ragnarok could only be the wonderwork of sorcerers; such was shadowy Nardath-Thool, with its alban walls hung with gardens, with the sinistrous ebon towers rising from its heart. And Hogar wondered that such marvels could be.

From the forest's deep came the chattering of a myriad birds, some to be seen rising now and then in brilliant-plumed flight. Ominous, black-winged Skulthurs circled vulturelike over the twin cities, ever watchful, returning at last to the grotesquely carved black towers.

At the hour of worship, Tha landed the Moonrath at the temple and descended the seven sacred steps to be adored as the White Goddess of the Oirrin-Yess. Hogar nightly drank of the elixir-filled chalice and again ascended to where the nuptial couch awaited him and the insatiable sorceress queen. So it was that for Hogar all else was forgotten, and the Ark of Tha rose each night like a horned moon in a starless sky.

One night, when they had made love and were spent, Tha whispered, "Ah, lover, thus always shall it be with us. I shall make thee king. Together we shall rule Nardath and lead the Oirrin-Yess against the Khthon, the White Gods against the Black. Together, my Hogar, we shall beard the Fire Lords in their den of iniquity and win to the secret place where lies hidden the Ravensword and the rune-ring of thy quest. With that fair blade in thy hand, my chieftain, and Tha in magic armor at thy side, holding aloft the rune-ring of Odin, then shall we bring down the Darkness upon Thool, and tumble her dark towers in the dust of battle." She rose from the couch, clenching her fists. "Then shall Nol Dragir fall!"

She stood transfixed in passionate anger; then suddenly the moment was gone, and Tha gave a startled cry. A hideous Skulthur settled itself on the deck rail with great flapping wings.

In a bound Hogar was upon the ominous creature, sword against gryffon claw. Never had he known such fierce parrying, nor quicker, than that of the Skulthur with its raking talons.

"Beware, O mortal! It is thy bane to slay my kind," croaked the monster. "Put up thy sword. I would not harm thee. Once before I spared thy life, remember? Hear me, O Tha! I bear thee greeting from thy royal brother."

Hogar fell back out of talon reach, a sword length between the heinous winged being and Tha.

"Dare thee violate the sanctity of the Moonrath, thou vulture?" cried Tha imperiously, her composure restored.

The creature inclined its grotesque beak.

"A thousand pardons, O Tha. I but serve my most worthy lord."

"Have thy say, Skulthur."

"Many nights now thy palace bedchamber hath not been slept in. Here, therefore, bring I Nol Dragir's message—nay, his command. Thou and thy paramour are summoned to stand in the Doom Ring, O Tha, and answer to the charge of treason and blasphemy against the gods."

Delivered of its burthen, the Skulthur unloosed its talons from the rail to wing skyward. The sorceress queen's spell-casting gesture caught the monster midair; it hung there momentarily, futilely beating its wings; then emitting an agonized croak, it plummeted to earth.

"Let that be my answer to the dragon spawn my mother whelped," cried Tha, splendid in her anger. "Nol Dragir, my half brother, is a monster out of my mother's womb by a loathsome Thalmanda. She was forced by a Fire Lord. She went mad, knowing she was with dragon child. The Fire Lords kept her alive until she birthed the vile thing; then they slew her in the Doom Ring."

"And what of thy father?"

"My father was High Priest of the Oirrin-Yess, hereditary Nemed, king of his people. When Nemed First fled Tor-a'Mor before the dreadful Fomors, and settled here on the rubble of ancient Asgarth, this was a desolation swept with the besom of destruction, a dwelling place of dragons. Such were the Thalmandas, who crawled amongst the ruins and worshiped a flame from out of the bowels of the earth. They were the last of a venerable lineage, the Old Ones, the once-powerful Dragonfolk, who ruled the world before the coming of the gods who dwelled in Asgarth. Nemed blasted the Thalmandas with spells and, having reduced them to the impotency of lizards, won from them the rune-ring of Odin, the source of their god-power. With the ring and their own wizardry, my forebears raised up Nardath of the White Walls on the wasteland of Ragnarok. All save for the Black Citadel. This was the later work of the Fire Lords, once back in power. On the death of my father, the ring again fell into the claws of the resurgent Thalmandas. They brought forth the black towers of Thool out of the heart of Nardath; and so the city of the sorcerers became Nardath-Thool. What thereafter became of my mother, I have told thee. I was but a child then; still, the Thalmandas chose me, my father's only heir, to sit the throne of Nardath as queen, and White Goddess of the Oirrin-Yess. Nol Dragir, because he was born with dragon wings, they later made Archon of Thool and High Priest of the Khthon, the Black Gods of the Old Ones. Thus did Nardath-Thool come to be twin cities, one within the other; a diarchy of the White and Black Gods and their Lords Temporal and Spiritual, yet ruled in fact by the Archon of Thool alone. I am but a puppet queen, with no powers but the sorcery inherited from my forebears; for magic runs in my Nemedian blood; even as it does in the dragon blood of my half-human sibling, who would destroy me to rule Nardath and Thool without a queen.

"Come, my lion. I must teach thee to fly if we are to outwit the Fire Lords. To my palace, then. We shall armor ourselves to stand in the Doom Ring."

XXX

The Doom Ring

The luxury of Tha's palatial quarters staggered Hogar's imagination from the moment the Moonrath touched down on the landing terrace. Tha laughed gaily at his openmouthed wonderment. At the clap of her lovely hands, slave girls appeared to prepare the bath he and Tha were to share.

Later, when toweled and anointed with spices and oils, they were robed in the finest of silks and damask, interwoven with threads of silver and gold. Tha walked with Hogar beneath the starless night. From the hanging gardens on the palace walls, they looked out over the blue-tiled rooftops and across the Field of Nardath to the shimmering blue-black waters beyond. Slaves set a sumptuous repast before them, with the rarest of wines and the most delectable of viands to tempt their palates. The thought of arming themselves against the Fire Lords was long in coming to mind.

Hogar marveled much at Tha's sorcery, at the armament she brought forth out of thin air, how she busked him and herself in ring mail of elfin-forged excellence, and in feathered cloaks that took flight as mighty eagle wings on command. All this Tha conjured by the utterance of Nemedian runes. The tarnhelms she kept for the last.

"These, my Hogar," Tha told him, "are caps of darkness. The wearer of one becomes invisible to all eyes. Behold!" Helming herself, she vanished before him; as he stood in wonder, Tha's voice spoke to him seemingly from out of nowhere.

"Put on your helm, my chieftain. 'Tis well," she said when he had done so. "I cannot see thee with thy tarnhelm on. Don now thy cloak of woven feathers. Spread thy wings. So. Thou art an eagle, my Hogar. Lift! Lo, we are airborne!"

They practiced flying together, hand in hand; soaring, circling, and landing, then taking off in flight again, until Hogar had mastered the skill to wing it alone.

"Thou art ready," said Tha, pleased at last. "Wear these as thy reward." She buckled on his own sword and dagger, taken from him by Nathas Klar. The heft of *Skull Breaker* again in his grasp gave Hogar new heart. Despite his enchantment, certain memories returned. He knew this was only because Tha willed it so.

"This was my father's sword," he said with grim rememberance. The memory of how *Skull Breaker* came to be his, and of what had passed at Grimmswold keep before that, of why he sought the Ravensword and the rune-ring of Odin, and how his quest for the fabled pair had brought him to Nardath-Thool—all this again he knew. But of Ragnahild he remembered nothing.

"I have knowledge of all this," said Tha, when he would have told her. "It is given me to read these things in your mind, as I read the runes. The future and what it holds is not mine to say." More than that, she said little. But she was aware of a cloud over Hogar's past that made his heart unreadable. Of his love and devotion she was certain; for she held him with the power of Nemed, which ran in her blood.

"Come, my Hogar" said Tha, clearing her mind of all else but the purpose at hand. "This night we shall bring the Darkness down, and win the Ravensword and the ring of Odin. This, then, is the plan, my warrior."

When she had told him, she cautioned, "Do exactly as I bid thee. Now, take wing!"

Soon they were circling above the sinistrous black towers that housed their objective. Tha guided Hogar, so that they settled together on the ledge of the open-air Temple of the Flame. Overhead, the sky was crimsoned by the glow of the sacred fire that rose from the Doom Ring below.

In the center of the eerie sanctuary, forming the dread circle of judgment, stood the Twelve Runestones of the Law. In their midst lay the Doom Stone, where offenders stood trial. If such was the will of the Fire Lords, the Ravensword was brought from its secret place into the Doom Ring to behead the victim, whose heart was then cut out and consumed in the Well of Fire, while the hot lifeblood was drunk in heinous rites.

Tha pressed Hogar's hand in the prearranged signal. They rose from the ledge, circling high, then down on silent wings in a long spiral until they hovered over the stone-ringed fane.

It was an eldritch, fire-lit scene they witnessed. On the Doom Seat, with his dragon wings folded behind him, sat Nol Dragir, Archon of the Fire Lords, and hereditary Doomsman of Thool. Two black-armored Skulthurs guarded him on either side, their short swords at salute in fierce gryffon claws. Before each of the Twelve Runestones there was posted another of the hideous creatures. Others stood like shadows where shadows were not. In the center of this eerie circle, between the Doom Stone and the Archon's throne, flamed the Well of Fire, tended by four green-robed Thalmandas, the Fire Lords of Thool. From their movements, Hogar sensed the hooded figures to be something less than human. Others of their ilk sat within the stone ring.

Hogar could not see Tha. According to plan, she would now be standing on the Doom Stone, about to unhelm and reveal herself. He hovered there, waiting for her to speak.

"I am come at thy summons, my brother," cried Tha, lifting her tarnhelm upward into Hogar's ready hands, dramatically disclosing her presence. "Behold, Tha stands before thee in the Doom Ring. I am come to answer thy false charges of treason and blasphemy against the gods."

Amid the startled assemblage, she appeared as an

eagle-winged goddess. She partially let drop her feathered cloak, to reveal herself armor-clad in a black ring-byrnie and war girdle, leaving her thighs and legs bare from the tops of her black leather half boots in a most provocative manner, with her lustrous raven tresses capped in a close-fitting black coif.

Gods! She is incomparable! thought Hogar, with a catch in his throat at the awesome spectacle.

Nol Dragir recovered at last.

"Thou art brazen in thy coming, thou Skulthur slayer," he said. "Where is thy barbarian, with whom thou would bring down the Darkness?"

"Hogar Bloodsword is he named," cried Tha. "At my call shall he come. For though he is a god in his Nordland"—here she lied a little—"he doth worship at my shrine, and drinketh of my cup. When he cometh, beware, Lords of the Fire, thou dwellers in evil ways, for he shall cut a swath of blood amongst thee with his mighty sword, and of thy skulls and bones shall he build a great tower reaching up to the heavens. Then shall Nardath give thanks to the Oirrin-Yess, with burnt offerings from the highest place upon that tower wall, for her deliverance from the Khthon and their minions. Thus shall fall the Fire Lords, and thou, their Archon, my brother."

Majestically drawing the feathered cloak once again about her shoulders, Tha stood with arms aloft, eagle wings full spread to symbolize her divinity.

"Behold," she cried out, "I am She-Who-Walks-the-Night. I am the Black Goddess of Doom, who taketh away the Light!"

From out of the starless night came the dire response.

"Hail, O Black Moon that bringeth down the Darkness!"

A gasp of horror ran through the assembled Thalmanda Fire Lords and their gryffon-taloned Guardians of the Ring. Stark terror shone in their eyes, as the dreaded invocation seemingly came out of nowhere, and Tha vanished into darkness.

It was all as Tha had planned it. It was Hogar who spoke the dire words and placed the tarnhelm back upon her head, causing Tha to disappear yet still be heard.

"I, Immortal Tha, walk amongst thee unseen. For behold, I bring down the Darkness upon thee! To me, O Hogar, to me! Let thy sword be seen through the Darkness like an avenging Light!"

Still wrapped in invisibilty, Hogar drew at Tha's command. The glow of the sacred well-fire touched his naked blade with flame. When they saw the fiery sword come out of the Darkness to fall upon them of itself (for no hand was seen to wield it), the Fire Lords and their Skulthur minions fell blinded by their fears. Nol Dragir, the Archon of Thool, cried out in his terror, "O Immortal Tha, thou hast brought down the Darkness; for my eyes no longer see."

Hogar would have slain them all, but Tha stayed his hand.

"Nay, the time for slaying is yet to come. Behold," she cried, "I have cast them down, and they are fallen as though dead in a swoon-spell." She lifted off her tarnhelm and stood glorified of herself for what she had done.

"Take now the Ravensword from its secret place, as I direct thee," said Tha. "There also thou will find the rune-ring of Odin. Bring them to me."

The secret place was concealed within the Doom Seat, where Tha told him it would be. Therein, wrapped in a cloth of black velvet, were the sword and the ring of his quest. When he had looked upon them in wonder, he brought the two treasures to Tha, as she commanded of him. Girding herself with the Ravensword and clasping the ring of Odin upon her right arm, Tha stood triumphant before him.

"It is rist on the Twelve Runestones," she told him, "one day the Oirrin-Yess and the Khthon must battle to the death. And that day shall be called the Last Day of the Gods. Then shall come one who will bring down the dark towers of Thool, with the ring of Odin worn on his sword arm upraised against his enemies. Thou art that one, and that day, my Hogar, will soon be upon us. Therefore did I stay thee from slaying the Fire Lords and their Archon this night; for the day of their night is yet to come, when Nol Dragir and thee are met with swords upon the Field of Nardath. Let us now begone from this place of evil."

Together they took flight unseen, as though on the silent wings of night, leaving the Fire Lords and their minions ensorceled in the Darkness Tha had brought down upon them—save for the glow from the Well of Fire, which crimsoned the starless night as before.

XXXI

"Put Not Thy Trust in Sorceresses!"

Hogar felt the mind-probe before he awakened. It was a voice in a dream, he told himself. He looked at Tha. She was curled beside him half covered, asleep.

"Do not disturb her," the voice commanded.

He was about to speak out, but could not; as though in a dream, knowing all the while he was awake. It was then he knew the voice that spoke within his mind was that of the Wizard of Lom.

"Hear me, Hogar. I am come to awaken you from ensorcelment. She with whom you lie in lust holds you in her spell. Forget not, Tha is a Nemedian sorceress, to he feared for her powers. Should I materialize before her in shadow substance, it would be my undoing. She would rip my shadow-self to shreds, and make of me a disembodied soul doomed to wander the Cold Waste of the Sorcerers forever. Therefore I have cast a binding spell upon Tha while she lies sleeping, until what I am come to say is said, and I am gone from here to await you on the Field of Nardath. Nay, do not attempt to speak. I have wrought you speechless for the while, the better for you to attend my words.

"Time passes quickly for you here, Hogar. Days become weeks, and weeks are soon months gone by. Ragnahild, meanwhile, has grown heavy with your bairn. The while you have lain spellbound by a sorceress, Hothir Longtooth and his cohorts have moved against Nardath-Thool by the River Skaa, to win the Ravensword and the ring of Odin to himself, and thus secure the Raven Throne. In Hothir's van rides the scoundrel Drakko. Nay, doubt me not, strange as this may seem. Hothir has sworn to deliver your head, and your queen mother in the bargain, to Drakko in repayment for Vandir warriors to man his longships. His own sworn karls have deserted Hothir one by one. Two bad apples are barreled together. Drakko, being censured by King Hern for his lecherous ways, did foully slay his king and claim the throne of Vandirheim. The two usurpers have put their evil heads together with that sly shaman, Klavun Thorg, and have pacted an alliance. On hearing this, the jarls who had cast their lots with Hothir Longtooth, went over to the queen. Rorik Bloodaxe alone keeps shield oath to the false-king; he wants you dead for slaying Blund, his brother.

"Meanwhile," the voice continued within his mind, "commanded by Starulf, Ermengard's flotilla fares hard on Hothir's wake, braving the Great Ice Marsh, up the River Skaa, where it winds its inky way to the inland Sea of Nemed.

"With sword, spear, and magic they come. Ragnahild stands with drawn sword in the bow of the queen's longship, armor-clad to protect your unborn son. It was Ragnahild who forced the march on Hothir's van by land and sea, saying she would storm the very walls of Nardath-Thool alone if none other rallied to your rescue, once it was known you were held here in ensorcelment.

"Ever at her side is Nels the Bowman, faithfully discharging his trust. With your queen mother also fare Fjaerlda, Ketil the Skald, and one-eyed Ari Oxmain, while overhead in full battle array, Queen Astrith of the Swans and her Hundred Shields keep watch in flight.

"Even as I speak, Hothir Longtooth beaches his forty ships along the river jetties, to raise his tents before the walls of Nardath-Thool. Go forth, Hogar Bloodsword, true King of the Asyr, and take the field against your foes.

"Lo, Tha stirs from the sleep spell. The sorceress queen can bind you no more. She has led you to recover the sword and the ring of your quest, but not to your advantage. It is Tha who holds them both. I warn you: *put not your trust in sorceresses!*"

With the Wizard of Lom's words ringing in his mind, Hogar rose to arm himself. The rustle of silks caused him to turn. Tha had awakened. Her green cat eyes burned into his with hurt and distrust.

"I loved thee, Hogar," whispered the sorceress, her anger rising.

"And I thee," he answered in the Old Tongue.

"Nay. Thou hast betrayed me."

"Thou doth stiil dream," Hogar replied calmly. "Whenever have I done thee harm?"

"Thou bringest an armed host against me," Tha accused.

"They who bivouac before the walls of Nardath-Thool are my enemies."

"Thy wizard doth lead them, and thou art come to destroy Tha, who helped thee win the treasures of thy quest. Deny it not. He hath told thee I would keep the sword and the ring for my own purposes against thee. I read his mind-talk," said Tha. "Thou shall die for thy treason!"

With these bitter words, she shape-shifted. Where her voluptuous body had lain naked in his arms, a green-eyed saber-toothed tigress rose ready to spring upon him from their love bed.

Reaching out for the weapon nearest to hand, Hogar's fingers closed about Tha's hunting spear, which stood propped against a bedside gong. He raised the spear to defend himself, and would have driven it home through the white beast's savage heart, had not Tha shape-shifted again to her own provocative self.

Hogar wavered.

How could he slay her with whom he had lain in ecstasy?

"Thou art a fool!" Tha taunted. Had she anticipated this very weakness in the strength of his love? The spear became a writhing serpent in Hogar's hand as Tha cast a changing spell. He flung it from him, looking for his sword.

"Guards!" cried Tha, striking the gong with an angry fist. From behind the arras sprang two hawk-visored kerns, brandishing great curved swords.

"To the pits with him—*alive*!" Tha commanded.

Hogar fought off the kerns with his bare hands. Ordered not to slay him, they were obliged to sheathe their weapons to grapple with the agile Nordsman, and found him more than enough for the pair of them to take alive. Tha seized the fallen spear and brought the butt end down hard on Hogar's head.

He crumpled.

"Buffoons!" she shouted at the hapless kerns. "Truss him quickly ere he recovers and strangles thee both with one hand."

Tha's eyes glistened with tears; mixed emotions tugged at the corners of her lovely mouth as she watched Hogar led away.

XXXII

The Smell of Dungeons

The great iron door creaked open. Hogar's guards shoved him forward, to stumble down damp stone steps into mildewed darkness. From the foul depths that awaited him below, the smell of dungeons rose like the noisome stench of an opened grave. Behind him came the sounds of the heavy door clanking shut, a bolt shot into place, and the turning of a key in the lock.

Hogar groped his way to the bottom of the steps; they gave onto a dim-lit open dungeon, partitioned by arched underpinnings of stone into low-ceiled alcoves and chambers of past and forgotten horrors. The time-picked bones of long-dead wretches still hung in iron cages; the dying slumped in rotting rags, fettered to a wall.

Coming toward him from out of the shadows, crutching a useless leg, he saw Nars Anthor, the kern he had crippled with a sword thrust through the thigh. The former queen's champion snarled his hatred.

"The quern of the gods grinds exceedingly small." He was gloating. "Because I am now fit for little else, Nathas Klar has made me dungeon master. You who destroyed me are now mine to destroy. A fitting revenge, eh, Hogar? Guards! Seize this barbarian. To the cages with him. The arena is not a pleasant place to die, alien, as you will soon discover, with a sword thrust in your guts."

Wrist-bound, Hogar had no alternative but submission; but not without putting a boot in a groin, and a shoulder against a nose, that sent two guards sprawling in pain. Finally subdued with a blow over the head, against which he had small way of defending himself, Hogar was roughly confined in one of the holding cells for those condemned to die in the arena. The cages varied in size. From the shadows of some there came anguished cries for mercy. The large cage into which he was unceremoniously shoved was full of surprises. The first was a voice that spoke out of the shadows in salty Nordish.

"Damn my eyes, if it's not Hogar Bloodsword! By Balor and Bress! I'd given you up for lost, mate."

Lon Thoddrach clapped him on the shoulder. Hogar was equally amazed to find the Fomorian pirate still alive. They embraced like brothers; then came the second surprise. Svadi, Frodi, and Lif showed themselves, declaring in unison, "We thought you were dead and gone, lord."

From the next cage came a cry of greeting from the surviving Fomors, their strange brogue made intelligible to Hogar by the amiable grins on their fierce faces.

"What sorcery is this?" he exclaimed in wonder. "With my own eyes I saw the lot of you perish. Swallowed up by the kraken that attacked our ship."

"Aye, sorcery it was, mate," said Lon Thoddrach, "and no sea monster did you ken. Damn me, it was an illusion, naught else. A bloody sorcerer's trick, to entrap foolhardy sea wolves such as ourselves, who dare venture beyond the Frozen Sea." He told how an eldritch light beam had struck them down, so that they were stunned and made defenseless against Nathas Klar's minions, who took them captive and burned the *Sea Raven*.

"When our heads cleared, here we were; and here we have remained awaiting our fate in the arena," he concluded.

"I, too, have been held captive by sorcery this long while," Hogar recited in half truth. "I awakened this day from the glamour cast over me by the sorceress queen, Tha. Accused of treason, I sought to escape, only to be overpowered and brought here for my pains." He found himself staring at the white-maned kern in the next cage with the Fomorian pirate crew, who now stood looking at him through the bars.

"Thaul of Tarthiz!" he exclaimed. "What ill fortune has silenced your tongue, friend Thaul?"

"I was biding my time, to get a word in edgewise," the Tarthizian replied, smiling. "As the old saying goes, I fell in with bad company, it would seem. I'm here because of my show of friendship to you in your brawl with Nars Anthor. Well met again, Hogar Bloodsword, though troubles seem to dog our paths. Have a care," he warned, at the sound of approaching footsteps.

Silence fell upon the cages as the turnkeys appeared to dole out the day's ration: a foul slumgullion, bread, and sour wine rudely shoved through an opening between the bars and the damp stone floor. Left alone, the prisoners fell to with their fingers. Wolfing down the miserable fare, they banged their metal cups against the cages for more wine.

The thump-thump of a lone crutch brought the dungeon master. Singling out the cage that held Hogar, Nars Anthor braced himself with one hand high on the bars, and shouted above the banging cups.

"Silence, dogs! Or it shall be the hot iron for every last mother's son of you! Queen Tha has ordered the games held tonight. I'll waste no more wine on dogs about to have their gullets slit. Through yon grating, Hogar, you may watch what goes on in the arena until your turn comes." He brought forth a shagreen-cased sword from the folds of his robe. "A bone for a dog from the Queen. Tha returns this to defend yourself." He handed *Skull Breaker* to Hogar through the bars. "Better you turn the point against yourself, alien, and spare your white-livered heart the death agony that awaits you on the sand." Nars Anthor hobbled off, racked with cruel laughter.

XXXIII

The Queen's Pleasure

By late afternoon, the cheaper tiers began to fill. The amphitheater came alive to the roar and smell of the bloodthirsty rabble scrambling for seats. They brought their own food and drink, against the long wait for the Queen's Pleasure to commence. To the effluvium of garlic, wine, sausage, and strong cheese, each added his own body stink; a heady offering to the gods of carnage.

From the menagerie, unseen but known of its presence from the choking emanations of animal waste, came the deep, angry cry of caged beasts brought from the queen's hunting preserve and tormented to man-killing rage, soon to be vented on hapless victims thrown to a dreadful fate on the smooth raked sand.

The dragon-pennon-draped boxes where the Archon of the Fire Lords and Thalmanda royalty were wont to sit remained conspicuously empty. The Lords of Nardath were seated in their loggias. The queen, girded with the Ravensword and wearing the ring of Odin on her arm, occupied the royal pavilion with her train. The games were opened at last.

The first event brought first blood. The crowd roared its pleasure as thirty black aurochs entered the arena. The great wild oxen, standing eleven feet at the withers, milled about nervously, uncertain of their surroundings, not liking the grassless sand upon which they had been turned out. A great roar rose from the stands as the lead bull of a hairy mammoth herd stood under the raised barrier, poised to trumpet its presence and sound the charge. Twenty bull mammoths thundered into the arena, and the barrier came down. The scent of the pachyderms unnerved the wild oxen;

although they stood shoulder high to one another, instinctively they sensed their prodigious horns were no match for the awesome curved tusks of the trumpeting mammoths. The aurochs panicked, goring each other in their confusion, making their slaughter a certainty.

At a sign from Tha, the barrier was again raised to admit a company of archers and spearmen. The crowd roared its approval as the lead bull was brought down with loosed shafts and spears. It was the first mammoth to perish. The remaining bulls fixed angry red eyes on their tormentors. Trumpeting their rage, they charged. A maddened bull trampled three spearmen and tossed their mangled bodies in the air with its trunk. The stands went wild. One well-sped arrow took a mammoth in the eye, dropping the great beast dead in its tracks. It rolled over slowly, crushing two hapless archers to a bloody pulp as it expired trumpeting. The gory struggle went on; carcasses of man and beast strewed the arena; the sand ran wet with blood. Finally the last arrow, the last spear were spent. Fifteen men and ten mammoths survived. The great pachyderms, pin cushioned by arrows and spears, charged. The unarmed archers and spearmen turned and fled before the terrible curved tusks. One by one they were gored to death, as the aurochs had been before them, or hurled against the stone wall encircling the stands. The crowd was delirious with blood lust.

Nars Anthor leered at Hogar between the bars.

"Your time has come, alien dog." He turned the key in the locks and opened the two adjacent holding cages. "Be ready when the barrier goes up. Laggards get a dagger in the back."

Each combatant was armed with a spear as he stood at the closed gate. Through the iron grating, Hogar saw Tha rise and signal the keepers. The barrier went up, and the Nordsman and his companions took the field to the roar of the crowd.

The maddened mammoths wheeled and charged, their small red eyes glaring hatred for their new tormentors. Spent from exertion and the carnage they had wrought, and the futile effort to dislodge the arrows and spears sunk deep in their blood-dyed hairy hides, they went down before the fresh wave of spears, and were quickly dispatched.

Clarions sounded. Hogar and his comrades-in-arms regrouped themselves to face whatever new peril waited behind the closed barrier. Again Tha signed to the keepers. The barrier was lifted. Onto the death-strewn sand charged a score and ten helmeted kerns, armed with swords and shields. Their trappings bore the white badge of Queen Tha, or the orange of Nathas Klar. Amongst them were warrior-slaves Hogar had seen but briefly in the Hall of Kerns.

"Go for the visors," Thaul said in a low growl. The word was passed from spear to spear. The kerns charged. The wall of spears against them held. For every kern unhelmed and run through the body or throat, a sword changed hands. The kerns fell back before the fierce attack. Trained to fight Nemedian fashion, they had never faced such warriors as the blue-skinned giants from Tor-a'Mor. They turned and fled. Well-thrown spears brought them down one by one. The crowd screamed its delight at the carnage.

Queen Tha was not pleased. Her green eyes sought out Hogar. Her lovely mouth curled in a cruel and heartless smile as the barrier lifted to admit a rush of twelve white saber-toothed tigers onto the sand and closed behind them. The smell of blood and death brought a snarling challenge from the great cats. Weaving uncertainly, they caught the living man scent. They crouched low, coughing; bellies dredging the sand, they slunk toward their quarry, their twelve-foot bodies a symphony of rippling muscles under sleek, gold-striped hides.

Before the walls of Nardath-Thool where Hothir's bivouac was tented, within the false-king's pavilion, three figures were huddled about a copper brazier. A wizard wind had whipped the Cold Waste, smoldering the reluctant fire that filled the tent with smoke-reek, but little warmth. At length one of the three spoke out harshly.

"Enough! By the gods, I have had a belly full of this. Back to the ships!"

"Nay, master," said Klavun Thorg. His shaved pate glistened as he poked at the slow-burning dung chips, with small hope of a blaze. "We await him who can gain us passage through yonder walls without shedding a drop of blood on either side."

Hothir shrugged.

"Who cares about shedding Nemedian blood?"

"A drop of one sheds two of the other," cautioned the shaman. The figure in Vandir armor made a deprecating gesture. "Patience, King Drakko," said the sorcerer.

"We must be within the gates before dawn, while Nardath sleeps," said the Vandir. "What keeps this perfidious Nemedian?"

As though conjured up by Drakko's words, the tent flap was parted by the sentry to admit their tardy visitor. The three figures by the smoldering fire turned their eyes on the saffron-robed Archpriest of Tha as he entered.

XXXIV

"Kill! Kill! Kill!

"By the nines!" shouted Hogar, taking command as the saber-toothed cats sprang forward. In closed ranks three across, three deep, he and his comrades-in-arms moved in phalanx formation to meet the bounding attack, spears resolutely set to impale.

But the sorcery of Tha intervened. The twelve charging tigers were spell-changed in midstride. Twelve exact counterparts of Tha beckoned seductively with open arms. The phalanges wavered.

"Sorcery!" cried Hogar. "Beware!"

Despite his dire warning, a few Fomors broke ranks to embrace the voluptuous clones who came toward them offering their bodies for carnal pleasure.

"Cast spears!" Hogar ordered. "They are phantom women! Beware! The tigers are upon you! Slay them, or be slain!"

Even as he spoke, even as the spears were loosed, those who had broken ranks were torn to shreds by saber-tooth and talon. The illusion faded then as the change-spell gave way to the reality of death, to reveal twelve snowy tigers lying dead on the bloody sand, impaled by spears.

From the queen's pavilion came a scream of rage. With a terrible gesture, Tha cast the darkest spell within her powers. At the utterance of the Black Runes summoning the Khthon, the Black Gods of Thool, shrieks of terror rose from the stands. On the field, faces waxed grim. For before the eyes of all, from the blood-wet sand there rose up the bodies and carcasses of the slain, man and beast alike, to do the will of the sorceress queen.

"Kill! Kill! Kill!" screamed Tha.

And the dead stalked the living in the bloody arena of Nardath-Thool.

Reclaiming a fallen spear, Hogar ran within a dozen paces of the royal enclosure, his weapon poised to hurl. From the queen-seat, Tha screamed her hatred.

"Thou shall die, Hogar! Thou hast slain the Twelve White Beasts of the Oirrin-Yess. By the Black Runes of the Khthon, I have risen up the dead to drag thee down to the Darkness."

Hogar drew back the spear, yet could not throw.

Tha laughed bitterly and shape-shifted. For a fleeting moment, Hogar saw a green-eyed saber-toothed tigress, sword-girded and snarling from the queen-seat, before the snowy beast sprang for his throat.

He barely had time to drop on one knee with the spear held firmly in both hands, the butt of the shaft dug into the sand, before the great cat was upon him. The spear took the beautiful beast below the heart in midair. The talons of one savage paw raked his shoulder. With a wild cry of anguish, the great cat lay dying at his feet, its green eyes glazing; he felt the warmth of Tha's perfumed breath in his face. The tigress was once more a beautiful woman, as the change-spell spent itself. With a blood-chilling cry, half tigress, half human, it was the sorceress Queen of Nardath-Thool herself who lay on the bloody sand, impaled by Hogar's spear.

Tha's green cat eyes held him in a reproachful glare.

"Thou art a fool, Hogar," she whispered. "Thou could have shared the throne of Nardath as thee did the queen's couch. Now thou hast slain the one for whom thy heart beats. Take the Ravensword and the rune-ring of Odin, which thou hast won. But beware Nol Dragir! The Darkness I brought down upon Thool was but an illusion, and is lifting. My powers ebb with the bloody tide that flows from the wound thou hast given me.

"Kiss me, my lion. And farewell. So dies Tha, thy tigress, who loved thee."

Hogar rose with the blood taste of her dying kiss on his lips. Taking them from her body, he girded himself with the Ravensword, and clasped the ring of Odin upon his strong right arm.

Tha had called herself immortal, incarnate. And yet she lay dead.

For a long moment there was a stunned silence. Then from the royal pavilion, the voice of Nathas Klar, the Queen's Procurer, rose shrilly above the confused outcry of the crowd.

"Guards! Seize him! He has slain the queen!"

Before a single pikeman could reach the arena field, Lon Thoddrach and his Fomors were vaulting over the stone wall into the royal loggia. His sword point was at Nathas Klar's fat throat. His sea wolves held sword and spear pressed against the hearts of the cowering Lords of Nardath.

Nathas Klar's hooded eyes widened with terror as he screamed for the lords to disarm themselves. They wavered, and the Fomors slew them to a man. So died Nathas Klar.

At that moment, the barrier was raised. Into the arena poured fifty Vandir warriors led by Drakko. The saffron-robed figure who had treacherously led them to their doom reached for the lever to close the barrier. Hogar waited, Ravensword naked in hand. At his side was Thaul of Tarthiz. Next to him stood Svadi, Frodi, and Lif, all eager for the fray.

"He with the notched ear is mine!" Hogar cried out. "The one in yellow is the Archpriest of the Oirrin-Yess. Mark him well. He has betrayed his gods and his goddess by leading my enemies through the sewers and dungeons to take the city within its walls. Let him not escape." He and his comrades-in-arms fell upon the Vandir, sword to sword, as they met in the bloody arena called the Queen's Pleasure. Drakko turned to flee, but Hogar barred his way.

"Die, Asyr dog!" cried the false Vandir king.

Their swords clanged.

"Drakko, I promised you your death when next we met, you swine!" Hogar parried.

With a wild cry, Lon Thoddrach and his Fomors poured out of the stands to take the field, attacking the Vandir in a frenzy of iron on iron. All fought furiously, each man knowing full well he battled to the death. Hogar wielded the Ravensword of Thorir Treefoot, and the rune-carved blade bit deep; from its wounds none would recover. In a flurry of sword strokes, Drakko fell, cloven to the eyes. Freeing his sword from the corpse of his enemy, Hogar cried out his vengeance.

"For my queen mother, and for Ragnahild of Wulfstane, mother of my unborn son, have I struck thee down, Drakko. For the wrongs done them, walk thou forever in the Darkness!"

He lifted high the Ravensword, still adrip with blood.

"And now, fall Hothir!" he cried out with passion; but his words were muffled by a great whirring of wings. The sky was darkened by a thousand Skulthurs settling to rest atop the amphitheater's outer walls.

"To the streets!" shouted Thaul of Tarthiz. "Hogar, make for the turnstiles with your warriors."

The Nordsman cast a quick look down the carcass-strewn arena. Those that Tha had raised from death again lay dead. The Vandir had fallen to the last man at the cost of three Fomors. A yellow-robed corpse lay on the bloodied sand before the half-open barrier. The archpriest had managed no further retreat before being cut down. Nars Anthor lay on his crutch, sprawled in death under the half-raised gate, dagger in hand. Where the incomparable Tha of the Green Eyes, Queen of Nardath, had lain in death, there now was naught but blood-soaked sand . . . and the carcass of a white saber-toothed tigress transfixed by a spear.

"To the streets!" Hogar bellowed, heeding Thaul's counsel. He and his men fought their way through the panicked crowd toward the main spectator gates. He used the flat of his sword where he could, not wanting to kill wantonly. Those in the milling mob who raised weapons against him took his point through the heart or throat. It was a bloody swath Hogar and his comrades-in-arms were forced to cut through the screaming masses scrambling to avoid the talons of the Skulthurs, as they swept down on the stands like barn owls upon scurrying mice.

The way to the streets was finally won.

"Well done, friend Thaul," said Hogar, kicking his sword free from a Nemedian corpse and wiping the blade on his breeks. "'We part here. My archenemy is landed at the river jetties in great strength, to storm the walls and wrest from me the kingsword of the Asyr. I leave you to take the field against him."

"You have just slain their queen. Every Nemedian is your enemy. You'll never make it to the city gates," said Thaul.

"How then?"

"This way. After me," said Thaul of Tarthiz. "To the Temple of Tha. It's the only safe way out of the city."

Of a sudden Hogar knew why.

"The Moonrath!" he exclaimed breathlessly.

"Quickly!" cried Thaul, leading the way.

XXXV

The Field of Nardath

Thaul led Hogar and his men on. Halfway down the mall into which they turned, they came upon a nine of pikemen. The night watch. They were cut down like tall corn, without the loss of a man. Presently the mall gave onto a perfume-laden garden which the Nordsman was quick to recognize. The circled path led them to the narthex of the temple they sought. The great orichalch doors stood open, unattended. The temple guards Hogar remembered were nowhere in evidence. Through the doors, the roofless fane showed empty, save for the lone scarlet-robed priest in the act of locking up. His soul was sped on its way, to dwell forever in the Halls of the Oirrin-Yess, before his old eyes had seen the first-drawn sword.

Racing down the nave past the coiled serpent lamps, Thaul led the way to the sanctuary Hogar knew well. Here he had first set eyes on the incomparable Tha; here she would sit veiled and exalted no more. As his eyes sought the Moonrath at the top of the seven sacred steps, Hogar stopped, stunned by what he beheld.

In place of the expected Ark of Tha, there stood a ship of singular crafting, with neither oars nor sail, yet slender and graceful of line and hulled of fine woods.

"What sorcery have we here?" cried Hogar in disbelief.

"It is my sky-ship," said Thaul of Tarthiz simply. "By means of which I came unwontedly to Nardath-Thool. And by which, please the gods, we will leave. Board quickly, before the Skulthurs smell us out."

As the sky-craft lifted off its mooring stage Thaul revealed the secret of flight: a rotor, buoyancy chambers, and a hull of feather-light but durable okram and lagopa wood from the forests of Tarthiz.

"To think," said Hogar, "I believed Tha had but to utter an ancient rune."

"The Moonrath is no more," said Thaul. "The binding spell Tha cast over my galley has spent itself."

"A sky-ship!" Hogar murmured in wonder.

"Have you not heard of the ships of Tarthiz?" asked Thaul with an amused smile.

"Ships that fly without sorcery?"

"In all sooth," Thaul assured him. "I am the royal artificer. Maker of many such craft, from one-man chariots to ships of war carrying a complement of a hundred swords and a score of archers." As he spoke Hogar saw they were passing over the queen's hunting preserve. In a few moments they would be clear of the city walls. Thaul told how he had been manning his flier alone when a witch storm swept away the auxiliary sail and mast, and hurled him mercilessly off course, like a straw in the wind.

"My controls were locked," said Thaul, "by eldritch beams of arcing lights. My ship and I were downed unharmed in the wasteland and taken captive. The rest you know."

Svadi hurried aft from the galley's forward rail.

"The battle rages before the city gates, lord," he exclaimed. Hogar stepped to the steerboard gunwale with his bosun. Below them, Asyr and Vandir fought to the death on a field windrowed with corpses and fouled with the reek of slaughter. The opposing hosts of the false-king Hothir and the Queen of Nordgaard were met in savage single combat, at sword point and ax edge; control of the sinistrous city whose walls were thrown up against them depended on the outcome. No seige was laid; Hothir's war engines lay unassembled on the jetties where they had been landed. In the queen's van, carrying the assault on the city gates was the Old Warrior, stouthearted Starulf of Skaane. At his side fought Lothbrok Forkbeard and his valiants from Skona, cheering his men on with a bellowed "Heave, ho!" as they rammed the gates with a ship's mast. Ardvarth's Jarl Urik and his stalwart karls protected the right flank; Orlaf of Thone and his warriors, lately won over to Ermengard's cause, defended the left. Backing them were the brave men of Grundergaard, bearing high their dead jarl's Blue Fox standard. Overhead, Queen Astrith and her Hundred Shields flew at the foe with bloodied swords and spears.

A pang of anger gnawed at Hogar's vitals, like an army of ants, to see the Raven of Nordgaard borne aloft in the ranks of the Vandir. How dare Hothir flaunt this brave banner as his own! Hogar's mind flared red with hatred as he beheld the tall, yellow-bearded Hothir wielding his sword against men of Asyr blood, striving to defeat the woman he once had loved and whom he had brought to sorrow, all for a throne that was not rightfully his.

"Yon yellow beard who leads the Vandir is mine!" was Hogar's fierce cry. Thaul landed the sky-ship in the thick of the fray. Asyr and Vandir alike scattered; some in fear, some in disbelief and wonder at a warrior-manned ship from out of the skies. Roaring the war cry of the Asyr, Hogar vaulted the deck rail into the midst of the melee. Lon Thoddrach and his fierce-faced sea wolves followed. Stalwart Svadi, Frodi, and Lif cut a red swath of death with sword and ax, until they fell in a gallant rush to take the Raven banner. Thaul of Tarthiz wielded a bold and bloody blade, his flying white hair contrasted with Hogar's unruly rusty locks, not unlike white and red-maned lions fighting side by side.

In the press of battle, Hogar caught sight of a mighty swordsman, deftly laying Vandir dead around him with a lightning-fast blade. A turn of the grizzled head profiled the familiar hawk nose of Ketil the Skald. Beyond the warrior bard, on a rise of marble shards, four valiant figures battled in defense of their queen against Hothir and his cohorts.

Hogar's pulse hammered at his temples as he beheld Ragnahild swording it side by side with Nels the Bowman. Flanking them, one-eyed Ari Oxmain swung his great ax in a bloody arc. Fjaerlda, too, he saw; armor-clad like Ragnahild, sword flashing in her agile hand. The valiant four formed a ring of iron around their queen. Ermengard stood drawn, one hand supporting her war banner, the White Boar of Skaane, proudly unfurled with its staff firmly planted amongst the shards.

Nearby, on a similar rubbled mound, blue-robed and fierce-voiced, gray beard and uncapped hair flying in the wind, the Wizard of Lom stood like Odin of old, casting rune spells against the incantations of the scarlet-cassocked priests of Tha. From atop the white walls of Nardath, where they lined the battlements animal-masked, there arose the Mantra of the White Runes . . . *"Y'a El-hi'u ma r'hl y'a . . ."* invoking their bestial gods to avenge their slain goddess.

Lightning lashed the darkened sky. The heavens trembled at the thunderous coming of those summoned by the utterance of their rune-spelled names. Amongst the burgeoning clouds appeared the heinous and terrible faces of the Khthon and the Oirrin-Yess, priest conjured, one against the other with bloodied spears and dripping swords, even as it was rist upon the Twelve Runestones.

Klavun Thorg looked into the skies from where he stood casting spells at Hothir's side; he cried out at what he beheld, and fell groveling in terror amongst the shards. Nor could his magic do him aught. His mind had snapped.

"Doomed!" he screamed. "For I have looked upon the Dwellers in the Darkness. I have seen the Unseeable. Doomed! Doomed! Doomed! I have looked upon the faceless faces of the Twelve in One."

"You have brought down the evil!" Hothir cried, running the raving warlock through. Klavun Thorg raised his dying eyes to those of his slayer and cried out with his last breath, *"The hand of thine enemy shall find thee!"*

"I would begone from such madness!" Hothir cried, drawing forth his blade from the Nemedian's dead body. "Back to the ships!" he shouted. Before he could sound a retreat, there came against him the swords of vengeance. In the van of those who opposed him came Hogar with the Ravensword raised aloft. And death stood between them, waiting.

"Ah, Hogar!" cried Hothir, rushing forward undaunted, with his falchion raised. "I will have thee dead at last."

They closed quickly, blade to blade, hilt to hilt. Countering furiously, each smelled the hatred rising in the other's sweat. With a great blow, Hothir drove Hogar to one knee. At that moment, Fjaerlda fought her way through the press with a cry on her lips.

"Die, false king!"

Her sword was swift. Hothir fell backward with the blow that took him between the neck and shoulder. As the crookback sister of the queen withdrew her blade, Hogar, regaining his footing, brought down the Ravensword and struck off the head of his father's slayer.

"Vengeance is mine!" he exulted, raising his eyes to the heavens. Tha had foretold this day.

"For Tha!" With the ring of Odin clasped upon his right arm, he lofted the Ravensword high for all to see, and cried out, "By the rune-ring of Odin, I command it! Fall ye towers! Tumble ye gates and walls! Let Nardath-Thool again be a dwelling place of things that crawl from under stones in the Cold Waste; for the sorcerers of Nemed and the Thalmanda Fire Lords shall rule no more. So say I, Hogar Bloodsword this day Master of Runes . . . Fall now, Nol Dragir!"

At his words, there came a wailing of priests from the battlements. The Field of Nardath was darkened by a myriad whirring Stygian wings as a legion of gryffon-beaked Skulthurs swooped down from the ebon towers of Thool. Over the garden-hung walls they swept low, tearing armor and flesh with raking talons. Leading his Black Legion, Nol Dragir flew at Hogar screaming his hatred, a great two-handed sword brandished in his dragonlike claws.

"With this, the true Ravensword, O Hogar, do I call down the fury of the Khthon upon thy head! By the power of the Black Runes, I summon the Black Gods of Thool to destroy thee!"

Hogar boldly strode to meet the Archon, true sword against false. So great were their blows, that sparks flew. They fought fiercely, man against wing-borne dragon spawn. Nol Dragir hovered, positioning himself to bring the great two-handed sword down upon Hogar's unhelmed head. The Nordsman parried deftly, strikinq upward in a countering blow that cut through the armor of Nol Dragir's right arm . . . yet failed to arrest the descending stroke that took him deep in the side, and drove him to his knees grievously wounded.

Ragnahild strove to win to Hogar's side. The distance between them was great; yet before the Archon's sword fell, she was borne aloft by Queen Astrith, her feathered swan maiden's cloak spreading into wings. She flew between Hogar and Nol Dragir with her sword upraised, parrying the fateful stroke meant to be Hogar's bane. Countering boldly, she smote the Archon of Thool such a blow that one dragon wing hung useless. With a bestial scream, Nol Dragir struggled to maintain flight, bringing the great sword down on his new antagonist one-handed as he fell. The blow rent Ragnahild's right side through her ring mail, from breast to groin. Hogar, recovering momentarily, brought the Ravensword down in a mighty stroke that clove Nol Dragir to the breastbone. He beheld the spurious sword fall from dying dragonclaws; then he crumpled from loss of blood. And all was black.

With the slaying of the Archon of Thool, one by one the surviving Skulthurs winged their way to kneel in an eerie circle around their fallen lord. With a piteous croak of despair, each of the hideous creatures drove its swordpoint upward through its inhuman throat.

Those who stood in arms before Nardath-Thool saw its white walls crack and crumble, its black towers fall. Out of the rubbled ruins of the shadowy city of the sorcerers, there arose a wailing and gnashing of teeth. The Last Day of the Gods was come. Nardath-Thool was no more. But the River Skaa flowed darkly on.

XXXVI

"I Have Given Thee a Son."

A small cry came from where Ragnahild lay with her swan-maiden cloak outspread, the crimson life tide flowing from her opened side. The sound brought Hogar back from the brink of unconsciousness. Ignoring his own dreadful wound, he dragged himself over to her still form.

"Ragnahild! Ragnahild!" he cried out in anguish, believing her dead until her eyes opened. She smiled weakly up at him.

"Hogar," she whispered with great effort. "Behold, my lord husband, I have given thee a son who shall someday be king."

Her eyes closed. She breathed a long, deep sigh. Hogar looked at the bairn in wonder, that with a death there should come a new life. He cradled Ragnahild gently in his arms, not disturbing the bairn, speaking her name in a soft whisper he was aware she could neither hear nor answer. He wept. The loss of blood made his head swim. He cried out, "She rides now with the Valkyrie!"

The blackness returned, blotting out sorrow and pain. In the mercifulness of his swoon, Hogar heard the sound of hooves thundering down out of the sky. Closer and closer they came, pounding, pounding, until they were brought to an abrupt halt with a great whinnying and blowing, like that of a stallion reined up sharply.

Before him stood the wraithlike figure of a tall, dark-mantled warrior of old, bearded gray and blind in one eye. From under his hood, his good eye glowed like a burning coal. A second rider reined up beside him. Hogar saw the horn-helmed face of a woman. Her golden hair flowed over her shoulders in a cascade, down either side of her ring-mail byrnie.

"Well done, Hogar Bloodsword."

Deep in his swoon, the words came to him as though from across a great distance. At first he could not distinguish the voice that welled up like a familiar echo. It was not the voice of Odin, that he knew . . . for the chief of the Nordland gods was doomed to silence since Ragnarok . . . Nor was it the Wizard of Lom, heard again in mind-talk . . . Nor Thorir Treefoot, come for the Ravensword . . . for the gray-bearded warrior had dismounted and stood before him with both feet firmly planted on the ground. He knew then it was neither wizard, nor saga king's shade, but Odin's god-wraith that unclasped the rune-ring from his arm, that lifted Ragnahild's slain body across the horn of his saddle . . . He heard the voice again, saw the armored woman's lips move . . . and knew it was the Volva who spoke, and that she spoke for the silent Valfather Odin. . . .

"Ragnahild shall henceforth ride with the warrior maids of Valhalla in the Wild Hunt. One day, Hogar Bloodsword," said the voice, "when you take your death blow in battle, look you to the skies. Then will you see Ragnahild come riding with Skuld and her Valkyrie host, to bring you to feast in the Hall of the Valiant. Till that day, fare thee well."

Again in his swoon, Hogar heard the thunder of hooves pounding hard into the sky, as though it were a road paved with stone. Then once more he was aware of nothing but blackness.

XXXVII

Fair Wind for Tarthiz

At Nordgaard, in the king's house, Queen Ermengard sat by Hogar's bedside, keeping vigil day and night until the fever from his wound passed. Sometimes she held Ragnahild's bairn in her arms, cooing to it absently while a pouting wet-nurse stood by. Other times she bathed her son's fever-drenched body with the help of her women, praying to the gods for them to spare the true and rightful King of the Asyr. She remained while the leech changed the dressings on the festered wound, turning her head away only because of the putrid stench that welled up from the mortified flesh the leech cut away, to keep the wound draining.

In his fevered brain, Hogar saw rise before him the faces of those numbered amongst the slain before the walls of Nardath-Thool. Tossing and thrashing in his delirium, he called out their names in his mutterings.

Svadi. Frodi. Lif.

Starulf.

Orlaf of Thone.

A sea of remembered faces crowded his mind, both Asyr and Vandir, as he relived the fierce hand-to-hand fighting.

Rorik Bloodaxe went down before his sword . . .

Hothir Longtooth's yellow bearded head rolled . . .

Ragnahild! Ragnahild! . . .

She flew to his defense, borne on swan-maiden wings, as Nol Dragir's heinous face appeared . . . the Archon's great two-handed sword came down . . .

Ragnahild! Ragnahild! . . . he saw her fall . . . then all went black.

Another time, he saw again the longships laden with

the slain put to the torch, and set adrift on the River Skaa . . .

Skoal, stout hearts!

The fever abated. The dead faces left him, and Hogar slept.

A twelve-month was come and gone before Hogar's wound was fully healed. Through constant care and the skill of the best leeches in the realm, but mostly by the magic of the healing waters brought at last from Dorn Woods by Hrapp the doughty reeve, he lived, once more to don his harness and buckle on the Ravensword.

Ragnahild's passing lay heavy on his heart, so that he ate but little and drank overmuch, until the day came when he went to find his son, where he found him at play with toys of war. Taking the young Hukert to his breast, he embraced him fiercely.

"Come, little king," he said; then calling together his jarls and his chieftains, he strode to the great hall. Carrying his son in his arms, he mounted the dais to the royal seat. There in the presence of the court and his new-sworn Vandir vassal lords, Hogar placed his son on the Raven Throne of Nordgaard and girded him with the Ravensword, with a "Skoal, Hukert, King of the Asyr and the Vandir!"

Turning to his assembled jarls and chieftains, he called forth Lothbrok Forkbeard of Skona; Urik of Ardvarth, and Ari Oxmain, newly made Jarl of Thone. Between them and Queen Ermengard, he delegated regents to rule in Hukert of Nordgaard's behalf until the boy-king was come of age.

To Ketil the Skald, the Wizard of Lom, and Fjaerlda, Hogar entrusted Hukert's learning.

"And what then of thyself, lad?" asked Ketil, still addressing Hogar as he always had.

"I am meant to win a throne elsewhere, good skald," Hogar told him. He turned to question one who stood amongst the jarls as the king's guest. "How blows the breath of the gods this day, Thaul?"

"He whom you call Tyr blows a fair wind for Tarthiz," was the white-maned chieftain's reply. "Come with me, Hogar. There will I build you a great ship such as no man has yet seen or commanded."

Hogar gave no answer for the moment. Instead, his eyes sought out Nels the Bowman.

"Nels," he said, "which will you have? The jarldom of Grundergaard, or the post of helmsman on the great ship that awaits me in Tarthiz?"

"By Thor's hammer!" boomed the burly Utgarthian. "Where you sail, Hogar, so sail I."

"By Balor and Bress!" cried a black-bearded, one-eyed Fomorian pirate, stepping forth boldly from where he stood amongst the lords. "Damn my eyes, Hogar Bloodsword, if you'll go a-roving without a fierce fighting crew of Fomor sea wolves, and Lon Thoddrach as your mate!"

"There is your answer, Thaul of Tarthiz," said the erstwhile Lord of the Asyr. Striding to his queen mother's side and kissing her farewell, Hogar turned to his jarls.

"I leave each of you to his sworn duty to Nordgaard's new and rightful king," he said. "I fare forth to follow the marches of the sun, to the far reaches and corners of the world, for such is the Norn-woven destiny of Hogar Bloodsword. A fair wind blows me to Tarthiz. From thence I shall fare wheresoever blow the winds of fortune."

He embraced Ketil the Skald as son to father and strode from the great hall in the king's house, turning his back forever on his right to the Raven Throne, which he had won at such great cost, where now sat Hukert, his son, where someday would sit his son's son. As for himself, a throne awaited him in a far-off and splendored land, where, too, there waited a breathtaking queen.

For so said the Weird of the Gods.

GLOSSARY

AALS = a seaport in Utgarth.
ÆGIR (eé-jir) = Nordland sea god; husband of Ran.
ANTEDILUVIAN WORLD = Hogar's world; the post-Ragnarok Age, circa 12,000 years ago.
ARCHON OF THOOL (ark-un) = Nol Dragir (drag-gur).
ARCHPRIEST OF THA = High Priest of the Oirrin-Yess.
ARDVARTH = one of the five fylkes of Nordgaard. See FYLKE.
ARI OXMAIN = an Asyr warrior; shield karl to Hothir Longtooth.
ARK OF THA = the Moonrath.
ARN = fortress of Astrith, Queen of the Swans.
ASA (aý-zuh) = gods of the Nordland, worshiped by the Asyrfolk.
ASA-THOR = the Nordland god of warriors and war. See THOR.
ASGARTH = home of the Nordland gods.
ASTRITH = Queen of the Swans. See ARN.
ASYR (aý-zur) = the Asyrfolk; Nordland Kelts; a warrior race said to be god-born descendants of Odin's seed. See GOD-BORN.
ASYRFOLK = the Asyr; a Nordic-Keltic race who settled the Nordland 1000 years after Ragnarok, circa 12,000 years ago. See NORDGAARD.
ATHELING = the heir of a royal or noble family.

BALOR OF THE EVIL EYE = the one-eyed Fomorian god.
BIFROST = the rainbow bridge over which the Nordland gods crossed from Earth (Midgarth) to

Asgarth; fell in ruins during destruction of the world at Ragnarok.
BLACK CITADEL = the black towers of Thool; stronghold of the Fire Lords and their Skulthur minions. See THALMANDAS. See SKULTHURS.
BLACK GODDESS OF DOOM = Tha.
BLACK GODS = the Khthon.
BLACK LEGION = Skulthurs; minions of the Fire Lords.
BLACK MOON = Tha, in her manifestation as the Black Goddess.
BLACK RUNES = runes chanted to invoke the Khthon, the Black Gods of Thool.
BLACK WOLF = Lon Thoddrach's pirate galley.
BLOOD OATH = one's most solemn oath of fealty.
BLUE DOLPHIN = a waterfront inn in Koben.
BLUE FOX = the blazon of the Grundergaard jarls. See GRUNDERGAARD.
BLUND = an Asyr warrior; sentry at Grimmswold keep; brother of Rorik Bloodaxe.
BORBAS CROOKBACK = a Nemedian slaver.
BRESS = a Fomorian god.
BRUGAR = an Utgarthian lancer who mistook Ragnahild for a Valkyrie while in his cups.
BYRNIE = a coat of ring mail.

CAT'S THROAT = a broad inlet of the Nord Sea between Nordgaard and Utgarth.
CHUGA = the great white wolf of the Frozen Lands.
CROMM CRUIACH = a Kymric god; invoked as an oath by Fomors.
CROWN-FYLKE = a dormant jarldom reverted to the crown.

DONAR = an Asyr warrior at Grimmswold.
DOOM RING = a circle of twelve runestones, in which offenders stood for judgment before the Fire Lords.
DOOM SEAT = the Archon of Thool's throne.
DOOMSMAN = a hereditary title of the Archon of Thool.
DOOM STONE = the center stone in the Doom Ring, on which offenders stood for judgment.

DORN = a steading above Loki's Rock, on the Utgarthian coast.

DORN HALL = same as Dorn.

DORN WOODS = the Thane of Dorn's hunting preserve; an ensorceled forest. See HULDREN.

DRAGONSHIP = a longship with dragon heads carved on stern and stem post. See LONGSHIP.

DRAKKO = the Vandir king's emissary.

ERMENGARD = Ermengard of Skaane; wife of Hothir Longtooth; mother of Hogar by Helmer Bloodsword; daughter of Ogmund, King of the Rhens; born at Skaane Hall; later, Queen of Nordgaard.

ELDRITCH = weird, eerie.

ENSORCELED = bewitched.

ENSORCELMENT = sorcery; a spell, or enchantment.

EY (ee) = island. See ORKNA EY.

FANE = a temple.

FENRIS-WOLF = a monstrous troll wolf kept chained by the Nordland gods; released by Loki, it slew and was slain by Odin at Ragnarok.

FEY = enchanted, or under a spell.

FIEF (feef) = a feudal estate.

FIEFDOM = a fief.

FIEFED = apportioned as a fief.

FIELD OF NARDATH = See VIGRITH.

FIVE FYLKES = the five jarldoms of Nordgaard: Valhelm, Thone, Skona, Ardvarth, and Grundergaard.

FINNAMARK = the dread Frozen Lands; also called the Great Ice Marsh; beyond which lies the Frozen Sea, the ice-troll caves, and the Cold Waste of the Sorcerers.

FINNUR = one of Svadi's four brothers.

FIRE LORDS = the Thalmandas; descended from the Old Ones, the ancient Dragonfolk who periodically sought to conquer the Nordland. Their stronghold was Thool.

FJAERLDA (fyerl-da) = the hunchback dwarf sister of Ermengard; called the Ugly Cygnet; a harpist and composer of staves; an accomplished swordswoman.

FOMORS = a woad-tattooed, fierce-faced pirate race from behind the World's Edge; averaged seven feet in height.

FOMORIAN = of, or pertaining to the Fomors. See TOR-A'MOR.

FORSOOTH = in truth; certainly.

FREY (fry) = a Nordland god. See RAVENSWORD.

FRIGGA = a Nordland goddess; wife of Odin.

FRODI (fró-dee) = one of Svadi's four brothers.

FROZEN LANDS = the Finnamark, through which winds the River Skaa. See GREAT ICE MARSH; see FINNAMARK.

FROZEN SEA = the ice floe and icebergs beyond the Finnamark.

FYLKE (filk) = a jarldom.

GATE OF THIEVES = the gate by which Hogar entered Nardath-Thool.

GARTH = an enclosed or walled estate; a steading; a stronghold.

GERDA = wife of Hrapp the reeve; thrall to Runulf of Dorn.

GLAMOUR = an enchantment or spell.

GLIKKA = an old Yukha she; befriended Hogar.

GOD-BORN = the Asyrfolk.

GOD-MAGIC = supernatural powers attributed to the rune-ring of Odin.

GOOM = an Ice Age glacier-entrapped hairy mammoth, worshiped by the Yukhas. See SNOW BEASTS.

GRAY-BEARDED ONE = the Wizard of Lom.

GREAT ICE MARSH = the Finnamark.

GREAT MIDDLE LAND SEA = the Mediterranean Sea. See TARTHIZ.

GREEN-ISLAND-UNDER-THE-WAVES = prehistoric Ireland; from which the Fomors drove the People of Nemed, the Nemedians; so called because it lay beyond the horizon. See WORLD's EDGE; see NEMED FIRST.

GRIMLIR = one of the berkerkers slain by Hogar at Dorn.

GRIMMSWOLD = an Asyr keep built by Helmer Bloodsword to guard the Marches; garrisoned by Hothir Longtooth; fiefed to Hogar as king's thane on his coming of age. See THE MARCHES.

GRUNDERGAARD = one of the five fylkes of Nordgaard.

GUARDIANS OF THE RING = Skulthurs who guard the Doom Ring. See SKULTHURS.

GWERN = a Fomorian pirate; Lon Thoddrach's oarmaster.

HAAKI (hah́-key) = one of Svadi's four brothers.

HALL OF KERNS = quarters for the warrior-slaves of Nardath-Thool.

HAVILAR = a fabled city of Hogar's time.

HEL = the Nordland goddess of the dead; her icy domain.

HELGI HOTBLOOD = an Asyr warrior garrisoned at Grimmswold.

HELMER BLOODSWORD = father of Hogar; second son of Thorir Treefoot; true Jarl of Valhelm; murdered by his younger brother, Hothir Longtooth.

HERN = King of the Vandir.

HIRED SWORD = a mercenary.

HOGAR (hoé-gar) = son of Helmer Bloodsword and Ermengard of Skaane; atheling of the Asyr King; called the king's thane; true heir to the Raven Throne of Nordgaard; banished by his stepsire, Hothir Longtooth; thereafter called Hogar Bloodsword.

HORD THE OLD = the name carved in runes on the lintel stone of an old burial mound in Dorn Woods. See HOWE.

HOTHIR LONGTOOTH = third son of Thorir Treefoot; slew his brothers to succeed as King of the Asyr; seduced the slain Helmer Bloodsword's bride by sorcery; planned the death of Hogar, the true heir to the Raven Throne; usurped the jarldom of Valhelm, and claimed Nordgaard's Raven Throne; called the false-king.

HOTT = a berserker slain by Hogar at Dorn.

HOWE = a burial mound.

HRAPP = reeve of Dorn steading; thrall to Runulf the Thane. Once a bowman; husband of Gerda.

HROKK THE HALFLING = a half-dwarf, half-elfin swordsmith.

HROMUND = one of Svadi's four brothers.

HUKERT = son born to Ragnahild and Hogar; heir to the Raven Throne. First King of the Asyr and the Vandir.

HULDREN = the troll wife of Dorn Woods. See WERBEAST.

HUNDRED SHIELDS = swan-maiden warrior maids defending Arn.

ICE TROLLS = an extinct Ice Age race.

ICE-TROLL CAVES = a glacial formation in the Frozen Sea; inhabited by sea-troll sirens, and the snow beasts. (See YUKHAS) Beyond the ice-troll caves lies the Cold Waste of the Sorcerers. See NARDATH-THOOL.

INGVAR = Jonker of Svend; nephew of Mulik the Unsteady, Jarl of Grundergaard.

JARL = an earl.

JARLESS = the wife of a jarl.

JONKER = a nobleman; a feudal lord ranking next to a jarl.

KARL = a warrior; a man.

KEEP = a fortress.

KERN = a warrior-slave. See HALL OF KERNS.

KETIL THE SKALD = Hogar's mentor and faithful friend; a Rhenish warrior bard, once court skald to Ogmund, King of Skaane; later skald to Hothir Longtooth.

KHTHON = the Black Gods of Thool; the seven bestial gods of the Old Ones, the Dragonfolk; worshiped by the Fire Lords.

KING'S FALCHION = the Ravensword; the King-sword of the Asyr.

KINGSWORD = See RAVENSWORD.

KING'S THANE = Hogar's title as atheling of the Asyr king.
KLAVUN THORG = a Nemedian sorcerer; thrall to Hothir Longtooth.
KNOTS OF DESTINY = one's fate or Weird, as woven by the Norns. See NORNS.
KOBEN = a seaport in Nordgaard.
KRAKEN = a frightful sea monster.
KYMRIC = of, or pertaining to the Kymry.
KYMRIC WILDERLAND = Prehistoric British Isles; land of the ancient Gaals, Brythons, and Cornish Kelts of the post-Ragnarok Age.
KYMRY = A pre-Pictish race of Kelts.

LAGOPA = a Tarthizian forest tree noted for its lightweight wood.
LAST DAY OF THE GODS = the fateful day when the Oirrin-Yess and the Khthon would battle to the death, and Nardath-Thool would become a desolation. See TWELVE RUNESTONES.
LEECH = a physician.
LIF = a red-bearded Utgarthian axman and sometime fisherman, who fared with the *Sea Raven*.
LIFE THREADS = one's life span as woven by the Norns.
LOKI = the Nordland god of evil.
LOKIAN = evil; of, or pertaining to Loki.
LOKI'S ROCK = a treacherous point on the jagged coast of Utgarth; said to be the habitat of troll fiends. See DORN.
LOM = a small fiefdom near Arn.
LOM WOODS = home of the Wizard of Lom.
LONGHOUSE = the main building of a steading.
LONGSHIP = a Nordland galley, usually twenty-oared, carrying one square rigged mast, with a crew of forty karls rowing in two shifts. See DRAGONSHIP.
LON THODDRACH (Thód-rack) = a Fomorian pirate chieftain.
LORD OF THE ASYR = King of the Asyrfolk.
LOST SWORD OF FREY = said by the skalds to be the Ravensword.
LOTHBROK FORKBEARD = Jarl of Skona. See FIVE FYLKES.

LUR = a battle horn. Also the weather horn sounded from a ship's bow.

MANTRA OF THE WHITE RUNES = an ancient Nemedian incantation chanted by the priests of Tha to invoke the White Gods. See OIRRIN-YESS.

MARCHES, THE = disputed borderland fylke between Nordgaard and Vandirheim.

MEED = reward.

METAL = one's armor, badge, or blazon.

MIDDLE LAND SEA = the Mediterranean Sea in antediluvian times.

MIDGARTH = the Earth.

MIDGARTHSORM = the monstrous serpent that slew Thor at Ragnarok.

MIRROR OF TRUTH = occult sands that foretold the past, present, and future.

MOONRATH = the Ark of Tha.

MULIK THE UNSTEADY = Jarl of Grundergaard. See FIVE FYLKES.

NARDATH OF THE WHITE WALLS = the rune-built city erected by Nemed First on the ruins of Asgarth. Ruled by Queen Tha.

NARDATH-THOOL = the city of Nemedian sorcerers; being the twin cities of Nardath of the White Gods; and Thool, the citadel of the Black Gods; stronghold of the Fire Lords and their Black Legion.

NARS ANTHOR = A Nemedian kern; Queen Tha's champion in the arena. See the QUEEN'S PLEASURE.

NATHAS KLAR = a Nemedian noble; Queen Tha's Procurer of Man and Beast.

NELS THE BOWMAN = an Utgarthian mercenary; hired sword to Runulf of Dorn. Comrade-in-arms with Hogar.

NEMED = hereditary title of the Nemedian kings.

NEMED FIRST = King of the People of Nemed, who fled prehistoric Ireland before the invading Fomors. See the GREEN-ISLAND-UNDER-THE-WAVES.

NEMED, SEA OF = the rune-spelled waters beside Nardath-Thool, into which flowed the River Skaa.

NEMEDIAN = of, or pertaining to the People of Nemed; a native of Nardath-Thool.

NEMEDIAN SORCERERS = the descendants of Nemed First; the priests of Tha; the Thalmanda Fire Lord rulers of Nardath-Thool.

NOL DRAGIR = the dragon-spawned Archon of the Fire Lords; High Priest of the Khthon; a Thalmanda halfling; Tha's sibling.

NORD = the North; one of the "god-born" forebears of the Asyr.

NORDGAARD = the kingdom of the Asyr; chief of the Nord kingdoms. See RIKE.

NORD GODS = the Asa.

NORDISH = the language of the Nordland; forerunner to Old Norse.

NORD KINGDOMS = kingdoms of the North; prehistoric Scandinavia.

NORDLAND = the Northland; the Nord kingdoms.

NORDLANDER = a native of any Nord kingdom.

NORDLAND GODS = the Asa.

NORD SEA = the North Sea of the post-Ragnarok Age.

NORDSMAN = a native of Nordgaard.

NORNS = the Fates; the Three Weirds.

ODIN = Chief of the Nordland gods; fell at Ragnarok.

OGMUND = King of Skaane and the Rhens; father of Ermengard and Fjaerlda. Long in his howe; fell at the battle of Skaane against the Vandir and the Fire Lords.

OIRRIN-YESS = the White Gods; the five bestial gods of Nardath.

OKRAM = a Tarthizian forest tree noted for its lightweight wood.

OLD ONES = the once-powerful Dragonfolk, who ruled the world before the coming of the Asa. The Thalmandas (see FIRE LORDS) were the last of their venerable lineage; reduced to the impotency of lizards by Nemed First, who won from them the rune-ring of Odin, found on the battlefield at Ragnarok.

OLD TONGUE = the archaic language of the Old Ones; the poetic language of the skalds.
OLD WARRIOR = Starulf's sobriquet. See STARULF.
OLEG = Lothbrok Forkbeard's captain of warriors.
OPHUR = a fabled city of Hogar's time.
ORKNA = a seal.
ORKNA EY (ee) = the seal islands off the northernmost tip of the Kymric Wilderland; a pirates' nest. See THAIRM.
OLAF = Jarl of Thone. See FIVE FYLKES.

PEOPLE OF NEMED = the Nemedians.
POST-RAGNAROK AGE = Hogar's era; 1000 years after Ragnarok. The antediluvian world, circa 12,000 years ago.
POTEEN = a pot-stilled liquor, the strong drink of the Fomors; called "the water of life."

QUEEN ASTRITH OF THE SWANS = the Swan Queen. Her fortress of the Red Swan at Arn was the realm of the Swan Maidens, called her Hundred Shields.
QUEEN'S PLEASURE, THE = Nemedian gladiatorial Games fought in the arena at Nardath-Thool.

RAGNAHILD = a swan-maiden novice; Hogar's bride; mother of Hukert.
RAGNAROK = the twilight of the gods; the doomsday of the world, preceding its regeneration.
RAN = the Nordland sea goddess; wife of Ægir.
RAVEN FLAG = flag of Nordland pirates.
RAVEN-MARK = three ravens: the blazon and standard of Thorir Treefoot. Adopted by Hogar as his own.
RAVEN OF NORDGAARD = the blazon and royal standard of the Asyr kings.
RAVENSWORD = Thorir Treefoot's runesword; dwarf-forged and elfin-fashioned by Hrokk the Halfling; said by the skalds to be the lost sword of the god Frey, graven with Thorir Treefoot's raven mark; the true king's falchion; the Kingsword of the Asyr.

RAVEN THRONE = the royal chair of Nordgaard.
REAVER = a marauder.
REDE = counsel.
RED GODDESS OF LOVE AND BATTLE = Tha.
RED LION = the blazon of the Valhelm jarls. See FIVE FYLKES.
RED MOON OF LOVE'S DELIGHT = Tha.
RED SWAN = an order of swan maidens. See QUEEN ASTRITH.
REEVE = an overseer of a steading.
RHENISH = of, or pertaining to the Rhens.
RHENS = a red-haired Asyrfolk from the Rhenish kingdom of Skaane.
RIKE = kingdom.
RING OF ODIN = See RUNE-RING.
RIST = marked; scratched; carved or engraved.
RORIK BLOODAXE = An Asyr warrior; shield-karl to Hothir. Brother of Blund.
RUNECRAFT = knowledge; the use of runes in sorcery.
RUNE LOCK = a lock opened and closed by runes.
RUNE-RING OF ODIN = according to the skalds, the ring Odin lost on the field at Ragnarok.
RUNESPELL = an enchantment wrought by casting runes, or by their utterance.
RUNESTONES = See TWELVE RUNESTONES.
RUNULF OF DORN = Thane of Dorn, a steading on the Utgarthian coast above Loki's Rock.

SAGAMAN = a skald.
SCOT = tribute.
SCOT-KING = a petty king in vassalage, who pays scot to the high king.
SEA RAVEN = Hogar's longship on which he begins his quest.
SEA-STEED = a Nordland longship.
SECRET PLACE OF THOOL = where the Ravensword and the ring of Odin were hidden.
SEER-OF-ALL = the Wizard of Lom.
SENNIGHT (sen-it) = seven days and nights; a week.
SHADOW WRAITH = the materialization of one's mind in visible form.

SHAMAN (shah-mun) = a warlock-priest; a sorcerer.
SHAPE-SHIFT = to change one's shape by sorcery.
SHARK'S BIGHT = a dingy shebeen in Thairm, in the Orkna Ey.
SHE-WHO-WALKS-THE-NIGHT = Tha.
SHIELD KARL = a warrior bound by shield oath to serve a lord.
SIXERN = a six-oared boat.
SKAA (skah) = the winding River Skaa; its Stygian waters flowed into the Sea of Nemed.
SKAANE (skane) = the kingdom of the Rhens; Ermengard's homeland.
SKAANE HALL = King Ogmund's stronghold.
SKALD = a Nordland bard.
SKALDCRAFT = the wisdom of the skalds.
SKEEG = a heavy lash.
SKONA = one of the five fylkes of Nordgaard.
SKULD = leader of the Valkyries.
SKULTHURS = grotesque winged beings, something less than human; gryffon-beaked and taloned; clad in black plate armor, armed with a short sword. They are minions of the Fire Lords of Thool; the Black Legion; the Guardians of the Ring.
SNOW BEASTS = the Yukhas; infrahuman troglodytes; inhabited the ice-troll caves.
SOOTH = truth; true.
SPELLCRAFT = sorcery.
SPELL RAG = a wind seller's talisman; a wind charm.
SPELL WIND = a wind raised by sorcery.
STARULF = the great Rhenish hero of Ogmund's reign. Watchdog of Skaane; called to arms by Queen Ermengard to levy an army and march against Hothir, the false-king. Known affectionately as the "Old Warrior."
STEERBOARD = starboard.
STORM MAIDENS = daughters of Ægir and Ran; said to cause men to drown at sea.
STREET OF THE WIND SELLERS = a street in Thairm, where sellers of wind charms were quartered.
SVADI (Svah-dee) = a runagate; later Hogar's valiant

bosun; eldest brother of Finnur, Frodi, Haaki, and Hromund.
SVEND = fiefdom of Jonker Ingvar.
SWAN MAIDEN = a warrior maid; one of the Hundred Shields at Arn. Ermengard's sobriquet.
SWAN MAIDENS = warrior maids belonging to an order. See RED SWAN.
SWAN-MARK = a swan maiden's identifying tattoo above the heart.
SWAN QUEEN = Astrith of the Swans.
SWORD AND THE RING, THE = two fabled objects of Hogar's quest. See RAVENSWORD; RUNE-RING OF ODIN.
SWORN KARL = a warrior bound by his sworn oath to serve a lord. See SHIELD KARL.

TARTHIZ = a great walled city and seaport on the antediluvian Iberian peninsula, within the Straits of Tarthiz on the Middle Land Sea.
TEMPLE OF THE FLAME = the High Place of Thool.
TEMPLE OF THA = the Nemedian fane where Queen Tha was worshiped daily as the White Goddess of the Oirrin-Yess.
THA = the sorceress Queen of Nardath-Thool; daughter of Nemed; half sister of Nol Dragir, the Archon of Thool.
THAIRM = a pirate stronghold in the Orkna Ey.
THALMANDAS = last of the venerable lineage descended from the Old Ones, the ancient Dragonfolk who ruled the world before the coming of the Nordland gods, the Asa. See FIRE LORDS.
THANE = feudal lord ranking below a jonker.
THAUL OF TARTHIZ = royal artificer to the King of Tarthiz. Hogar and Thaul met as fellow warrior-slaves at the Hall of Kerns in Nardath-Thool.
THONE = one of the Five Fylkes of Nordgaard.
THOOL = the sinistrous black citadel that rose from the heart of Nardath; stronghold of the Thalmanda Fire Lords; one of the twin cities of Nardath-Thool.
THOR = the Nordland god of warriors and war; maker of thunder and lightning. Also called Asa-Thor, which literally means "the god Thor."

THORIR TREEFOOT = legendary pirate king of the Asyr; lost an eye and a leg against the pirates of Thairm, where he won the fabled Ravensword. Fell at Skaane against the Vandir and the Fire Lords. Hogar's grandsire.

THORODD FAIRHAIR = firstborn of Thorir Treefoot; succeeded him as King of the Asyr; brother of Helmer Bloodsword, and Hothir Longtooth. Murdered by the latter.

THRALLSFEST = an annual three-day feast, when even the lowliest serf was granted leave from labor to carouse in the village on the largess of his lord. A Nordland custom.

THREE WEIRDS = the Norns; the Fates. Weavers of Life Threads, which they tied in Knots of Destiny.

THYLLA = a sea troll that inhabited one of the ice-troll caves.

TIGRESS MADE WOMAN = Tha.

TOR-A'MOR = the Green-Island-Under-the-Waves, as prehistoric Ireland was known to the Asyrfolk; the stronghold of the Fomors.

TWELVE IN ONE, THE = the Seven Khthon and the Five Oirrin-Yess. The bestial gods of Nardath-Thool.

TWELVE RUNESTONES, THE = rune-carved monoliths that formed the Doom Ring of Thool.

TWILIGHT OF THE GODS = Ragnarok.

TYR = the Nordland god of the wind and sky.

UGLY CYGNET (sig-net) = Fjaerlda's sobriquet.

URIK = Jarl of Ardvarth. See FIVE FYLKES.

UTGARTH = one of the Nord kingdoms; across the Cat's Throat from Nordgaard.

UTGARTHIAN = of, or pertaining to Utgarth; a native of that rike, or kingdom.

VAL = an Asyr warrior garrisoned at Grimmswold keep.

VALHALLA = the Hall of Odin.

VALHELM = fylke of the Valhelm jarls; one of the Five Fylkes of Nordgaard.

VALKYRIES (Val-KEER-ees) = the warrior maidens of Odin; choosers of the slain in battle. See SKULD; WILD HUNT.
VANDIR = the warrior race constantly at war with the Asyr; a native of Vandirheim. The Vandir were Northern Kelts like the Asyrfolk.
VANDIRHEIM = the rike or kingdom of the Vandir; traditional enemy of the Asyr kingdom of Nordgaard.
VIGRITH = the bloody battlefield where the Asa fell at Ragnarok. Renamed the Field of Nardath by Nemed First.
VOLVA, THE = the Weird of the Gods; the prophetess of the Asa; the sibyl who appeared to Hogar in his fey dream in the sea cave.

WASTING SICKNESS = a dreaded plague.
WATCHDOG OF SKAANE = Starulf.
WEEN = imagine.
WEIRD = one's own fate; one of the Norns; a prophetess.
WEIRD OF THE GODS = the Volva.
WELL OF FIRE = the sacred flame kept burning in the center of the Doom Ring.
WEOR (Weé-yor) = chief god of the Vandir.
WERBEAST = a man-beast; a human or troll capable of taking animal form.
WHITE BOAR = the blazon and royal standard of Skaane. Ermengard's personal badge.
WHITE GODDESS = Tha.
WHITE GODS = the Oirrin-Yess.
WHITE MOON OF NARDATH = Tha.
WHITE RUNES = runes chanted to invoke the White Gods.
WILD HUNT = the Ride of the Valkyries.
WIND SELLER = a witch or warlock who sold spell winds breathed into knotted rags called wind charms.
WIS = to know; believe.
WITCH FIRE = weird blue flames caused to burn by sorcery.
WITCH STORM = a storm raised by an enchantment or wind charm; also said of a sudden severe storm.

WITCH WIND = a wind raised by sorcery. See SPELL WIND.

WIZARD OF LOM = the most powerful mage of the Nordland. Not infallible, however, due to his penchant for forgetting. Court magician at Skaane during Ogmund's reign, when Ermengard and Fjaerlda were young girls. Called the Seer-of-All; the Gray-Bearded One. Resided in a modest hut in Lom Woods. Sought out by Fjaerlda.

WOAD = a blue dyestuff yielded by leaves of an herb of the mustard family; used by the Fomors to tattoo their bodies.

WOLF FLAG = the pirate flag of the Fomors.

WORLD'S EDGE = the horizon, which in Hogar's time was believed to be the brink of the Great Abyss. The sun was not said to set but to fall behind the World's Edge. Land beyond the horizon was believed to be under the sea.

WULFSTANE = a steading in Vandirheim; Ragnahild's home.

YOG = chief of the Yukhas.

YUKHAS = the infrahuman snow beasts inhabiting the ice-troll caves in the Frozen Lands.

About the Author

John Rufus Sharpe III is a professional writer of words to music, from the popular form to art songs, to works of an extended nature such as librettos for an oratorio, a light opera, and a jazz opera. His songs include "So Rare," one of the Great Ones, immortalized by Jimmy Dorsey. He is a writer/publisher member of the American Society of Composers, Authors and Publishers (ASCAP); a member of the Songwriters Guild; the Dramatists Guild; and is *Listed by Marquis* in *Who's Who in the West*. He was born in Berkeley, California. He resides in San Mateo, a suburb of San Francisco, with his wife, Josephine Tumminia, former leading soprano with the Metropolitan Opera. This is his first published novel.